LOVE & OTHER CURES
FOR THE RECENTLY UNDEAD

HJ RAMSAY

www.BOROUGHSPUBLISHINGGROUP.com

LOVE & OTHER CURES FOR THE RECENTLY UNDEAD

ISBN 978-1-957295-82-4

*As always to my husband, Nick, and my three children,
Gracie, Annie, and Bradley who support me unconditionally.
And to all my tennis friends at Sun Oaks,
and my coach, Steve Kinder, who gave me the love of tennis.*

ACKNOWLEDGMENTS

Novels don't happen in a vacuum. At every stage, there's always others who've helped it along and deserve thanks.

Love & Other Cures for the Recently Undead wouldn't have gotten its start if it wasn't for Ashley Rich who talked about zombies while we were golfing. It's because of her that *what if* questions crept into my mind. What if there was a cure? What would it be like for the people who came out of it and how would they cope? Those questions triggered the first steps to this story and led to multiple drafts read by not only Ashley, but also Eric Halpenny whose collective comments and suggestions were invaluable as I worked through its first drafts and learned who Derrick and CeCe were to the story and to each other.

Thank you also to Courtney Grela, a lover of all romance, who read the entire novel twice and whose thoughtful feedback and encouragement kept me going.

Thank you to Boroughs Publishing Group for seeing the uniqueness of this story and a willingness to help bring an idea that started on a golf course into readers' hands.

As with everything, I'm forever in debt to my husband, Nick, who's given me the space to write and encourages me to explore my passions. And to my children, Gracie, Annie, and Bradley, my biggest fans, who give me precious little space to write, but I love them just the same.

LOVE & OTHER CURES
FOR THE RECENTLY UNDEAD

Chapter One

Something twitches and the sound of teeth grinding in her ear annoys her.

Stop it, Teddy.

CeCe tries to push her brother away, but her arm scrapes against asphalt and the unfamiliarity jolts her awake. Her heart pounds as she opens her eyes to blackness. A tart scent and an overwhelming stench of rot fills her nostrils. She blinks, trying to focus her vision, but her eyelids itch like they're brushing across sandpaper.

Where am I?

Last thing she remembers she was in downtown Chico at Mason's Restaurant with her best friend Leyton celebrating her eighteenth birthday.

"L...L..." she calls and her throat stiffens as if encrusted from lungs to larynx. "L...Ley..."

A strained whimper answers.

Her fingers grope the darkness and her breaths come in burning terrified gulps. She drags herself closer to the noise until she presses against someone's back. She hears whimpering again.

Leyton? Are you okay?

She can't tell what, or who, it is. Her fingers tingle with numbness as she searches for any signs of her friend. Her palm brushes the short, cropped hair of a man and she lurches backward. Her muscles scream in agony as she knocks into another body, motionless and rancid with death. Then a wail erupts nearby, followed by another and another.

She tries to move, but every way she twists herself, she's met with flailing arms and legs that crush and squeeze. She tucks into a ball, her sobs joining the cacophony of the crying, and shrieks, and the unseen mass that slithers and moans around her.

***

CeCe wakes to the beeping and purring of devices. She hears other noises too. The creaks of metal, footsteps crisscrossing the floor, and low murmurs. Gauze covers her eyes. She wants to remove it, but can't lift her hand any more than a hover before giving up. Everything aches like a bruise that keeps getting pressed. She clenches her teeth and moans. A strange hand circles around her numb fingers. Out of instinct, she jerks away.

"It's me," her dad says. He's trying not to cry. She can tell by the way his voice cracks. "I'm here."

She tries to say, "Dad," but all she manages is a raspy exhale.

His hand squeezes tighter. "You should sleep," he says. She hears him get to his feet, the clink of a tray moving, and the flicking of his fingers against metal. He leans next to her. "You might feel a sting."

When he's done, she hears the rattle as he sets down the syringe.

Feel what sting? She didn't feel anything.

She doesn't want to sleep. She wants to know where she is, what's happened, and why her body is numb. Was there an accident? Is Leyton okay? She wants to ask, but a fog creeps along the edges of her mind. She tries to hold on to her thoughts, but they slip away as her eyes close.

"N…" Her lips form a word, but her throat burns with the effort.

Over and over again, her father puts her to sleep like a hypnotist's spell she can't escape. She has no idea how long she's been out. The next time she wakes her eyes are unbandaged. She blinks.

Everything's blurry, as if the world is underwater, and she manages to see what looks like a spider's web of tubes running into her arms.

She turns her head. Her dad is sitting nearby working on a laptop.

"D…D…Dad," she says in a voice she doesn't recognize.

He shuts the computer and grips her hand. She's still numb and uncomfortable, but his face is close, and tears roll down his cheeks.

"W…w…where?" she asks, her throat aching.

"You're safe," he says, but she doesn't understand why he'd say that. Why *safe*? She looks past him. *Where's Mom? And her brother? Was Leyton hurt too?*

"M…m…" The word sticks against her cracked lips, but it won't come out. "W…where?" she manages again.

"A hospital. Kind of a hospital. We had to make do with the Costco."

She tries to sit up, but her dad gently pushes her back down. "Not yet, Cees. Your body's been through a lot. Let it rest."

"Wha…what…h…h…hap…" Her voice gains strength, but the words she wants to say won't come out.

"You were Infected."

So, not an accident. She listens as he explains a parasite, so tiny it could pass through the blood-brain barrier, embedded itself in her neural tissue. It took over all conscious thought and nearly shut down her internal organs.

"Cysticercosis-Lyssa, CC-L," he says. "Most call it the Kill Virus because the transmissions are, well, they're violent. Bites, mostly. Like your hand. Do you remember?"

She clenches her right fist, and she's met with a dull throbbing. Her dad tells her how the Infection spread, how for some it was immediate, others several hours, and some a day, but all she can think of is her birthday dinner at Mason's Restaurant.

"I was out with friends," she whispers. She swallows in discomfort and her father pushes a glass against her lips and makes her drink water. Lubrication makes speaking easier. "We…we saw this guy outside. He looked really sick. I tried to help him and he—"

She swallows as the memory floods back and the vision of the sick guy flashes into her brain—she'll never forget what he looked like. "He fucking bit me." Her voice rises as panic sets in. "Like a rabid dog."

Her father nods, his face drawn. "He was Infected."

CeCe closes her eyes in fatigue. The college guy she'd tried to help was the person responsible for how she felt now? This was what trying to do a good deed had cost her?

"Where's Leyton?" she whispers. "Is she here? And what about Riley, where's he?" Her boyfriend would be around somewhere, waiting to see her.

Her dad looks at her. "There's still a lot of people missing."

"H…how… l…l…long have I been like this? Where's Mom and Teddy?" *And where's Riley? Why isn't Dad answering me?*

He doesn't respond at first. Her heart thumps in her chest as he leans in and grasps her hands; his warmth doesn't seep into her ice-cold skin. "CeCe, you've been Infected for two years."

Her breath catches and something starts beeping wildly. She must have misheard him. There was no way she could've been gone for years. That was impossible. He'd said two weeks. It had only been two weeks.

Her dad squeezes her numb fingers. "I know this is a shock, a lot to take in. But you're back now and once you're feeling better, I'll take you home. I've tried to keep everything the same… As much as I could."

Why was he talking like that? A few weeks was nothing. She stares at him. His hair is grayer at the temples than before. New worry lines etch his forehead. He *looks* older.

"Maybe I should've waited to tell you," he says. "But I would've wanted to know in your shoes. It's a long time, but things will be better now. You'll see."

No. No. No, she screams inside her head. *I can't have been gone years.* Her body twitches and the hospital mattress squeaks like gum bubbles popping.

Her dad stands. "Let's rest a bit and allow things to settle," he says. "We'll talk more later."

She shakes her head. She can't breathe and gulps for air. Dry drowning as her dad moves around her. An alarm goes off on one of the machines.

"It's going to be okay," he says. "It'll all be okay."

***

CeCe lies in her hospital bed, unable to register the sounds around her. She replays everything her dad had said, trying to make sense out of the impossible—out of the nightmare she'd woken up to—but it's like something out of a horror film.

For two years, she'd been in "stasis," as her dad called it. Two years of shuffling in place. Two years while the world imploded and fed upon itself. Two years of time moving unseen. Dead, but not dead, within a horde of other Infected. That was where she'd been this whole time as they worked on a way to kill the parasite. It took longer than anyone thought, but then again most of those who specialized in disease control were Infected themselves.

He'd found it a month ago. Her dad, once the neighborhood veterinarian, discovered the cure for CC-L and formulated it for mass inoculation via a gas he called Nitrociptine. Black Hawk helicopters dropped canisters of Nitrociptine like bombs all over Chico and the surrounding areas. The fumes entered the bloodstream, killing the parasite and triggering paralyzed immune systems to attack whatever remained.

The drug physiologically restarted those who'd been Infected, no matter the extent of the injuries before and after transmission. The worst cases didn't survive the jump start.

Her mother hadn't made it. She'd known from the look on her father's face when she asked him. He'd found her mom's body thirty yards from CeCe in the same mall parking lot.

The knowledge of that blurs along the edges of CeCe's skull where it clings like a film. Her mom can't be gone. She'd been making her and Teddy pancakes that morning before school and had smiled with tears in her eyes as she handed CeCe her birthday card.

"My baby isn't a baby anymore," her mom had said.

That is what CeCe remembers. For her, it'd only been yesterday that everything was normal and right until she and her mom were Infected, unaware, lost and cured together, whether they'd survive it or not. How this happened, CeCe has no idea, only that she'd been carried away and her mom hadn't.

In one breath, her dad tells her this, and in the next, what happened to her brother.

"Teddy and I got separated when the Infection first hit. I was trying to get him out of the city, but then I couldn't and I lost him. I'm going to find Teddy, like I found you."

She takes all this in, as well as the news that Riley and Leyton haven't been found and are presumed Infected or dead somewhere.

It's too much.

Her mom, her brother, her friends… How is she supposed to adjust to this? How can anyone? She pushes what she's learned deep inside, unable to absorb any of it and not wanting to either.

She needs to cry, only nothing comes out. In its place, a void opens inside her rib cage that folds onto itself and takes whatever remains of her with it.

She should've never left that parking lot.

Chapter Two

The air inside Costco grows stagnant by the hour. A curtain divides her space into a coffin-like rectangle. She knows she's not alone, but she doesn't know how many others are with her. At night, she hears crying and some pain-filled moans, but mostly crying.

Three days after waking, she's taken off the monitors and IVs. Her dad holds a straw to her lips, and her throat burns as she manages only the smallest amount of water, but once it feels more like flesh than scab, she can swallow more at a time.

Picking up the glass is another issue. Her bitten hand stiffened into a claw, and there isn't anything she can do about it until the stitches she needed two years ago come out.

She's given a mountain of medications and vitamins, and every four to six hours, her dad gives her pain injections from a needle she still can't feel. Looking at her body now, she finds it hard to believe she once glided around a tennis court.

By day six, she leaves her bed for the first time. It takes her dad, and another woman named Lauren, to help her.

CeCe's legs shake and she groans in agony as pinpricks cascade in waves through her abs and down to her quads, hamstrings, and calf muscles. Every part of her wants to lie down, but she wants this. Needs this. She pushes through, and eventually she's on her feet, gasping for air.

After her dad counts to ten, they lay her down. They do this three times a day—the counts extending to fifteen, twenty, and thirty—until she can get up on her own with the help of a pulley she uses with her good hand.

This is her new reality. She's stuck in a body that doesn't feel like her own.

Lights flicker overhead. It could be morning or the middle of the night. Time doesn't really exist here.

She's been awake for hours thinking about her mom and Teddy. A hollowness opens in her chest when she remembers the last morning before the Infection. The last day of school with Riley and Leyton. The last time she'd heard her brother's laugh or seen her mom's smile. Her eyes burn with impending tears and the moments she'll never have again.

Her dad comes through the bleached curtain.

"How'd you sleep?" he asks.

"Not well," she says, wiping her eyes as she sits up. Her throat's still sore, but at least her voice has stopped cracking. "Whoever's next to me kept screaming."

He lowers his voice. "She wasn't as lucky as you. Her injuries are much worse. She's in a lot of pain and…other things."

CeCe glances toward the curtain, the thin sheet that separates them. Her bitten hand throbs. She understands the "other things." The injuries that broke the inside. A creeping despair that coats her bones and pulls at her veins. She feels that too.

Her dad sets a walker next to her bed. "Think you're ready for this?"

Part of her isn't. Once she sees what's outside, she can't unsee it.

But she has to know.

He helps her up. Her legs shake and prickles shoot up her thighs. She plants her hands on each side of the walker; her stocking feet seem so far below her. Her triceps ache as she pushes toward the curtain, and inch by inch, she moves outside of it.

When she does, her breath catches.

Lines of curtains stretch along the warehouse, disappearing around corners where she guesses are even more rows of ex-Infected.

So many. How could this have happened to so many?

***

As the weeks turn into months, CeCe has seen men, women, and children. Many with deep scars and missing limbs. They pass each through the rows, most often without a glance.

She spends most of her time in the physical therapy room, which was once the loading dock. Her dad's friend, Lauren, leads the sessions, and there CeCe learns to use her hand again.

She's gone from picking up a pencil, to a glass, to dressing herself.

Every day, she's getting stronger and her muscles scream from the exertion. The constant numbness makes everything feel off. Her dad says it should subside. He can't know for sure. It's only a hope. Like everything else in this place.

Her dad meets her at the entry of her physical therapy session. Today, Lauren says, is the squeeze test. CeCe has to pick up squishy balls and grip each one as hard as she can. Even numb, it feels like razor blades are slicing through her flesh. She hates Squeeze Day.

"I have news," he says.

She thinks of Teddy and clenches her bitten hand.

"You're getting discharged. You're coming home."

It isn't the news she was hoping for, but it's good news nonetheless.

Her dad pauses for a moment. "Nothing is going to be like how you remembered. You'll have to prepare yourself as much as you can for the shock."

She tries to understand, tries to be ready.

When she thinks of home, she sees the Luken boys riding their bikes up and down the winding cul-de-sac, and Mrs. Morgan outside with her rose bushes.

But when she finally sees what's left of her hometown—storefront windows busted out, puddles of dried blood on the sidewalks, smoke billowing in the distance, and the abandoned houses on her street—no amount of preparation could've ever been enough.

Whatever this is, it isn't home anymore. It's only a warped version that has been twisted and shaken and discarded like a broken toy. If this is all that's left, then why come back? The Infection should've taken it all.

A few days after she's home, her dad takes her to the City Center Mall parking lot where she and her mother were both gassed, along with countless others. Her mom didn't have a funeral. No one did. All the bodies were burned together.

It's the closest she'll get to her mother's final resting place.

They pick roses that overrun the backyard and make bouquets with ribbon they find in her mom's craft room. Her mom's body was found about fifty yards from CeCe. Close enough that if she knew, she would've crawled over the dead and dying to get to her mom.

And now, a dark stain is all that remains of her, one among so many others.

Her mother died in front of Divine Nails Salon, where posters of perfect acrylics still cling to the glass windows. CeCe and her mom used to go there every four weeks for their mother/daughter date. This is where she'd come as an Infected, and somehow CeCe had made it there too.

Like somewhere in their fevered brains, they were still connected, even then. The Infection took everything, but it didn't take that.

"How'd she die?"

"She was bitten in the neck," Dad tells her. "The virus kept her alive, but the cure…"

"Killed her," CeCe says quietly. "Did she…did she…"

She chokes on the last word:

Suffer.

He shakes his head. "I don't think so."

She sets the flowers down. They stand together in a parking lot larger than five football fields that once held thousands of the Infected.

Its desolation is as bottomless and expansive as the emptiness in her chest. A circling black hole of the person she used to be.

Chapter Three

Cannons boom in the distance in three ten-minute intervals. They go off every morning to draw the Infected from their hiding places in a chain that leads them to the gas fields of Folsom Prison. It used to bother her, but like everything else, she's gotten used to it.

CeCe stretches out her arm as her dad tightens the rubber tourniquet. He presses his finger down, looking for a vein. This has become their routine. Once a week for the last one hundred and twenty-two days since she'd been cured.

Her half-eaten bowl of bland oatmeal cools next to her. Her dad puts the needle against her skin. She looks away out of habit, anticipating the sting of the needle even though she never feels it. Lingering numbness is common among the Cured and might even be permanent.

"Done," he says.

He sticks a cotton ball to her arm and wraps it in place with medical tape before gathering the tubes and labeling them with a Sharpie.

"I should have the results later today, but I don't expect any change. I'm sure you're perfectly normal," he says with a smile she doesn't return. "You have everything?"

Her GED textbook is on the counter. It's out of place here. A relic. "Yeah."

He reaches over and takes her gloved hand, the one hiding her scarred bite mark. The glove is a cheap blue mitten of which she'd cut off the top. The material probably cost no more than a nickel and it'd sat at the bottom of her dresser drawer for years, ever since she pulled it out of her Christmas stocking.

Now she can't take it off.

Without it, she feels untethered, like a balloon caught in a crosswind.

When the smell of over-wear forces her to put it through the washing machine, her hand opens and closes, as if by some reflex, until it's back on.

"This is a good thing, CeCe," he says. "Back to normal. That's what we all want, right?"

He releases her hand. She glances at the family picture on the wall next to the dining room table. Her mom, dad, and Teddy. The photo was a few years old even before the Infection.

Her dad follows her gaze.

"Your mom would want this for you. You know she would."

"Yeah, probably."

Her dad gets up and attaches his CAVE badge to his shirt pocket. Center for Applied Virology and Epidemiology. It's a big jump from his days at Westside Pet Hospital.

She watches him gather his things. His coffee, his laptop, his keys, her blood, which goes into a Styrofoam cooler. He turns to her when he's done. "You ready?"

Slinging her bag over her shoulder, she follows him out the door, passing her tennis racquet propped in the corner where it's stood since her eighteenth birthday.

Dust coats its black strings, and she has to stop herself from reaching out to grab it, still forgetting sometimes that tennis doesn't exist anymore.

No tennis team, no tennis friends, no tennis scholarship.

That part of her life is over.

She shuts the door behind her and gets in her dad's silver sedan. They pull out of the driveway. The street she grew up on stretches before them. The once pristine lawns are dried and yellowed or overgrown. Planks of plywood cover the windows of most of the houses. Only two other families live here now: the Morgans and the Lukens.

The Morgans are Survivors, but the Lukens are like her, the Cured. They had five- and seven-year-old boys, Connor and Hudson. CeCe used to babysit them on date nights. Only there's no Connor and Hudson anymore on their bikes, and Mr. and Mrs. Luken avert their gaze every time they see her.

Her dad turns onto the main road. Traffic lights blink at the intersections where they've been stuck red ever since the power grid was turned back on. They come to a stop next to Ed's MiniMart where in the past she'd grab soda, gum, candy—anything really—just to see Mack.

He was a senior when she was a freshman and she had a crush on him, but told no one, not even Leyton. He'd flirt with her, or she liked to think he did, but Mack was like that. Friendly with everyone. He had a lot of girlfriends.

All the windows of Ed's MiniMart are busted out now. The shelves are turned over, spilling into the parking lot. In red spray paint, someone had written the word "Repent" in large letters on its cinder blocks.

Parked out front are white vans with a crew from the Sanitation Department going in and out in hazmat suits, cleaning, getting it ready to reopen. For what this time? Household supplies? Medicines? They carry a body bag out from the store. Before the Infection, such a thing would have shocked her. Now, she watches. What if it is Mack in that bag?

Her dad drives on and she turns her gaze forward, the tires humming underneath her feet. Franklin High School isn't much farther. In her memories, it's like before, but it won't be. She's been cured long enough to know that. The car comes to a stop next to the stairs of the school, its red brick front towering above them.

She only had three months left of her senior year. The best year of her life, everyone said. Only it wasn't. On her last real day, she remembers taking a final in chemistry. And how she worried about it because science didn't come as easy for her as it did her dad. Sometimes, she still wonders what she got on it.

Her dad turns to her. "I know you must be nervous. First day jitters, but it's going to be all right."

Nerves have nothing to do with it. She doesn't want to go in. In there is every good memory she ever had, and if she goes inside, it will be replaced with her post-Infection existence. She'll never have it back. Not ever.

She wants to tell her dad this, that she can't lose another good thing, but he wouldn't listen. For him, this is part of the road back to humanity, as if that were even possible. It's all pointless. Pointless like this GED program. As if a GED would make a difference in anything.

As if it could make her forget.

"You have your phone?" he asks.

She runs her hand along her pocket and feels the bump of the flip phone. Cell service was one of the first bullet points in the Human Race Reconfiguration Initiative. Next is expanded Wi-Fi. The Department of Rehabilitation has been aggressive in Silicon Valley, curing the Infected by the hundreds only to shove them behind computer screens so everyone can get back online to watch YouTube.

Her dad has been an integral part of it all. He used to deworm dogs and cats on a daily basis. Now he meets with government officials, goes to debriefings, monitors the cure-versus-Infection rates, and works in a lab.

The Savior of the Infected.

Only she misses the local veterinarian with his samples of the latest prescription diets for animals with IBS.

"Yeah," she says. "I have my phone."

"Make sure it stays on you, okay?"

"Sure."

She watches a few students make their way up the stairs past the Rehab Caseworkers in their black pants, white shirts, and clipboards. They came to her house a week ago with paperwork for the program.

"Reports from the Sanitation Department indicate that the school's on track for reopening next Monday," they told her, but they were addressing her dad.

She hadn't wanted to go, but he was too enthusiastic about it to be deterred, and she didn't have the energy to argue. She didn't have the energy for most anything since the moment she woke up with her face pressed against asphalt.

She gets out of the car and shuts the door. Her dad rolls down the window.

"I'll pick you up after school."

"Okay."

"Have a good day, sweetheart. I love you."

"Love you too."

She turns for the stairs. The caseworkers watch her as she climbs toward them, a man and a woman. The woman moves in her direction. CeCe doesn't remember her name. Emily or Lilly. "Good to see you," she says. "You'll be in Room 114. Do you need help finding it?"

Room 114 was Mr. Wilcox's class. She'd taken freshman algebra with him and then calculus her junior year. She shakes her head. "I've got it."

Emily or Lilly smiles, but it isn't genuine. It's part of her job. CeCe doesn't hold it against her. Being here is a show, and they all have their parts to play.

Inside the school, the floors are swept clean, and walls are naked with new paint. It smells of cleaning solution and bleach, and her shoes squeak on the linoleum.

She stops at the display cabinets near the school office. The glass has been broken and shards of it still linger along the edge where the broom had missed them. She hovers where her team tennis photo had been and all her friends were smiling in their green-and-black uniforms with the Franklin Falcon on their chest.

They'd taken State that year. Right after, she'd gotten a scholarship offer from Ohio to play for the Buckeyes. It was one of the happiest days of her life. Now it seems like a joke.

She walks past the display toward the gym. A chained padlock snakes around its handles with a "Do Not Enter" sign pasted on the front.

Then she turns down the hall where deep scratches etch many of the classroom doors and metal lockers pucker with dents. A man in a sanitation suit wipes down a wall where there once had been a bloodstain, work left over from the Sanitation Department, she supposes. He looks at her and then dips the sponge into a bucket by his feet.

She stops at Room 114 and opens the door. A few of Mr. Wilcox's posters still cling to the walls, a kitten holding on to a rope with a "Hang in There" slogan, and a goldfish wearing a shark fin with "Mindset" as the caption.

Five students are in the class. They keep their gazes down as she walks past them. One boy has a long scar along the side of his cheek. Another girl is missing an ear and part of her nose. Others hide whatever scars they have under layers of sweatshirts and pants. She stretches out her gloved hand. The skin aches with the strain.

With her GED book still in hand, she heads toward her old desk, dropping her bag by her feet. Inside is one notebook, one pencil, one pen, an old graphing calculator her dad scavenged from storage, and her lunch: a peanut butter and jelly sandwich and a packet of fruit snacks.

A girl comes in, sees CeCe, and takes the desk next to her. She has a shiny bald spot the size of a tennis ball where her hair had been yanked out.

"I know you," she says and smiles. "Not really know you. I was a sophomore, but I watched a few of your games. You were amazing."

"Thanks."

"I'm Savannah."

"CeCe."

"I know." She smiles again. "And your dad is Dr. Campbell. My aunt lights a candle for him every day like he's a saint. I suppose he is in a way."

The door yanks open and another girl hurries in, taking a seat the farthest from the other students. She hunches over the desk, her whole body pulling together as if it were held by rubber bands, ready to snap at any moment.

"Oh my god," Savannah whispers. "I thought the Survivors never left their houses."

"A Survivor?"

CeCe's never seen one up close. Her dad, she supposes, is a Survivor, but he'd been in the CAVE for most of the Infection. She feels bad thinking that way, minimizing it, but he was inside a heavily guarded military compound, while outside Infected hordes roamed in packs of twenty, fifty, sometimes even by the hundreds, or so she'd overheard from talk at Costco when they didn't think she was listening.

She looks at the girl, wondering where she'd been, how she'd done it. Where she hid, got food, stayed unbitten. Was she with others? Like the Morgans, who had each other? She keeps wondering about this until she realizes she's staring and the Survivor locks gazes with her.

CeCe turns away, self-consciousness washing over her at getting caught gawking. But the feeling wilts as quickly as it comes, absorbing back into the numbness.

Savannah, though, doesn't seem to care about staring at the girl.

"My aunt says the Survivors are still scared of us," she tells me. "Like we're going to go all Hannibal Lecter again. *Hello, Clarice.*"

The door opens and closes and then opens again. An older woman backs into the classroom. She struggles with her crutch as she makes her way inside.

"Hello," she says and moves to the front of the class. The bottom of her left trouser leg is clipped tight where her foot is missing. "I'm Ms. Dobson. I'll be helping you prepare for the GED test in three months."

Ms. Dobson's face is strained, as all their faces are, but she's youngish, CeCe realizes, and had been happy once. She can tell by the way the lines around her eyes and mouth still want to curl up, except they don't.

"I'm thrilled to be back teaching," she says. "Even under these circumstances. Perhaps I should say *especially* under these circumstances. I was a professor in the English department at Stanford. I was teaching there before this whole mess and then I came here to visit my... Well, I suppose that doesn't matter." She takes a breath. "This is my first time teaching high school students and I can't wait to get to know all of you. Why don't we go through introductions?" She turns to the boy closest to the door. "How about we start with you?"

"Brandon," he replies without looking up.

"Nice to meet you, Brandon. And you are?" she says to the girl near him.

"Amelia."

Ms. Dobson goes around the room, addressing each student. Everyone mutters their names. There are a few CeCe thinks she recognizes, most she doesn't. Ten in all are in the class. Last is the Survivor.

"Olivia," she says.

"Olivia." Ms. Dobson nods. "Happy to have you here."

CeCe wonders if Ms. Dobson can also tell Olivia's a Survivor. Or if she already knows because the caseworkers told her.

"Now that we all know each other's names," she says, "why don't we turn to the English section of our books. We might as well start with that, seeing it's what I know best. It looks like it begins with some poetry."

Shuffling pages fill the silence that's almost deafening.

Ms. Dobson begins reading a poem by Emily Dickinson. "Because I could not stop for Death, he kindly stopped for me...." She pauses for a long time, long enough to draw attention. CeCe glances up. Ms. Dobson's lips are tight and the book trembles in her hands.

"I think..." she says, going through the pages. "I think we...here...let's start with Part One of 'A Rose for Emily' instead and complete the questions at the end. We only have a few hours today and that'll be a good transition into our new schedule for all of us. We can read quietly on our own and discuss our answers tomorrow."

Mrs. Dobson moves behind the desk where she sits and stays.

CeCe finds "A Rose for Emily" and stares at the first paragraph, at the first sentence, unable to go any further. She tries. Sometimes she hears a page turn, and she wonders how they're able to do it, to focus. She listens to Savannah taking long deep breaths as she rubs her fingers along the bald spot of her scalp.

Minutes tick by as CeCe keeps trying to read, but it seems so meaningless. What does it even matter anymore?

She looks up from the page to Ms. Dobson, to the clock, to the door. She can't stay in this room like a leftover in a Tupperware container. She gets up to go to the bathroom. She expects Ms. Dobson to ask her where she's going or maybe glance in her direction, but she stares out the window.

Pushing open the door, CeCe leaves the class. The bathroom is up the hall where signs in glitter and big block letters announce homecoming, football, and baseball games. Many she'd put up herself. The years of tape and thumbtacks had taken pieces of the paint and drywall, pockmarking them into something of a dot matrix.

She stops at a familiar locker. She doesn't want to, but it's as if her feet won't move any farther.

It's not hers. It's Riley's.

She'd thought of him so many times these last few months and being here, next to where they'd meet after class, was like coming across his ghost. She'd known Riley nearly all her life and like everything else, he's gone.

They met at a tennis camp when they were in first grade. They couldn't hit a single ball the entire time, but they became friends and then their parents became friends, and every weekend was spent at each other's houses.

When Riley had moved on to baseball, she was devastated, but they still remained close. For a time, she looked at Riley as another brother, but as they got older, she started looking at him differently. Only, he never noticed, and she thought he never would.

Her junior year, he asked her to the Winter Dance. She thought maybe it was a friend thing, but he kissed her that night and they'd been together ever since.

She stares at Riley's locker. At the new and the old scratches. It's been dented. *When?* She wonders. *How?* She runs her fingers along the curved metal and toward the combination lock. She knows what it is and twists to the first number, hearing the familiar click, but unable to go any further.

All that's left of Riley is inside. Pictures of them, his notebooks, his things. And she can't. She's not ready.

Leaving the combination on the first digit, she hurries to the bathroom to shut herself away from memories of Riley. She expects a sanctuary, but it's worse—a vault untouched by the Kill Virus.

The tarnished mirrors, the stalls with names engraved into its doors. The too-thin sheets of toilet paper. She closes her eyes and can almost hear the voices of students out in the halls, a sound of nothing and everything at once. The life of the school bleeding through from the past and washing over her numb skin. She can't escape, not even here.

Her heart wallops in her chest like a fist punching her insides. It's too much being back at Franklin. She shouldn't have come. She shouldn't have let her dad talk her into it.

She braces herself against the white porcelain sink, trying to force away the pressure of the past. Of Riley. Of Leyton. They don't exist anymore.

She unrolls her glove. The scar from the bite mark glares up at her, red with puffy edges and an outline of the teeth that sunk deep. It's still painful. Almost fresh. She turns on the water and runs her hand under it to cool the burning, leaving it there for a long time.

When her breathing returns to normal, she turns off the faucet. She doesn't know how long she's been gone. It could've been fifteen minutes or an hour. The pads of her fingers are puckered and waterlogged. She gets a paper towel, dries her hand, and drops the used towel in the trash.

She avoids looking at Riley's locker when she goes back to the classroom. When she opens the door, Ms. Dobson is still staring out the window. No one pays any attention as she comes back in, no one but Olivia, who clicks her pen in and out.

Savannah is already writing in a notebook. She's made it to the questions at the end of the section.

CeCe sits back at her desk and stares at the first sentence again. She forces herself to concentrate. She manages only the first paragraph before her mind wanders again. She thinks about eating her sandwich. She opens her lunch bag, but it's gone. Has she already eaten it? She can't remember.

Eventually, Ms. Dobson stirs, reaching for her crutch. "We did it," she says. Hearing her voice in the room feels strange after so much silence. "Our first day is complete. We should all be proud of ourselves. Please finish the questions for tomorrow."

CeCe grabs her bag and leaves the classroom. Savannah hurries up after her.

"I only have two questions left," she says. "How'd you do?"

"Not good."

They pass the empty display cabinets, the dimmed school office, and through the front doors into the gray light. Clouds have gathered since they arrived, and she can smell rain in the air. Even now, even after everything that has happened, her first thought is that the tennis courts will be wet, and she won't be able to play. It's like an impulse she can't control.

"There's my aunt," Savannah says, pointing to a minivan. "See you tomorrow?"

CeCe can't imagine having to go through another day of this, but worse, tomorrow it's five hours instead of three.

Five hours of sitting, unable to think, unable to read, unable to do anything. Everything is a reminder of what it was before. Always the "before" and what will never be again. But it isn't her choice. She'll be back at Franklin and its room of strays whether she wants to or not.

"Yeah," she says. "See you tomorrow."

Savannah bounds down the stairs and over to her aunt. She gives a final wave as they pull away. CeCe waves back and watches until they disappear down the street.

She searches for her dad's car among the few idling, but he's not there. The other students shamble off. Some down the street, others to waiting vehicles. Olivia darts down the steps and jumps into the passenger side of an old Toyota truck. Olivia looks up at her as the driver takes off, black smoke erupting from the exhaust, and vanishes around a corner.

CeCe's the only one left.

Ms. Dobson comes out the front doors. "Are you still waiting for your ride?" she asks.

CeCe nods.

"Would you like me to take you home?"

CeCe can almost see the battle within Ms. Dobson: the person who she was before the Kill Virus and the one after. Ms. Dobson post-Kill doesn't really want to give her a ride. It's not the lack of concern. It's the prospect of having to do it.

"My dad will be here."

"Are you sure?"

"Yeah, I'm sure."

"All right then," she says. "Have a good afternoon."

Ms. Dobson places one hand on the railing, the other holding her crutch. It takes her a while to get to the bottom. When she does, she turns back to CeCe, giving her a final wave before going down the sidewalk to wherever her car's parked.

CeCe gets out her phone and calls her dad. It goes to voicemail. She texts him. It takes her longer than it did with her old phone. She leaves a simple, "School's out," and then puts it back in her pocket. She sits on the steps as the first sprinkles of rain blot the concrete.

Once her hair starts to cling to her face and the dampness grows stickier through her sweatshirt, she checks her phone. It's been an hour. She thinks of calling again and then changes her mind.

Her house isn't far. Only two miles or a little more. She used to run that at least three times a week. But now she doubts she'd be able to run half a block without getting winded.

As she stands there, the open space presses against her. She's been outside longer than she has in months. Clutching her GED study guide and notebook, she goes down the stairs and turns for home.

Trash clogs the gutters of the streets. Photographs, a wallet, a broken cell phone, a stained baby sock. It's quiet and still early, but no one is out.

There used to be joggers, people walking their dogs, but now it's empty. No one stays out longer than necessary. They either closet themselves in their homes, or in the community centers for those who have no surviving family. It's against the rules to be alone.

Seems counterintuitive, considering.

A man watches her from his front window. It would've freaked her out before, having him standing there, unmoving, but nothing will happen. He won't come out. He won't speak to her. He won't do anything. The need to hurt, to harm, to take—it's gone. The only thing left is existing, and most don't even want that.

Her dad has talked about the suicide rates when he didn't think she was listening. The higher-ups hadn't planned for that. They thought the cure would be enough. There'd be a transition period, sure, but they counted on an eagerness to rebuild once the Cured had physically healed.

It was the opposite. Even though they'd been brought back, this was not a world anyone wanted to return to. The Rehabilitation Program became their solution—its aim getting everything and everyone back to normal.

As she approaches Ed's MiniMart, a movement catches her attention. She thinks it's a cat, but it's only a plastic grocery bag scraping against the asphalt. That's one thing she hasn't seen much of since returning. Animals. Sometimes at night, she hears the random bark of a dog and wonders if it's okay, if it's happy, or if it's trying to make it to the next day like everyone else.

She hears something, and her feet stop mid-step. Her heart thumps in her chest as she listens. She hears it again. It's chuckling. Someone's chuckling. She glances over at Ed's where a Sanitation Department van sits outside, but the others that had been there earlier are gone. The outside windows have already been replaced, and a fresh coat of paint covers "Repent" even though the outline is still visible.

The laughter comes again, followed by low, animated voices. She heads toward the store and peers inside. The shelves have been righted and pushed against a far wall and the counter cleared, but no one's in there.

There's an excited shout and she jumps, almost hitting the glass with her face. She moves along the front until she can see down the side of the building. There, she finds three guys huddled together over a tablet. Their hazmat suits are unzipped with the arms hanging around their waists. They look so normal as they hover together, and her stomach twists in irritation, in jealousy.

She's about to turn around when one of them glances up at her, a sloppy grin still on his face. A jolt of familiarity thrums down her spine. She recognizes him from somewhere. Her mouth opens and shuts as his smile fades.

He stares at her in confusion.

"Hey." He stands. "Hey. Do I know you?"

His friends abandon the tablet, turning their gazes on her.

CeCe takes a step backward. Then another.

It's him. The college boy.

***

Leyton arranged dinner at Mason's as a surprise with her entire tennis team. Riley was supposed to be there but had baseball practice.

They sat around the table laughing, gossiping, enjoying the moment because it would be their last year together. CeCe had a tennis scholarship for Ohio State, and Leyton was already set to go to UCLA. The others were attending Chico or Reno. They'd get to be together on the West Coast—close enough to drive and plan trips—while she would be nearly on the other side of the country. At least she'd have Riley with her. He was going to Ohio State too.

After dinner, Leyton and CeCe waited for an Uber, shivering in the cool spring air as police sirens shrilled in the distance. Leyton followed the Uber's progress on her phone.

"Going up D now," Leyton said, winding a lock of her blonde hair between her fingers as she studied the screen. "And…he's stopped again. Jesus. Has this guy hit every red light?"

Someone groaned behind them and CeCe turned. Outside of the lights of the restaurant, a young guy in a Chico State sweatshirt stood hunched over, gripping his stomach. He groaned louder.

"I think he needs help," she said to Leyton. "We should call someone."

Leyton looked in his direction. "He's probably just wasted and got ditched by his buddies."

CeCe had seen her fair share of wasted college guys, but this was different. Like he might need some medical help. She didn't want to be responsible if he died of alcohol poisoning on the side of

Mason's. She could already hear the newscast playing out in her mind: *College Boy Dies while Franklin Falcon Tennis Players Catch Their Uber.*

Before she could get her phone, a howl wrenched her attention back to the guy. The sound didn't seem human.

"Call an ambulance," CeCe ordered.

"Where are you going?" Leyton asked. "The Uber's almost here."

The click of CeCe's stilettos sounded like gunshots as she approached him.

"Are you okay?"

He didn't answer.

"We're getting help. Hold on."

His eyes were squeezed shut. Sweat trickled down his temples and he stumbled forward. CeCe reached out of instinct to pull him up.

In one quick movement, he twisted his head and sank his teeth into her hand. She screamed as pain ripped through her skin. For one nauseating moment, he turned his eyes on her, crazed and bloodshot, as he clamped down like a rabid dog.

CeCe screamed for Leyton, who clocked him with her elbow as if swinging the perfect forehand. A loud crack echoed in CeCe's ears, and he finally let go. He reached for her again, his jaw hanging crookedly, as Leyton pulled her away.

CeCe cradled her hand, blood spilling onto the street as restaurant patrons funneled out to help. She tried to form a fist, but her gnarled flesh was already swelling and turning purple. Even while the night filled with screams, all she could think about was her scholarship, and that once Ohio State found out about this, they'd take it away.

***

But she'd lost so much more.

Seeing his face and his teeth embedded in her skin is the last real thing she remembers before waking up. She'd thought of him often.

Hoped he hadn't made it. But even on the off chance that he had, she never expected to see him again.

But here he is, staring at her from the side of Ed's MiniMart.

She totters backward, her heel catching on the side of a curb. Her notebook slips out from underneath the GED study guide and falls to the ground like a broken bird's wing. She goes to pick it up, but he's coming over to her. She abandons the notebook and hurries down the street, walking at a pace she hasn't attempted since before the Infection. Her leg muscles burn with the exertion.

"Hey," he calls. "Wait."

She keeps going.

"Hey," he says again. "Do I know you?"

She shakes her head.

He keeps calling her, but she doesn't stop and doesn't turn around.

Her hand throbs underneath her glove, aching from the teeth that had pierced her flesh.

The teeth that had turned her into a monster.

Chapter Four

CeCe slows when she gets to her street, her hand still throbbing. Her mind circles around the guy next to Ed's, the guy she'd tried to help that night at Mason's. The one who'd Infected her. Why? Why had she run into him, of all people? Why not Mack? Or Rowan from Spanish class? Literally anyone else but him. She closes her eyes, squeezing them shut, squeezing him out.

She passes the Morgans' house. The blinds crack open. It's the only sign they're still alive. Mrs. Morgan used to walk the sidewalk with her basket, giving everyone clippings of her roses like the ones growing in her family's backyard. But CeCe hasn't seen her once since coming home. Her or her husband. Savannah had said the Survivors are still afraid of them. Maybe that's why.

Coming up her walkway, CeCe gets the spare key from under the mat and opens the door. She goes in and drops her backpack on the counter, then flexes her gloved hand.

Her phone rings. It's her dad. She picks up.

"Oh god, CeCe," he says. "I forgot today was an early day. I was on my way to come get you when I saw your messages."

She's not mad. The walk was nice until it wasn't. Seeing that college guy again brought all the horror back. Not only when she was Infected, but everything he took from her in that moment. Her friends. Her family. Her world. It's a pain that goes away only by forgetting.

"It's okay. I'm home," she says.

"You walked?" His voice rises. "Are you okay? Did anything…"

"No," she says. "It was fine."

"There's still Infected out there."

"I thought they were out of the city?"

"Mostly, yes, but not all. It's not safe. You should've waited at the school—"

"Dad. I'm home. Nothing happened."

He sighs. "I'm coming now. See you in a few."

"Yeah, okay."

CeCe hangs up. Her legs ache and her stomach is telling her to eat. She goes into the kitchen and makes another peanut butter and jelly sandwich with bread her dad makes in her mom's bread maker.

It hurts to spread the peanut butter with her hand, but it's the easiest thing to make. All they have in the cupboards are mostly things that could be preserved: canned vegetables, canned meats, canned everything. And for the things that weren't, expiration dates sort of went out the window. Frozen two-year-old butter still tasted pretty much the same as fresh.

She's about to take the sandwich to her room when she glances at her dad's computer. He's had his finger on every project since the cure, including the Sanitation Department, and she wonders if he has information about the college guy.

Even if he does, does she even want to know? Will it make a difference if she knows his name? It's not like it'll change anything.

Sitting her sandwich next to the computer, she jiggles the mouse. Her dad hasn't let her on it since she's come home, not exactly saying she can't, but making it obvious he doesn't want her to go searching. Once, when she wanted to look at some old photos, he came rushing in, all flustered, saying, "Hey, hey, I've got important work things on there. Let me close some files first."

And even then, he'd hovered over her, watching every file she opened. It was odd. He'd never been possessive over his computer. Not even when Teddy had downloaded a virus and nearly wiped out the entire hard drive because he clicked on some ad for a game he thought looked cool.

The screen lights up and asks for the password. She enters the one he uses for everything, a combination of their birthdays and first initials. It unlocks to a screenshot of them at Disneyland in front of Cinderella's Castle. She and her mom had their arms wrapped around each other, wearing mouse ears. Dad was holding Teddy. She stares at the picture. What she wouldn't give to go back. To relive that moment. To feel her mother's embrace one more time.

Opening the documents file, she starts pulling up folders. She's not sure what she's looking for, but her dad will be home soon and when he does, this hunt will end.

Most of the files are saved under a series of numbers. Or numbers and letters. She clicks on one and it opens a pdf. It's lab work results with no name or anything else connected to it. She's not sure what she's looking at. Numbers and lists of ranges, and numbers that say abnormal, but it means nothing without context.

She goes through more folders, clicks on more random files, but it's more of the same, nothing about people or departments, or guys found wearing a Chico State sweatshirt.

She jolts at the swoosh of an incoming email, and she shakes from the adrenaline rush. She pulls up her dad's mailbox. The message has a red flag with a bolded subject line saying, "Classified P73-7 Briefing."

If this were any other time, something labeled "Classified" wouldn't've been sent over email, but then again no one had email anymore except for the Initiative, the new government running things and all its factions, including the CAVE.

She's never heard her dad talk about P73-7. Obviously, he wouldn't if it was classified. She can't open the email. He'd know. But she goes through his other emails. He never deletes them. Not even before when he'd have over a thousand unopened emails from Pottery Barn to VetMeds. She does a search for P73-7. She finds at least fifty of them. They're all labeled with the same "Classified P73-7 Debriefing." But those he's read and so can she.

Update on ongoing observation. No change.

She goes to the next.

Results. Stable.

She's about to open another when keys jangle in the door. Dad's home.

She clicks out of his email and closes the screen as he comes in, carrying two large bags from the food bank. He smiles as he sets them down on the counter. "We'll feast tonight. And…" He digs into one of the bags and pulls out a can of peaches. "I have dessert."

They make spaghetti. He heats the sauce and CeCe does the noodles. They use a little bit of Crisco for butter, to give it an extra burst, but it wouldn't have mattered. Everything's bland like unflavored rice cakes, and no amount of seasoning changes it.

The peaches, though, they still have the sweetness she remembers. It's nice to have a little of what used to be. As she rolls the noodles around her fork, she thinks of the latest P73-7 email. She watched her dad read it while he was cooking, his face expressionless.

He slices a piece of bread and offers it to her. "Outside of me dropping the ball at pickup, which will not happen again, how was your first day?"

She takes it from him, thinking of the guy from Ed's, along with the ache in her hand. She shrugs. "It was okay. I have homework."

"That's fast."

He shovels a forkful of noodles in his mouth. "How was it like being back at Franklin?"

"It was Franklin."

"Was it, you know, strange?"

Strange is not the word she'd use. Foreign, perhaps. As if the school had been moved to an alternate universe where the guy from Twilight Zone provides narration. But those are her thoughts and best to keep them to herself.

"A little."

After dinner, she helps with the dishes before going up to her room. She opens her GED book and tries to read the story again. It's easier. Maybe because she's in her own space, but it still takes her a long time. She opens her backpack to get out her notebook and then curses herself when she remembers she dropped it at Ed's. But inside her pack is a single piece of folded paper. She takes it out and opens it.

It's a Xeroxed copy of a demon-looking creature with a goat's head and bat wings and hooves standing on a pile of bodies. Its eyes are wild, and something like blood drips from its fangs. In blocked letters underneath, someone had written: Judgment Day of the Unclean.

CeCe stares at it. It should bother her, and maybe somewhere in her brain it does. But right then, it's more of a surprise. She wonders who put it in her bag. Savannah was the closest to her desk, but it seems really unlikely, since the "Unclean" is obviously Infected. That rules everyone out in the class by default, leaving only Olivia. It had to be her.

That might not be fair, but who else could it be? She must've put it in her bag when she left to go to the bathroom, except Savannah was right there. She would've noticed. *Someone* would have noticed. Wouldn't they? She thinks back at how Ms. Dobson's gaze never left the window or Savannah's eyes from the textbook. Maybe they hadn't and Olivia slipped it in her bag while everyone was lost in their own thoughts.

She holds the picture in her hand, debating whether to show it to her dad. But she has no definite proof it was Olivia and doesn't want to start something if it wasn't. Instead, she places it back in her bag and finds some paper in her old binder and begins answering the first section questions. Her hand aches when she's done.

Getting in her pajamas, she turns off the light. It's quiet in the house. She can hear her dad clicking the keyboard on his laptop. Was he writing about P73-7? She'll have to check his Sent folder tomorrow if she can get a chance. Maybe there's more information in there.

She lies in bed, stretching out her fingers, bending them as far back as they'll go. She thinks of the guy at Ed's and his teeth permanently etched in her body as he laughed with his friends like nothing mattered and everything was A-OK.

She falls asleep with him in her thoughts and wakes with him still there when her alarm goes off. The bright light of the morning filters in through her blinds. It's going to be a nice day. Her sheets are damp with sweat from another round of nightmares.

She's had them every night, and she's come to expect them. The screams, the jostling of bodies, teeth, always teeth, and everything tinged in blood like a movie filter.

Before she gets dressed, she strips her sheets and her pillowcases and puts them in the wash. She takes out the spare set and makes her bed, tucking the corners, and knowing that tomorrow she'll have to do this ritual all over again.

Savannah smiles at her when she arrives. Olivia is also there, watching her, but CeCe's watching her in return. She doesn't know whether to confront Olivia about the picture and get some kind of confirmation. She would've done it before without a second thought.

Of course, then she'd have her friends with her. Now she was alone, and everything was too overwhelming to care about almost anything.

CeCe sits at her desk, and before Ms. Dobson comes in, Savannah gives her a full account of what she did yesterday.

They've been watching her aunt's *Friends* collection and she gives her the highlights. Ms. Dobson arrives, cutting off the punchline of Joey's joke, and gets right in discussing the first section of "A Rose for Emily."

She makes the class read the answers they wrote on the discussion questions. Unlike yesterday, she feigns an attempt to get some kind of conversation going about the story, but most don't offer anything other than what they'd put in their answers.

"Any other feelings you had reading this piece?" she asks, looking around, before turning to Brandon. "What about you, Brandon, isn't it? Any other thoughts?"

"Seems like she should pay her taxes."

"Okay."

Ms. Dobson turns to the rest of the class, perhaps hoping someone else will chime in, but no one does. One person rips out the page from their notebook to hand in. Then another follows suit, and another, until the sound fills the classroom.

"Oh," Ms. Dobson starts. "We don't need to turn anything in. Let's hold on to our work until we finish the story. How about we start on Section Two? I'd like to finish it today and maybe skip to the chapter on definitions and grammar usage."

Books open and pages turn. The room goes quiet. Ms. Dobson is back to looking out the window. Savannah to her bald spot. CeCe stares down at Section Two. She gets almost to the end of the page before she stops. The thought won't leave her alone, and there's something she needs to do before she loses the nerve.

She gets up, this time taking her bag with her. She checks to see if Olivia is looking. If she is, she's pretending not to.

She heads toward the bathroom, but that's not where she's going. The college guy wasn't the only one on her mind last night. Riley was too.

She makes it to his locker and before she can think too much about it, she puts in the combo. The lift of the latch echoes like the snapping of bone. Slowly, she swings the door open. Their pictures are still posted on the inside. A selfie of her and Riley taken at lunch. His arm around her, her face buried into his neck.

There's one of all three of them, her, Riley, and Leyton. She thinks of her and Leyton, laughing together in the hotel rooms at away games. Begging Coach Myer to let them be doubles partners. Talking crap to each other during practice.

Leyton would be able to handle all this. It wouldn't be hard for her as it has been for CeCe. But she doesn't know if Leyton's alive or Infected, or Infected and dead and a pile of ash in a crematorium. She might never know, and that's the worst part. She takes the pictures and puts them in her bag.

One of Riley's shirts sits on top of a stack of his books. She brings it to her face. His cologne wafts around her as if he were right beside her and her insides crack and tremble. Her eyes sting, but she tells herself *not here*. She can't lose herself here.

She puts the shirt in her backpack and looks back inside his locker. On top of his algebra book is a nicely bound present in polka-dot wrapping with a teal bow. She picks it up.

"For CeCe," the tag reads.

She stares at his familiar handwriting and jumps as the door to Room 114 opens and shuts.

It's Olivia.

CeCe puts the gift into her bag and zips it up. Shutting the locker, she turns as Olivia comes toward her. If she's going to ask Olivia about the picture, this would be the moment, but she doesn't want to. Not with the memory of Riley's ghost hovering so close.

She stands there as Olivia walks past. The expression on Olivia's face is not quite a smirk, not quite a scowl, but somewhere in between and there's a twinge of animosity in it. Even in her desensitized gut, CeCe senses it.

Why, though? She hasn't done anything to Olivia, but she supposes that doesn't matter. Olivia is going to be a problem, and while she's no stranger to dealing with problematic girls, she didn't think she'd have to be dealing with them now. *At least some things haven't changed.*

Olivia continues to look at her until CeCe averts her gaze and heads back to class.

Ms. Dobson is at the whiteboard, writing sentences. CeCe gets to her desk and starts hunting for some extra paper in her bag, carefully moving Riley's present, when Olivia comes back into the room. She glances at CeCe with a grin on her lips. Obviously, Olivia knows she made her uncomfortable in the hall, and CeCe hates that it was so obvious.

"Let's talk about semicolon usage," Ms. Dobson says. "It's really not all that difficult once it gets broken down."

CeCe gets the paper out and a pen. She keeps her eyes on the front of the class, focusing on Ms. Dobson instead of Olivia.

Ms. Dobson lectures in a way she must have done a hundred times before. Somehow, she manages to pull out some interaction from the students as they nod their heads yes or no. She even gets some volunteers to answer if a semicolon is used or a comma. It feels natural, ordinary even.

CeCe looks over at Olivia. She's sitting back, pulling at her bangs, not paying attention.

After school, CeCe walks out with Savannah. Her aunt is already waiting by the curb when they get outside. Her dad is parked right behind her. She's about to head down the steps when she sees another familiar face, one she would rather stay unfamiliar.

The college boy is leaning against the railing. He has her notebook. When he sees her, he moves forward and climbs the steps toward her.

"See you tomorrow," Savannah says and rushes off, leaving her by herself. CeCe tries to tell her, "No, not yet," but her words are mumbled, and Savannah's already gone.

She looks at her dad and then back at the guy.

"Hey," he says. "I'm Derrick. I, uh, I saw you yesterday. You dropped this. I wasn't sure if it was important or anything, but thought I'd bring it back."

CeCe takes it from him, staying silent. Derrick. She's not sure if she likes him having a name. It makes him a person, and she prefers not to think of him that way.

Even though he looks like any other regular guy in jeans and a long-sleeved shirt. Tallish, fit, sandy hair brushed back and curling around his ears. But she can't help seeing the monster who took everything away from her.

He holds something in his hand and keeps running his thumb over it like maybe he's nervous.

"When I saw you," he tells her, "I got this feeling like I know you or maybe I should know you. Does that seem weird? After everything that's happened..." He shrugs. "I don't know. It might be really weird, but I— Do we?"

She stares at him. Not saying a word.

"Maybe not." He shrugs again. "It was kind of a long shot anyway."

Her dad gets out of the car. She looks over at him. Derrick follows her gaze.

"That's Dr. Campbell, isn't it?"

She doesn't respond.

"He's the guy who discovered the Cure. He's like the closest thing we have to a celebrity these days."

Derrick keeps rubbing whatever he's holding. He turns back and notices her watching.

"Oh," he says and holds it out. It's a large, polished rock with veins of turquoise and gold running through it. It used to sit on the counter at Ed's.

"I found this yesterday," he says. "Sanitation Department, but you probably already figured that out with the suits. Do you like it? Here." He motions to her. "Take it."

She looks at his open palm but doesn't move.

"It's okay," he says and smiles with those teeth that are scarred in her hand. "I won't bite."

She cringes at the words. He sees it on her face.

"Oh shit," he says. "Sorry. I didn't mean it like that. You know, considering. Sometimes I'm such an ass. Here. Please. Take it."

He motions at her again. She reaches out and slowly takes the rock from his grasp. She feels the warmth of his palm on the stone. He puts his hands in his pockets and looks at her as if he's waiting for her to say thank you, but he'll have to wait forever for that.

Her dad waves at her.

She moves past Derrick and down the stairs to her dad's car. Each step is slow and tortured like she's wading through a strong current.

She feels Derrick's eyes on her as she holds on to the rock like it's a hollowed egg.

"Do you know that boy?" her dad asks her when she gets in.

"No."

Her dad puts the car in drive as she looks over at Derrick.

He waves at her.

She doesn't return the wave.

Chapter Five

CeCe sits at the kitchen counter while her dad makes dinner, moving the rock over and over in her palm. Her GED study guide lies open, her returned notebook beside it. She should be reading the second section of "A Rose for Emily" but can't take her eyes off the polished stone.

It reminds her of Derrick. The monster with a name. The monster who apparently returns dropped items and offers gifts.

She glides her thumb over its rich threads of blue. The stone doesn't feel exactly right, like there's a slight dullness. But she's not as numb as she has been. Maybe the feeling in her hand is coming back after all.

Her dad is at the counter. He's mixing soup and canned milk for a broccoli casserole. Frozen chicken boils in a pot on the stove. It's an elaborate meal for them. Almost a delicacy.

"Lauren's coming over for dinner," he says.

That explains all the effort. Lauren is her dad's new "friend." He doesn't have the guts to straight out tell her that Lauren's his girlfriend, but she's known for a while now. She'd hoped Lauren would eventually go away, but she keeps coming around.

He looks at her. "Can you help me with the biscuits?"

"Biscuits?"

"Yeah, they're in the fridge. I came home a little early and made the dough. They're actually pretty easy. I found the recipe in one of your mom's old cookbooks. Had to substitute some. Let's hope it turns out okay."

She gets off the stool, leaving the rock behind. It feels odd parting with it. She opens the refrigerator and gets out a stainless-steel bowl.

Her dad says, "You need to roll it out and cut them. Here." He hands her a cup. "Use the rim of this."

She does as he asks, her fingers tingling with the pressure. It's like they're always half-asleep. She pushes the dough flat as her dad drains the chicken and starts shredding it.

"What's all this for?" she asks.

"Can't a guy make a nice dinner?"

"Yeah, I guess so. But you've never made one with biscuits."

She glances over at him. Something's on his mind. She can tell by the way he digs into the chicken a little too intently.

"Were my test results all right?" she asks.

"What?"

"My blood work. The vials you took yesterday?"

"Oh, that. Yes," he says. "Everything was fine. Stable."

The word used in the emails about P73-7. Stable. A thought works its way into the back of her mind. Was he talking about her? Is she P73-7?

As far as she knows, her dad is the only Survivor in the CAVE living with an ex-Infected. Maybe she's the topic of all those confidential briefings.

The doorbell rings.

"That's Lauren," her dad says and dries his hands on a dishtowel.

She watches him go down the hall and open the door. Lauren comes in, carrying a bottle of wine. Her hair is pulled back, and she's wearing a little makeup.

Lauren's younger than CeCe's mom, and pretty, she supposes. But her features have hardened around the edges. She has the same scarred weariness her dad has from years of trying to stay alive. But when Lauren's with him, she smiles a lot. So does he.

"I didn't know what to bring," she says, holding out the wine. "They had a few bottles at the BX."

Her dad takes it. "It's perfect. Maybe CeCe can even have a little." He turns toward her. "Why don't you set the table, sweetheart?"

"The table?"

"Why not? It'll be nice to eat at the table for once, don't you think? I can finish the biscuits."

"Biscuits," Lauren says. "What a treat."

"That's pretty much what I said," CeCe grumbles under her breath.

She washes the leftover dough from her hands and goes to the cupboard. She gets three plates and carries them to the dining room. They haven't eaten at the table since she's come home, opting for the kitchen island, even when Lauren's here. Why all the effort tonight?

She does a shoddy job. The forks are plopped down. The dishes skew off the mats. The napkins unfolded. Maybe she's being childish, but it doesn't feel right eating in here with her dad and his girlfriend with their family picture hanging above them.

Her dad and Lauren are still in the kitchen. She watches them talking, a conversation that's stilted and full of nerves.

"Was the drive over okay?"

"Oh, sure, it was fine."

"Did Steve get his paperwork turned in?"

"He did."

Their uneasiness laces in the air. Something is off about this. It's more than her dad making a nice dinner. She senses a feeling hinting at the anticipation of trouble.

Her dad uncorks the wine and gets the glasses. He pours a little for CeCe and hands it to her. She brings it up to her mouth. It tastes sour as it rolls around her tongue. The scent of the cooking casserole and the biscuits fill the kitchen. She picks up Derrick's rock off the counter.

"It smells amazing, Shawn," Lauren says.

He smiles. "We'll have to see how it tastes. I was never the cook. It was more—"

CeCe glances up. He doesn't finish his sentence.

Her mother's ghost hovers between them, thick like the haze of heat and oil. Mom was a self-proclaimed foodie. She spent hours watching cooking shows and re-creating the dishes with perfection. Casseroles were emergency meals. She apologized every time she made one.

"I'm sure it'll be amazing," Lauren says.

They continue talking about work. Spreadsheets, data, this sector, that sector, until the timer goes off and the casserole comes out of the oven steaming in melted cheese. The biscuits come next, beautifully golden brown.

Her dad arranges the food on the table and gives each of them a generous portion. She picks up her fork, still holding the rock in the other.

Lauren turns to CeCe. "Your dad told me you're back at school. How is it?"

She shrugs. "It's okay."

Her dad laughs. "That's the only answer I get from her too."

"It must be difficult though," Lauren says, "being back and all?"

"You could say that."

CeCe moves the broccoli around on her plate. It came from a frozen bag and tastes funny. She pushes it from side to side, sensing their eyes on her. It makes everything worse. She finishes her wine.

"More, please."

Her dad looks at her for a moment and then pours her a thimbleful before diving back into work talk with Lauren, turning it into a two-way conversation. CeCe doesn't mind. It takes the focus off her.

"The briefing went well, don't you think?" he says to Lauren. "We're finally making sustainable progress, as long as the results remain stable."

CeCe looks up.

"Oh Shawn," Lauren says. "You worry too much. There's been no deviation. You of all people would know before anyone."

Lauren glances over at CeCe. Did she mean to do that? Or was it a reflex? It's hard to tell. Their conversation is too coded, saying enough, but not too much.

She wanted to go through more of her dad's emails when she got home, to find out what she could about P73-7, but he was in the kitchen the whole time. But if it's her, if she's P73-7, she has a right to know. The smart thing would be to wait, dig into her dad's stuff. Only she doesn't want to, and deep down, she wants to ruin these easygoing, happy-go-lucky vibes her dad and Lauren are sharing. It's spiteful, but the idea feels good.

CeCe grips the rock. "Who is P73-7?"

They both turn to her.

Her dad's playful grin morphs to a clenching jaw. "You went through my emails?"

"No," she lies, and he knows it.

"Then how do you know about that?"

CeCe shrugs.

An awkward silence grows between them.

"CeCe," her dad says. "That's classified information. We could…" He looks at Lauren "We could get in a lot of trouble."

"What more can they do? Whoever *they* are," CeCe says. "Take away my mother? Take away my brother? Or, God forbid, kick me out of my GED program? Yeah, so scared."

He shakes his head. "What is the matter with you?"

"This," she says, motioning to the table. "This is the matter. What is this? Your fancy dinner with your fancy biscuits. You're already trying to replace Mom, is that it?"

"CeCe."

Lauren stares at her dad, the skin around her already strained face pulling tighter. CeCe doesn't care if this is making her uncomfortable or she's ruining whatever expectations Lauren had of this evening.

Her dad gets really quiet. Lauren doesn't move. It doesn't even look like she's breathing.

"You're right," her dad says. "This isn't only having Lauren over for dinner. It was supposed to be special because..." He takes a breath as if to get the nerve. "Because we were going to tell you that Lauren and I are getting married."

CeCe recoils as if her dad had reached across the table and smacked her. She gapes at him, her stomach turning inside out while her mom smiles down from the picture.

Her mother's things still surround them. Her French confit pots, a Mother's Day vase scribbled on by Teddy from second grade. A blue box where she kept all the flameless candle remotes. And in one declaration, it's like she never mattered. Like she was never the glue that kept their family together.

CeCe wants to cry, the pressure aches behind her eyes, but she can't.

She stares at her dad. "I was right. You *are* replacing Mom."

"No," he says. "It's not like that."

"Then what the hell would you call it?"

She can't deal with this. It's too much.

First her mom. Teddy. Riley. Leyton. Her entire world. And now this.

Doesn't he realize that for him it's been two years, but for her, it's like it all happened yesterday? She can barely function, get out of bed in the morning. She hasn't even begun to process everything that has happened, and then he dumps this on her.

Pushing away from the table, she storms to her room. She wants to break something, punch a wall, anything, but they'd hear her, they'd wonder, and she wouldn't be able to stand the thought of them thinking of her as a monster.

Instead, she flings herself on her bed and grips the comforter until she hears its threads snapping.

Her dad and Lauren are talking downstairs. They're trying to be quiet, but she can hear the rise and fall of their voices. Her dad laughs and Lauren joins him in whatever stupid joke or comment he'd said.

They've already moved on, CeCe's reaction a momentary hiccup in their celebratory dinner.

She leans over and grabs her backpack. She unzips the top and takes out Riley's shirt, bringing it to her nose. It makes her feel like he's here with her, and while it breaks her in two, it also relaxes her.

Carefully, she folds his shirt and sets it by her pillow. Next, she takes out the pictures and arranges them on the corkboard over her desk where she'll always see them, where they'll always be present.

Last is Riley's gift. Her fingers start to unwrap the bow, but she stops herself. This is the last thing Riley ever gave her and will ever give her again and she's not ready to let that go yet. She places it on her nightstand.

Lying next to Riley's shirt, she listens to her dad's and Lauren's voices downstairs and rolls Derrick's rock over and over in her hand. Half of her wants to throw it out the window, but she likes the weight of it in her palm. Maybe he did too.

Eventually, she hears the front door open and close. Lauren must be going home. Soon, this will be her home. Her mother's house where she made pancakes in the morning, decorated the entryway every holiday, and hovered in the doorframes to talk, to comfort, to be.

Her dad's footfalls come toward her room. He taps lightly on her door before coming in to sit on the edge of her bed. He looks at the present.

"Who gave you that?"

"I found it in Riley's locker. He was supposed to meet up with us later that night and give it to me."

He picks up the gift, the wrapping paper crinkling with the movement. "I'm so sorry, CeCe."

"Yeah, me too."

"I, uh, I was hoping that tonight would have gone better. I knew you wouldn't be happy about it. I guess it was wishful thinking on my part that maybe you would. I suppose I really messed that up, huh?"

She shrugs. "Maybe."

"I figured so," he says, setting down the present.

"How could you do this to Mom?" she asks. "She just died, and what, you couldn't wait for an upgrade?"

"It's not like that, and I'd never upgrade your mother. She was, *is*, irreplaceable."

"Then what do you call it?"

He turns toward her. He's not angry or frustrated. Only sad. "CeCe, for me, your mother's been gone a long time."

"I was gone a long time too. Were you going to replace me as well? What about Teddy?"

"That's different, and you know it."

"I don't see any difference. New world, new life, new *wife* apparently."

"You're not being fair."

Maybe she isn't, but neither is he. He should've given her more time. At least waited until she could figure things out, found her place in all this, before he dropped his marriage on her.

He looks at her for a moment. "We've never talked much about what it was like for me, without your mom, without you or your brother. But those days, they are indescribable. Horrifying, mostly. Lauren and I, we were all we had. The chaos, the death. The unspeakable terror. Never being sure the gates and the doors would hold.

"Looking back, I don't know how we didn't crumble from the shock. None of us were meant to see those things. Weren't meant to experience something like that. It's a miracle any made it out, but even for those who did, we all lost people."

He let out a weighty sigh.

"I did. Lauren did. She lost her son. He was only six months old. She's not okay, neither am I, but the time we shared, it created a bond between us. Starting a relationship with her, it wasn't something I was planning, or she was planning. It just happened. I don't regret it and I won't apologize for it. I love her, and with everything that's happened, it's a gift I never expected to receive."

He takes her hand. "The virus taught me one thing. If you find happiness, you fight for it. You hold it tight. And I want that for you too. I want you to be happy."

Happiness doesn't even feel like a real concept. How can she ever be happy again? Her mother is dead. Her brother is missing. Her friends and boyfriend were ripped from her life. And, on top of all that, her dad is getting remarried. He's moving on. Without her. Like she's supposed to be ready because he is.

"Can you try to accept my marriage to Lauren?" he asks. "Maybe a little?"

What does it matter if she does or doesn't? It's not going to change anything. It's not going to bring anyone she loved back. It's not going to change her.

"Yeah, sure."

"Thank you," he says, squeezing her hand. "That means a lot to me. I love you. You know that, right? I don't want there to be any more secrets between us. Especially not now."

She nods and he gets up to leave, but she stops him before he gets to the door.

"Am I…" she starts to ask. "Am I P73-7?"

"No, and that's all I'm able to tell you."

"But you said no more secrets."

"That's not one between us. That one is much bigger than you."

Chapter Six

The cannons go off as CeCe comes down to breakfast. She thinks of the Infected, lumbering their way to the noise, drawn by the Pied Piper's lute. How many of them will wake up in the next few weeks and be like her? Numb, detached, and expected to participate? Expected to deal with it?

Her head aches, pressure building within the fissures of her brain. She didn't sleep well. That isn't a surprise, she's used to that, but this time it was the thoughts of her dad and Lauren and how everything will change again that kept her awake.

"Good morning," he says when she comes into the kitchen.

"Morning."

"How are you doing? I know it was a lot yesterday."

It wasn't *a lot*. *A lot* is being asked to run to the store after a full day of school and practice. *A lot* is being asked to clean the house after no one's picked up for a week. This isn't *a lot*. This is tilting the world's axis. It's a reminder of everything she's lost.

She's grateful to Lauren for being there for her dad when none of them could, but that's the most she can offer.

"I'm all right," she says.

"Good." He nods. "That's good."

He sits another Eggo with some peanut butter before her. What she wouldn't give for some eggs and bacon. She cuts off a piece and sticks it in her mouth as he fills up his coffee and settles before the computer. He tilts the screen away so she can't see it. She supposes she deserves that.

"Damn," her dad says.

"What?"

"They scheduled a status briefing at one thirty and you get out of school at two. I'll have to duck out early to come get you."

"I can walk home."

"I don't think so."

"Why? I don't mind walking. Really."

He looks at her, his jaw setting. "I already told you. It's not safe."

"Because of the Infected?"

"Yes, because of the Infected. How is it that doesn't seem to bother you?"

"I've seen other students walk home after school."

"But I'm not responsible for them. I'm responsible for you." He sighs. "Listen, CeCe. People went everywhere after the Infection. We don't know how many got Infected while they were in hiding. We're finding new ones all the time. You're cured now, *immune* to the virus. A bite. An attack. It could kill you. To be honest, those other students shouldn't be walking either."

If she came across another Infected, it would be different this time. She wouldn't be so blind as she had with Derrick. The wild rage in his eyes. Her flesh between his teeth. Her blood seeping from his mouth. Her dad doesn't need to warn her, she already knows what they're capable of doing, and she'd never let another Infected get close to her again.

"I'll leave the briefing early," he says.

"Don't." She shakes her head. "You said you wanted normal, right? Walking home from school is normal. I used to do it all the time. Instead of creepers and weirdos, I'll keep an eye out for the Infected. In a way, it's pretty much the same."

"It's not that simple."

"You want me to adapt. You want me to adjust. This is a start. If I let the Infected frighten me, they'll always frighten me."

Her dad gets really quiet. "They should."

She thinks of what he said last night about the terror, the nightmare of it all. She didn't have to see that part because *she* was the nightmare everyone was running from. Perhaps she's being naïve. She doesn't know. She never had a chance to know. Derrick took that from her.

"What if there's more than one Infected?" he asks her. "What would you do then?"

"What? Like a horde?"

"Yeah, exactly like a horde. That's how it used to be. There was never only one. More were always close by."

She shrugs. "I guess I'd have to run then, wouldn't I?"

Her dad makes a noise in the back of his throat.

Before, it wouldn't have even been a question. She used to be fast, sprinting around the tennis court, but she was so deconditioned now. She doubted she could run down the block without getting winded.

"I can do this," she says. "I promise."

Honestly, she's not sure why she's even pushing so hard. The easy thing would be to let him leave his meeting early, but this is bigger than a ride home from school. She wants the independence. Some control over what's left of her life.

Her dad sighs. "Let me see your phone."

She gives it to him. He punches in a number to her contacts.

"This is the direct line for the RRT. You see anything, you call them. They'll come and deal with it. Infected or not."

He hands the phone back to her. She puts it in her pocket.

"I mean *anything*," he says. "Understand?"

"Got it."

He grabs his bag. "I guess you're walking home today."

She smiles as she follows him out the door and into the car. They drive to school, talking about nothing. What to have for dinner. If she can move the laundry into the dryer when she gets home. If she needs another notebook for school. He drops her off at the steps, reminding her to call RRT if she has any problems, then takes off to the CAVE. She makes her way to the front doors of Franklin. The caseworkers are in the office again. There's more of them. At least seven total. They must be making it their headquarters.

Savannah greets her as she comes into class. Savannah's wearing a beanie that covers her bald spot and has makeup on. Only a little. Some mascara and lip gloss.

"You look pretty," CeCe says.

Savannah smiles. "I thought to myself, why not?"

Ms. Dobson already has a lesson plan on the whiteboard. More "Rose for Emily" followed with grammar rules and exercises.

She starts with the discussion of the second section questions. The mood is different today. Most everyone's gazes are forward instead of resting on the tops of the desks. Maybe it's a touch of time eroding walls. Mostly she thinks it's being in an actual classroom. It's reassuring and unsettling at the same time.

It's too soon, isn't it? People can't move on after all they've been through. They can't get into a routine after a couple of days. But maybe they can. Maybe this is how they start.

After about an hour, Ms. Dobson stops for a break. They can stay in the room or leave as long as they stay on campus. Some take her up on the opportunity, notably Olivia, but most stay. Savannah takes out her lunch and offers an apple to CeCe.

"My aunt has an apple tree in her backyard," she says. "I brought two."

It's smallish and dimpled, but she hasn't had an apple since before the Kill Virus. She takes a bite, and it fills her mouth with a tart sourness.

Savannah leans toward her. "That girl's always looking at you."

"Who?" she asks, even though she already knows the answer.

"Olivia. I overheard the caseworkers talking about her."

"Oh? And?"

"They called her a Revie."

"A Revie? What's that?"

She shrugs. "I don't know. I was hoping you'd might. Your dad being Dr. Campbell and all."

CeCe shakes her head. "He hasn't said anything about Revies. But I did find something in my bag after the first day of school. I think Olivia put it in there."

"What? Really? When did she pull that off?"

"When I went to the bathroom. You didn't see her come over to my desk, did you?"

"No," she says, "but I was a little out of it. What was it?"

"A picture."

"Can I see?"

CeCe fishes it out. Derrick's rock is at the bottom of her bag where she put it last night. She's not sure why she did. Why she hasn't thrown it away or stuffed it somewhere behind a stack of books. Probably for the same reason she's still lugging around her demon picture. She takes it out and hands it to Savannah.

"Well, that's creepy," she says. "Does she think you're some kind of demon spawn?"

"Clearly."

"If you are, then I must be too," Savannah says, giving her the picture back.

"Aren't we the popular ones?"

"Except she seems to be really into you and not, like, in a good way."

As if on cue, Olivia comes back into the classroom. She stares right at CeCe, her face twisting in disgust.

"Yeah," CeCe says, "she isn't making it obvious or anything."

Some more students return. Ms. Dobson gets up, her crutch under her arm, and goes back to the whiteboard. Not everyone is at their desks yet, but she continues with her lesson plan, picking up from where she stopped.

The rest of the day crawls along. CeCe thinks of Olivia more often than she wants. When her dad gets home, she wonders if she should talk to him about her. Ask if he knows what a Revie is. Maybe it can get Olivia kicked out of the program. And if not, her dad can insist. He's one of the Big Shots now.

And as much as CeCe wants to, as much as it gives her a sense of comfort to have that power, Olivia's here. She chose to sign up for the program. She chose to be here. Maybe she's trying to move on and is struggling. Who knows? But they all deserve the chance, including her. Without knowing Olivia's reasons, she can't take that away.

After school, CeCe and Savannah walk out together like they've done the last two days. It's casual. Normal even. A slow build to a possible friendship. It will be nice to have a friend again. Someone to talk to other than her dad. Someone who understands what it's like to once be Infected.

They leave out the front doors.

"Where's your dad?" Savannah asks. "He late again?"

"No. I'm walking home."

"Lucky. I wish my aunt would allow me to. She'd never."

Savannah's aunt is in her usual place, eyes before her, knuckles white on the steering wheel. CeCe is about to follow Savannah down, maybe introduce herself so that they can walk home together if Savannah lives nearby, but then she sees Derrick on the steps and stops mid-stride. He's in jeans and a hoodie. He looks up to her and waves.

What's he doing here? Again? Why can't he leave her alone? It's already hard enough knowing what he did to her. Does he have to rub it in her face?

Savannah glances back at her. "See you later," she says and hurries down toward her aunt's van.

CeCe opens her mouth to call after her, to see if her aunt can give her a ride, but by the time she realizes she should, Savannah's already at the van door and jumping in. Derrick looks at Savannah and then back up at CeCe. He smiles. It's probably meant to be friendly, but all she can see are those teeth.

He takes a few steps toward her.

Why did she have to push walking home? She should've let her dad leave his meeting early. If she had, she'd already be in his car, and she wouldn't be stuck in this impasse with Derrick blocking her path.

She turns back to the school.

She'll wait him out then. He'll have to leave eventually. Just as she's about to grab onto the handle, the door opens and Olivia comes out, slow and squirming like a snake released into the wild. The door shuts behind her and her gaze fixes on CeCe. They're so close she can see every strand of Olivia's bangs and something underneath. A scar? Maybe she isn't a Survivor.

Olivia smirks at her as she moves out of the way and CeCe takes the opportunity to grasp for the handle. She pulls to yank it open, but it doesn't budge. The damn thing has been set on auto-lock. She tries it again, but it's useless.

CeCe stands there, face against the door, feeling Olivia's eyes crawling over her. But not only hers. Derrick's too.

She can't deal with this. Can't deal with *them*. She keeps her hand clasped around the handle, unable to move, unable to think. She wants to go home.

"Hi again," she hears Derrick say from behind her.

She groans. "Are you going to be here every day?"

"Ah, she speaks. I wasn't sure if, you know, there was something wrong with your voice."

"I speak," she snaps as she turns, half expecting to see Olivia standing beside him, but she's already down the stairs, heading toward the same rumbling truck. At least that's one problem solved.

"I didn't mean anything by it," he says. "You never know though."

"Why are you here?" Her eyes narrow on him. "I'm pretty sure stalking is still a thing."

"I'm not a stalker, I promise."

"Could've fooled me."

"Yeah, okay." He runs his hand through his shaggy hair. "I mean, I thought it could come off that way, but I wasn't trying to."

"Then what do you want?"

"I don't want anything," he says. "I'm trying to be friendly I suppose." He looks behind him. "Is your dad picking you up?"

"Why do you want to know?"

"Whoa, I was asking. Wasn't trying to make it a big deal or anything."

CeCe looks down at the truck. Olivia and her friend are still there, and they keep glancing at her. What are they doing? Why haven't they left yet? Pinpricks stab her numb skin. Something is up.

Derrick says, "If he's not here, can I, I don't know, walk you home? I swear I'm safe."

She almost laughs, but it's suffocated by the thought of being left alone with Olivia and her friend in a vehicle while she's on foot. Exhaust smokes from the back of the truck as it sits there, idling. Waiting. She can't explain it, but it's a threat so palatable she tastes it in the back of her throat.

"Okay," he says. "I can take a hint. Sorry to have bothered you. Have a nice day."

Derrick starts to turn.

"Wait."

He looks up at her.

She doesn't want this. She doesn't want to spend another moment near him, but with her dad not coming, Derrick is all she has. At least she already knows what he's capable of. Olivia and her friend are another story.

Better the monster you know.

She sort of shuffles her feet. "Yeah, okay. You can walk me home."

He smiles at her with those teeth. "Yeah?"

"Yeah."

He holds out his hand. "Lead the way."

She goes with him down the stairs. Olivia eyes Derrick as they get closer and then leans over to the guy next to her, saying something. He puts the pickup in gear, and they drive off, disappearing around the corner.

CeCe exhales a long breath. They're gone. But now that they are, she wonders if she was being paranoid and volunteered for a walk home with Derrick for nothing.

Not to mention she's not sure if she likes the idea of him knowing where she lives. He already shows up at her school.

Will he start popping up at her house too? She's about ready to tell him to forget it, but then her paranoia creeps back in.

Olivia and her friend might have driven off, but it doesn't mean they've left. They could be waiting somewhere else. CeCe has the number to RRT, but all sorts of things could happen while she has to wait for them to show.

"This way," she says and hurries down the street.

Derrick catches up, matching her stride. "So, what's your name?"

"CeCe."

"CeCe, well, it's nice to actually meet you."

She looks at him. "How did you know where to find me?"

He motions to her GED book. "I saw you with that. I figured there was only one place you'd be carrying it. I helped clean up the school."

Now it seems fairly obvious. She might as well have been waving her whereabouts around like a flag. Why does she keep carrying it anyway? Old habit, she supposes. She never had room in her backpack for books. It was filled with cans of tennis balls, makeup, and an extra change of clothes. She even packed a blow-dryer most days. She removes her backpack and slips the book in. She sees his rock and debates giving it back to him, but decides not to. It's hers now.

"This is a one-time thing, okay?" she says as she zips her bag back up. "This walking me home."

"Sure, if that's what you want."

"I do."

"All right, all right. I get it. So if this is my only chance to talk to you, this being a *one-time thing* and everything, we don't, for sure, know each other, right?"

The ache in her hand returns. Like a phantom pain, but not.

"Why do you keep asking me that?"

"I don't know. I have this feeling that we do."

"Well, we don't."

It's the truth. They don't know each other. Their only interaction was CeCe trying to be a good person and him being an Infected.

"Huh. I'm usually good at remembering faces."

"Guess not all the time."

"Guess not."

A weird silence grows between them. The only sound is the rhythm of their steps in sync. No rumbling of a truck. No glimpses of red behind oleander bushes. Olivia and her friend must really be gone, and she wishes Derrick would take it upon himself to shove off, but he doesn't. He stays beside her.

"So, your dad is Dr. Campbell?"

"You already know that."

"I'm trying to make conversation. We don't have to. I'm fine either way. I'm a guy out walking. Enjoying a stroll."

Derrick starts to hum to himself.

She sighs. "Yeah, my dad is Dr. Campbell."

"He must be a really smart guy."

"Something like that."

"If it wasn't for him, we'd all still be like those mindless zombies."

"Yah, zombies."

She hasn't used that word yet, neither has her dad, but she supposes that's what they were. Nothing can stay undead like that for so long in a state of endless animation not eating, not drinking, not sleeping.

That's what zombies do. That's what they are known for. And for two years she'd stood in the same place. Two years. How could her body even do that? Remain stagnant like a pool of water growing bacteria? It's impossible, but she did.

They did. Stood in place.

Or shambled until they found a place.

Zombies. Every last one of them.

"I was in my apartment when it happened to me," Derrick says. "I was studying for my art history exam when—bam—my roommate bit me."

He pulls down the side of his shirt. There's a bite mark on the back of his shoulder.

"I didn't even hear the guy come in. He was just there. I figured he'd had too much to drink or something. But hell. The jerk bit me and I was bleeding all over the place. I pushed him off and the way he looked? I knew he wasn't right. He kept coming at me and the bite was burning. I could actually feel it going through my veins. I'd never felt anything like that before. I ran from my apartment and out the building. Next thing I knew I was on Pike Street."

The same street where CeCe had been celebrating her eighteenth birthday. Where she'd been waiting outside for an Uber with her friends. The same street where Derrick had turned her.

He says, "I don't even know how I got there. That's like ten blocks from my apartment. I only remember seeing the street sign. I don't remember much after that. It's pretty much a blur, until I woke up with what felt like a massive hangover and a dislocated jaw."

CeCe gets a flash of a macabre memory, a vivid picture of Leyton swinging her elbow at Derrick while he had his teeth in CeCe's flesh. She chuckles a little. *Payback is a bitch.*

"What?" he asks, smiling along with her. "Why are you laughing?"

She shrugs. "No reason."

He rubs his hand along his jaw. "They had to wire it for like two weeks. It still aches."

Good, she thinks to herself. She's glad it hurts.

"It was probably for the best though," he says. "Can't bite anyone when your mouth doesn't work. At least, that's what I'm hoping."

"Yeah," she says, and clenches her hand.

"When I saw you the other day," he continues. "I don't know, something clicked. This is going to sound way off, but I feel like I remember your face when I was in it, you know? Like when it was happening."

She says, "I already told you—"

"Yeah, I know. I heard you and I believe you. It must be something else. Like maybe I saw you at a Starbucks or something and I'm mixing it up in my head. I mean, who can remember what was what anymore? I needed to know for sure and now I do, so thank you. It means something to me."

They pass by Ed's MiniMart. They both become quiet as they do. There's no reason for it, but it's like sacred ground. More of a graveyard than a place where people bought Cheetos and slushies. It throbs with memories and past lives and death.

CeCe says, "I saw a body getting taken out of there."

He nods. "Yeah, some guy. Not sure if he was young or old. He'd been in there for a while."

"Was he Infected?"

"I don't think so. He, uh, he looked like he might have committed suicide. There was a gun right next to him."

She swallows as she thinks of Mack. Thinks of him lying on the floor even though she can't know for sure if it was him. If it *was* him, if Mack did kill himself, at least he made that decision and didn't have it made for him. Like Derrick did to her and his roommate did to him.

She pauses at that thought.

Like his roommate did to him.

It shocks her. The idea that maybe Derrick, this monster who took everything from her, had everything taken from him too. She doesn't like the feeling that they share something in common. That they're more alike than different. It's much easier to despise him for who he was after.

They continue past Ed's. Only a few more blocks to home.

"Do you find that a lot?" she asks. "Bodies?"

"Oh yeah, all the time. Either Infected, who'd been shot, or people, you know, like the guy in there, who'd killed themselves. I can't really blame them. If I'd known what was going to happen to me, I probably would have done the same."

She looks at him. "Would you?"

"Of course. To think that's what I was. That I might have hurt—" He shakes his head. "I can't think about that because that's the crap you never can get away from, this whole *what if*."

Like what if CeCe had hurt the Luken boys, Hudson and Connor.

It's something else CeCe and Derrick have in common. How it feels to not know and also not wanting to know because the truth would be unbearable.

Derrick puts his hands in his pockets. "I guess that's the only good part about not remembering."

She doesn't say so, but he's right. If she had to remember, she doesn't know if she could live with herself.

"What about the Infected?" she asks. "You ever find them?"

"Sure. We're not allowed to kill them or anything. All Infected are considered Resources by the Initiative. I guess you never can tell which one was once a rocket scientist or like an architect or whatever. They're not really dangerous on their own, I've dealt with a few, but when they're in packs, it can be a problem. When I saw you by yourself the other day, well, it isn't safe."

"You sound like my dad."

"He's kinda right though."

She glances over at him. It's getting easier to look at his face. "What do you do, you know, when you find the Infected?"

"We call the RRT. They gas them and take them away."

The same contact her dad had put in her phone. It does make her feel better knowing she has them on speed dial.

"How long have you been working for the Sanitation Department?" she asks.

"Since they stamped me with a clean bill of health."

"Are you staying with anyone?"

He shakes his head. "Nah. I don't have family here. All my people are in Montana. I came here for school. I, uh, I don't even know if they've made it or where they are. It's not like we can go online and find them on Facebook, you know? I can only hope they're okay."

"Who all is in Montana?"

"My mom and dad, grandparents, my two younger sisters." He turns to her. "You'd like them, and they'd like you."

She snorts. "They don't even know me. You don't either."

"Yeah, but I can tell, you're a good person."

She thinks of the Luken boys and isn't sure if she can agree with him.

They take the next turn onto her street. They come up to the Morgans. She wonders if they're watching from the curtains. If she has to guess, they are. She stops in front of her house.

"Well, this is me."

He points to the mailbox with Campbell in gold lettering. "Yeah, I figured."

Derrick stands there, looking at her. He's hesitating and for the first time since meeting him, she is too. She should be getting out her key and running into the house, shutting the door, but she doesn't.

"One second," he says and pulls a flip phone from his pocket. "I know you said you didn't want me to walk you home again, but I have one of these and if you have one of these too, maybe we can get to know each other the regular way. It'll make me more of a friend instead of, you know, a stalker."

She doesn't say anything. She's not sure how she feels about him still. It's a mix of everything. Like too much paint bleeding into each other. "I," she starts to say, "I don't know my number."

"Okay, I get it," he says, putting the phone away. "I thought I'd give it one last shot. Can't blame a guy though, right? It was nice to meet you, CeCe. Take care of yourself."

He turns and starts to walk away. Part of her wants to let him go. Neither one of them had had a choice when they'd been bitten. But *this* is a choice. The first one she's been given since he'd bitten her.

"Derrick," she says. She hasn't said his name aloud before. It sounds odd in her mouth.

She gets out her phone and holds it out to him.

"I really *don't* know my number. If you give yours to me, I can text you sometime, maybe."

He grins as he takes the phone and begins typing in his number. When he's done, he shuts it and hands it back to her.

"I'm available anytime you're bored or whatever. I guess not always if I'm working, but no pressure or anything."

"Okay," she says.

"Okay," he repeats. "Well, I hope I'll hear from you soon." He puts his hands in his pockets and steps back.

She glances at her empty house, her empty room, her empty life. "See you tomorrow after school?" she asks him. The words are out of her mouth before she realizes what she's saying. "I mean," she says, "I don't want to mess up your stalking routine or anything."

"Yeah," he says and smiles. "We wouldn't want that."

Chapter Seven

Derrick meets CeCe the next day on the steps after school, and again the day after that, and the day after that, until it's become routine.

Since Derrick started coming around, Olivia and her friend haven't waited in the truck in that weird way again. Instead, Olivia hops into her ride with her usual scowl and she and her friend take off without a glance back. It hasn't stopped Olivia from eyeing CeCe every chance she gets though.

On their walks home, CeCe has gotten to know Derrick and the more she does, the more the "Derrick of Pike Street" disappears. He's nice, genuinely, and she likes him. A fact that takes her by surprise. But it's easy in his company, and outside of Savannah, he's her only friend.

Her friend.

It's an odd thing to think about, but that's what they are. Somehow, she's become friends with the guy she hated. Only he still doesn't know that.

She's thought of telling him, several times, but she likes the way things are. Even if she did tell him, there's nothing he could do about it anyway, other than offer a meaningless apology. It's not like he could take it back. Not ever. And instead of this casual, easygoing friendship, there'd be a void of awkward silence. She doesn't want that, at least not right now.

Besides, she looks forward to her walks with him. It's been a break in the monotony. A break in pretending she's okay. She likes to listen to him talk, which he does with ease as if they weren't in a post-Infection world, but in a regular one.

He tells her about his sisters, Nora and Lila. His mom and dad. The horses his family had on their fifty-acre property, and the supply store they owned in Whitefish, Montana.

He says, "We sold all kinds of survival stuff, and I grew up hunting and shooting. My dad was always a better shot than me."

His world was different than hers. She'd grown up close to the city, playing tennis since she was in second grade after her parents realized she hated dance class.

But Derrick grew up in the country. Fishing by the time he was a toddler, stomping around the mountains with his sisters, wrangling cattle, and bagging his first deer when he was ten years old. He was like someone out of a Western movie.

"If anyone could survive the Kill Virus," he says, "it would be my dad. It's the one thing that makes me feel like maybe they're all okay."

"When do you think you can find out?"

"Probably once the barricades are down."

"But you can get past them, right?"

"Yeah. I did. Once. The barricades aren't the problem."

She looks at him. "What *is* the problem?"

"The horde. It was about two weeks after I left the Center. I was ready to go home, check on my family. I packed as much as I could scavenge and climbed over the barricade, but I didn't get far. There were at least forty Infected on the other side and that was only what I could see. I had no idea how many more were out there. One or two Infected, maybe even three, aren't really an issue, but anything more than that, it's suicide. It forced me back over."

"What about now? More and more are cured every day. It could be clear."

"I've thought about that," he says. "Actually, I think about it all the time."

"What's stopped you?"

He looks at her and smiles.

Her head jerks back. It can't be *her* keeping him here. They barely know each other, and he certainly doesn't know much of anything about her. She always lets him do all the talking.

CeCe clears her throat, not sure how to reply.

He nudges her in the shoulder. "Relax," he says. "I'm not some weird guy that sticks around for a girl. Well, maybe only a little weird."

"Okay," she says, feeling her cheeks getting warm. "So what is keeping you here?"

He takes a breath and lets it out slowly. "I guess it's the guys at the Sanitation Crew. Being part of something like rebuilding and helping the Infected. I don't know. I feel like I have a purpose, like I'm doing something to help fix what happened. It's not forever. It's only for now. I worry about my folks and my sisters all the time. Someday soon, I'm going to have to leave, but that day isn't today so I'm going to enjoy the time I have left here."

She looks at him. It must be nice to have a plan. And a purpose. What was that anymore? With her dad all about Lauren, all she'll have left when Derrick leaves is the few hours at school with Savannah. That'll probably stop too when they take the GED test and then what? She'll take Derrick's place at the Sanitation Department?

"You should think about maybe getting out too," he says. "Seeing something of the world, or what remains of it anyway."

She adjusts her backpack on her shoulders. "Unless by some miracle everything goes back to how it was, which I doubt, I wouldn't make it far past the barricade. Not even if every Infected was cured. I don't have much by way of survivor skills. I've never even gone camping."

"What?" He looks at her, his eyes wide. "What do you mean you've never gone camping?"

"My parents weren't into it. I mean, we stayed in cabins, but never, you know, like in a tent and a sleeping bag. Mom said she couldn't be anywhere without a shower. We did take a motor home once to the Grand Canyon. That was the most roughing it we've ever done. It was my mom's idea. I think toward the end, she regretted it."

"Where is your mom?" he asks. "She at the house with you?"

She swallows. "She, uh, she didn't make it."

"Oh, damn. I'm such an asshole to have asked like that. Sometimes I put a giant foot in my mouth."

"It's okay," she says. "It's not like you knew. My dad is actually getting remarried."

"Oh?" he says, surprised. "And how do you feel about that?"

"A little like my mom never existed."

"I'm sorry," he says and puts his arm around her.

She tenses. She might've stopped wishing that Derrick had died during the Infection, but she's not sure how she feels about his touch, even if it's only meant to be sympathetic.

As if a habitual twitch, her mind goes to Riley and what he'd think of another guy having his arm around her shoulders. Or maybe it's not Riley at all that's bothering her, and that thought bothers her even more.

Before she can dwell on it too long, he removes his arm. She lets out a breath, unclenching the knot in her chest, one that she'd clearly passed on to Derrick. An awkwardness thrums between them like the vibration of guitar strings that only gets stronger with each passing second.

"So," he starts to say. "If you never went camping, what did you do, you know, before the Kill Virus?"

It's a standard enough question to detour from the weirdness she'd caused, but it's another thought bomb that sends her rocketing to the past, a place she doesn't like to be. She thinks of her friends. She thinks of Riley. Of tennis. Of her life. Of her mom and her brother. Their trips to Disneyland. The vacations to Hawaii. Sleepovers. Away games. Senior Prom. Only she never had a chance to experience that one.

She shrugs. "Just the normal stuff, I guess."

"And in all that time, you never went camping and slept under the stars?"

"Nope."

"Man, that's kind of horrible."

She laughs. "That's dramatic."

"Yeah, maybe. But seriously, we'll have to change that, won't we? Everyone should sleep under the stars at least once."

He always talks like that. *The One Days*, the *I Can't Wait for Whens*, the *As Soon as I'm Ables*. Derrick sees a future she can't. How can there ever be a future that doesn't involve the Kill Virus and what it's done, what they've lost?

"You're really optimistic," she tells him.

"And you're seriously pessimistic, which is why we get along."

"I'm not pessimistic. I like to think of myself as more of a realist."

"Things will get better," he says. "It already has. There used to be nothing. There was only the Costco and the Housing Center. Now the hospital's been opened, some gas stations, grocery stores, your school. It's all happened pretty fast."

"I suppose so."

"Come on, you've got to admit it. I thought for sure it would have taken years to get to where we are. You must've been a later Cure then."

"Actually, I was in the first phase."

"Say what?" he says, stunned. "Me too. They dropped bombs of the gas all over downtown and they found me at Washington Park. Me and my buddies used to hang out there and drink on the weekends. You know it?"

"Yeah, I know it."

Washington Park was only a few blocks away from Mason's. Her hand aches again. It does every time he brings up anything that reminds her of that night.

"What about you?" he asks. "Where were you found?"

"The mall."

He laughs. "Classic. What was it? H&M?"

"No, worse. Nail salon."

The moment she says it, she's reminded of her mom and there's another ache to replace the one in her hand. Only this one is deeper, and along with it comes the scent of roses and asphalt, and the memory of her mother's last resting place.

She should go back there. If anything, to at least replace the dead roses with new ones, but she can't. If it'd been CeCe who'd died there, her mom would go every day. Nothing would've stopped her. Not pain, not the hurt, the feeling of being left behind by dying. But CeCe isn't as strong as her mom was.

They come up to Ed's MiniMart. Fresh spray paint bleeds from its cinder wall where "Repent" had once been. This time, someone wrote, "The cure is a lie."

"Great," Derrick says as they get closer. "We just fixed that. The city is trashed everywhere, you'd think those guys would want to help us, not make it worse."

"Those guys?"

"Yeah, the Revies."

She looks at him. She'd meant to talk to her dad about what Savannah had told her about Olivia. But that plan got lost in a series of texts with Derrick that started with a simple *thanks for walking me home*, and then didn't stop. The distraction was like a drug. She was unable to stop the back-and-forth, despite not really wanting to talk to him, but too deep in the anticipation for the dings that signaled an incoming message.

"Who are the Revies?"

"The Followers of John. They think they're the 144,000 sealed by Jesus in Revelations. They're extreme to say the least."

"Revelations, as in the Bible Revelations?"

The only knowledge she had in the Bible is what she learned when her grandparents used to drag her to Sunday School. But then they moved to Arizona and that ended.

"Yeah. Armageddon and all that. The cure really put a dent in their plan for the second coming of Jesus. They hate us. All the Infected and ex-Infected, but your dad even more. To them, he's the Antichrist."

"My dad? Come on. He's about as evil as a butterfly."

"He came up with the cure. They blame him for, you know, stopping God's work in letting us kill each other."

She thinks of Olivia's smirks and glares. The way Olivia's eyes are constantly following her every movement. Is that why Olivia has it so in for her? She hates CeCe's dad and hates her too. But is she a Revie? CeCe remembers seeing glimpses of a scar under her bangs. Maybe that's how Olivia hides what had happened to her. Like Savannah does with her beanie. And she does with her glove.

"I think there's a Revie in my class," she says. "I don't know for sure, but I'm pretty certain she put this in my bag. I mean, I don't have proof she did, but she's been acting weird toward me since day one."

CeCe opens her backpack. His rock is still hanging out on the bottom. She wonders what he'd think if she knew she carried it around with her. Or that sometimes she holds it until she goes to sleep at night, so she has something to grasp onto. She takes out the paper with the demon on it and shows it to Derrick.

"Yup," he says and nods. "This has Revie all over it. She's in your class?"

"Yeah."

"Do the caseworkers know?"

"I think so. My friend said she overheard them talking about her."

"And she's still there?"

"Yeah. Every day."

"Is she the one who drives off in the red pickup?"

"The one and only."

"I thought that girl seemed off, but so does everyone."

"Hey," she says. "What about me?"

He smiles. "Especially you."

CeCe grins despite herself and her cheeks get warm for the second time that day.

He hands her back the paper. "You probably don't have anything to worry about. The Revies aren't really a threat or anything. They're mostly a pain in the ass doing crap like this," he points to the building, "but you're Dr. Campbell's daughter, and they have it in for him. It's odd that she's there and they haven't done anything about it."

"Maybe she's not a Revie. Maybe she's a regular run-of-the-mill jerk."

"Yeah, maybe."

She remembers that encounter in the hallway with Olivia, the menacing air of it, the feeling that she was on the other side of the bathroom door ready to jump out like a spider. It could be nothing or it could be something. Or some kind of strange fascination. Like haters who can't stop obsessing about their least favorite celebrities. She hopes it's that. Some kind of sick interest.

Derrick says, "You should stay clear of her."

"Already do."

They continue to her home, changing the conversation. Derrick talks about what he's been doing on the Sanitation Crew. The places they're getting into and the cool stuff they've found. They've been working in a Best Buy and have stacks of new PlayStation games that keep them occupied. She tries to pay attention, but she can't stop thinking about Olivia and the Revies, and if Olivia is one of them at all.

They stop in front of her house. Her dad's car is in the driveway. Derrick looks at the door. She wonders if he's waiting for an invite. She hasn't invited him in yet. She probably should introduce him to her dad so he can meet the guy who's been walking her home every day, but she doesn't.

She doesn't have any reason why she hasn't. Maybe it's still some loyalty to Riley that stops her, but she's not sure. Derrick is a friend. She can have guys that are friends.

"Text me later?" he asks her.

"Yeah," she says.

"Okay." He smiles and turns away. She watches him for a moment before heading inside, regretting not asking him to come in. Next time, she tells herself, but if she is being truthful, she probably won't then either.

Her dad is in the kitchen. He gets off the computer as soon as he sees her and takes off his glasses. His face is bright, brighter than she's seen in a while. He's amped up about something. "I have a surprise for you in your room."

"Okaaay," she says slowly.

"Go look."

He follows her up the stairs. There's a dress on her bed. A simple navy-blue satin gown. There's a handwritten card on top. She picks it up.

For my best man.

She turns to her dad.

"Well, what do you think?" he asks.

"About the dress?"

"Yes, about the dress, but also about being my best man? We're doing it, Cees. Tomorrow."

A weight presses against her chest and she has to suck in a gulp of air.

"Tomorrow? Isn't there supposed to be, like, a date, you know, in advance?"

He'd told her about the marriage like a week ago? Two tops. She's barely begun processing that it is going to happen and he's already forcing it down her throat. She sits on the bed, the note still in her hand.

"Sure," he says, "but me and the guys at the CAVE have been talking about it. Tomorrow's perfect. We've reached a breather in our workload if you can believe it. Plus, you have your dress. So does Lauren. And General MacGregor is coming for an inspection. He's become a good friend of mine and he's actually a licensed officiant. I want you to meet him. He's a six-star general. There hasn't been one of those since 1919."

She stares at her dad, her heart thumping fast. She's not ready for this. It's like she's in a parallel universe and somewhere in another dimension where she's with Riley and Leyton, and playing tennis and coming home to her mom's cooked dinners. And, somehow, she got stuck in this universe where she's been asked to be her dad's best man when he marries another woman.

"You're going to really like him," her dad says, unaware of the panic building inside her.

"Is Lauren going to start living here now?" she blurts out.

"No." He shakes his head as he comes to sit beside her. "I mean, not right away. We thought it would be better if we waited until you were done with the GED program and settled and doing your own thing. You are nearly twenty-one years old. I figured you wouldn't want to be living with your old dad much longer anyway."

He can't know what she wants because she doesn't even know. The one thing she knows is she doesn't want *this*.

He says, "Why don't you try on the dress while I get dinner started. Call you down in a few, okay?"

CeCe doesn't say anything and keeps holding on to his note. He's acting as if they've been talking about what movie to watch that night, without any clue of what this news is doing to her.

Tomorrow. Tomorrow her dad is going to get remarried, snuffing her mother out of their lives for good.

He leaves and she stays there, unmoving, unable to process, until her phone dings in her pocket. She pulls it out. It's Derrick.

D: Hey. You have a sec?

She stares at the screen. She wants to respond but can't bring herself to. At that moment she's jealous of him. He has his family still out there, still together. Even if they aren't, he has the luxury of ignorance. He can keep living with that hope. She doesn't have that. She puts the phone on silent and slides it back in her pocket.

She eats dinner at the kitchen counter. Dad's made rice with some refried beans mixed in. He talks. She doesn't. She thinks of her mom and Teddy and the family picture on the wall. Her chest feels hollow. Like a pit left over where her heart should be.

Her phone vibrates. It's Derrick again.

D: *I have an idea.*

"Who's that?" her dad asks in mid-bite.

"No one," she says, putting the phone away. "A friend from school."

She finishes her dinner and goes upstairs. She lies on her bed, her backpack next to her. The dress is hanging on the back of the door. She sets her phone on her nightstand. It buzzes the moment she does.

D: *Me again. Seeing what you're up to.*

She looks at the screen. She should text him back. It's not Derrick's fault her dad dropped the wedding on her like he did.

C: *Nothing.*

Her fingers hover over the send button. She contemplates telling him about the wedding, but saying it makes it more real, and he'd probably ask her about it and then she'd have to respond. She doesn't want to.

C: *Doing schoolwork.*

D: *It's Friday. You can't do schoolwork on a Friday. I'm pretty sure there's a rule somewhere written down by the first kid who ever went to school.*

He's trying to be clever, but she's not in the mood.

C: *Nothing much else going on.*

She had planned to do her work. Planned to be productive, be more of a student. Focus on something other than her insignificant existence. They're doing math now in class. It's not her favorite subject, but it's been better, easier to process, but now she's thinking of tomorrow, and her dad and Lauren, and her mom.

D: *You want to hang out?*

C: *And do what?*

D: There's something I want to show you. It's kind of a surprise.

The dress was also a "surprise," and it wasn't all that great. She looks at the clock.

C: Curfew?

D: It'll be okay. Me and my friends go out all the time.

The phone hovers in her hand. Outside of school, she hasn't left her house since coming home from Costco, and she definitely hasn't gone anywhere at night. Is she ready for that? She isn't sure.

D: Please.

She glances up at the navy-blue gown on the door.

C: Okay.

D: I'll pick you up in an hour, cool?

He adds an old-school smiley face.

C: Cool.

She spends the next forty-five minutes doing her math and avoiding the dress. She hears her dad go into his room. It's quiet. He's reading. He always reads before bed. Fifteen minutes before Derrick is set to arrive, she goes to the bathroom and brushes her hair. She sees her makeup bag on the shelf next to the sink. She hasn't touched it since she's returned. She thinks of Savannah and unzips the bag and rummages through all the eye shadows and eyeliner. It's all over two years old now and probably gross. She finds a tube of mascara and puts a little on her eyelashes. It goes on okay. Not clumping or anything so she guesses it's still all right. She digs into the bag some more and finds a Chapstick and puts that on too and then a bit of blush.

She peers into the mirror. A glimmer of her old self stares back.

What am I doing?

She gets a hand towel and runs it under the water until it's warm. She scrubs at her cheeks and her eyes until all the makeup is off. She's not her old self and there's no use in pretending she ever will be.

When she's done, she heads toward the stairs, creeping past her dad's door. She can hear him snoring on the other side, probably dreaming of marital bliss. Her stomach turns at the thought. She continues on, laying her feet carefully on the floorboards.

She tiptoes down the stairs. Her phone vibrates.

D: Here.

C: Coming.

She goes to the front door, quietly opening and closing it behind her. She takes the key from under the mat and locks it before heading down the walkway to Derrick. He's sitting on a sleek black motorcycle that looks like something out of a videogame. He watches her with a smile.

"Sneaking out?" he whispers as she gets closer.

"Guilty," she says. "But this isn't going to help." She points to the bike.

"This?" He runs his hand along the top. "This is the perfect sneak-out bike. It's an Energica Ego Plus. All electric. Doesn't make a sound. Found it behind a mechanic shop and hooked it up to a generator."

"Still, you don't expect me to actually get on that thing, do you?"

He holds out a helmet. "It'll be a really long walk otherwise."

She gives him an *I'm reluctantly doing this* look before she takes the helmet and slips it over her head. She adjusts the strap under her chin, making sure it's tight. Her hair presses flat against her face. There was probably a better way of doing it, but she's never ridden on a bike. Riley had a truck. Sensible and less of a death trap.

Derrick moves forward, an invitation to get on. She hesitates. It'd been awkward today when he'd put his arm around her, and now she's about to snuggle him from the back.

He looks at her. "I'm ready if you are."

She takes a breath and hoists her leg over. Slowly, she puts her arms around his waist. She hasn't touched anyone like this since before the Kill. And while her impulse is to let go, he's warm and smells a little like vanilla and clove.

"Hold on," he says.

The bike lurches forward, and she tightens her grip. They circle around and take off down the street and soon they're far from her house.

Everything is dark. No light emanates from the windows. No glowing auras from shops. Outside of the occasional blinking traffic light, a cloak shrouds the city. It's unsettling to see it this way. Like it's been abandoned and left for dead.

Derrick navigates toward downtown, taking streets that once were so familiar, but now unrecognizable without the usual traffic.

In the distance, tall buildings shadow the skies, reaching up like darkened tree trunks. She wants to ask him if it's safe to come here, but she stays quiet, feeling the vibration of the bike underneath her.

They veer off into Old Town District. Old Town was a favorite hangout for locals and tourists alike. Any given weekend, its sidewalks ballooned with shoppers perusing the stores for handmade goods. Blown-glass knickknacks, candles and soaps, regional art, and crystals and jewelry.

On the corner of Maple and Ninth was Madame Lu's Palm and Tarot Readings. It had been there since she was a kid. She and Leyton had even gone in there once. Madame Lu told her she'd get married and have three kids. Seems like such a joke now.

Derrick slows down and pulls alongside a redbrick building.

"We're here," he says.

Shattered glass spreads like dandelion seeds on the vacant sidewalks, and broken chairs and shelves hang outside the shop windows.

She sees Big Al's Brewery down toward the end. They'd had the best burgers in the city. She'd go there with her parents all the time. But like everything else, it's become another wasteland.

She gets off the bike, her legs and arms sore from holding on to Derrick for so long. But now that she's away from him, she misses the closeness. It's an ache, an emptiness. The desire to be with another human being taking over her good sense. She shakes away the feeling as she follows Derrick to a glass door.

He dangles a key in his hand. Brick walls stretch on either side. It's not a store. Or not one she recognizes as one. There are no large bay windows or anything, but on the door is a Store Hours sign so it must be.

"I found this place last week," he says.

He unlocks it and pushes it open to a jingle of bells.

Soft light pours from the inside. He gestures for her to go before him, and she steps in. It's a music shop. Guitars of all types and sizes hang next to neon signs that say, "Rock 'n Roll" and "Up All Night."

Flushed against the walls are wooden tables with dusty headphones still resting on top, cords neatly coiled. And dividing the space are shelves full of vinyl records and cassettes in yellowed plastic.

CeCe drinks it all in. The framed album covers, the well-worn carpet, the color-coded box of guitar pics. It's untouched. A time capsule unspoiled by the Kill Virus.

"Amazing, right?" he says, coming beside her.

"How'd you find it?"

"I was driving around. Exploring. I jimmied the lock to get in. Wasn't sure what I'd find. Infected, mostly, but instead I got this."

He turns to her. She isn't sure if it's his face shining from his excitement or the neon lights, but she feels the energy too. Like they've stumbled into a treasure chest.

She walks around, running her fingers along the shelves. Hints of patchouli oil still linger in the air even after all this time. People came here to listen to music, to play. It feels so foreign now that such a thing existed. That people used to enjoy themselves like this.

Derrick points up a set of stairs. "There's an apartment up there. I'm still cleaning that part up. Found an extra set of keys behind the counter. As soon as I get permission, I'm going to move in. You know, as long as the girl it belongs to doesn't come back."

"Girl?"

"Yeah, I found some of her stuff upstairs."

She picks up a No Doubt CD and looks at the cover.

"I wonder what happened to her."

"What I could tell, she left fast. The dresser drawers were out, the closet kind of a mess. She could've stayed, there was food in the fridge and the water still works. I really don't know. Only that she locked it up. Glad she did. Otherwise, who knows what it would have looked like."

He goes over to a record player and flicks it on. It hums with electricity. He sets a vinyl on the spinning table and puts the needle down. A slow guitar riff begins playing and then the light sound of drums and finally a man's voice. It's older and reminds her of something her dad might listen to.

"Who's that?"

"Who's that?" he scoffs. "It's Eric Clapton. He's a genius."

She tilts her ear to it. The music is nice. She wants to like it. Though, it's not the song that's bothering her, but the sound. It's from another time, another world, and it's pulling her back like the bathroom did that first day at Franklin.

She can feel the past on her numb skin. Its ghosts chattering in her mind. She almost tells Derrick to turn it off, but when she sees his face, his joy, she can't make herself do it.

"Let me show you the surprise," he says.

"I thought this was the surprise."

He smiles. "Nope."

He takes her to the back where there's a ladder. He climbs up first and pushes open a trapdoor.

"Come on," he says, gesturing to her to follow.

She goes up. At the top, he holds out his hand. She takes it. This time without hesitation, without awkwardness. He hoists her out onto the roof.

"This is the surprise," he says.

Candles light up the dark rooftop, flickering like fairy lights. She gasps at the sight of it. It's beautiful, and she hasn't seen anything she could define as beautiful since waking up in the Costco. She takes a step forward, staring at the flames dancing in their glass holders. With the sound of the music still coming from downstairs, it's almost magical.

"You did this for me?" she asks.

"Well, yeah."

She looks at him. For the first time since that night, she sees him without the memory of Mason's tainting it.

She sees Derrick.

No monster, no teeth. Only him.

She didn't think that could be possible, but somehow, he made it possible.

"There's more," he says.

He goes to the other side of an air-conditioning unit and holds up a wicker laundry hamper. He says, "It's the closest I could get to a picnic basket. It's clean, I swear. I mean, at least I think so."

She smiles. "I'm sure it's fine."

She goes with him to the center of the roof and helps him lay out a blanket. She runs her hands along the sides, making sure they're flat.

"Why did you do all this?"

"I don't know," he says, as he takes out a box of Triscuits and two water bottles from the hamper. "It's kinda that no one really knows what's going to happen and I wanted you to get a chance to lie under the stars. I hope you're okay with Triscuits. They might be stale."

He looks at her, and the way he does, she feels it. A skip, a flutter. The seed of something growing. She can hardly believe it, and yet, there it is, like a tickle warming her insides.

Happiness. And it's because of him.

He's made her feel this way.

She almost wants to laugh with the irony of it. The guy who took her happiness is bringing it back to her.

"This is really nice," she says. "Definitely a surprise. A good one."

"Come on then," he says and pats the blanket. "Let's check out some stars."

She gets beside him and lies on her back, looking up at the sky. The stars are bright and clear. There's so many of them dotting the blackness like the freckles that used to cover her nose and cheeks when she was little.

She doesn't remember it ever looking like this, or maybe it's because she's never really looked.

Derrick opens the box of Triscuits. He takes a bite of one.

"Definitely stale," he says.

He offers the box to her, and she digs in for a few. She puts one in her mouth. He's right. Two-year-old crackers don't age well, but it's not like either one of them can taste it properly anyway—another side effect of the Kill Virus. Temporary, so her dad thinks.

"What do you think?" he asks, motioning to the night sky.

"It's beautiful. So this is what it's like camping, huh?"

"Not quite, but I don't know, I might like this better."

The music drifts up from downstairs. It's peaceful, no longer bothering her. It makes her feel like she could stay like this forever. Her and Derrick staring up at the night sky with a box of stale crackers. And that maybe for once she could fall asleep without nightmares.

Derrick leans on his side. "Tell me about yourself."

She shrugs. "There's not much to tell."

"Oh, come on," he says. "I've told you practically everything about me. Tell me something about you. What were you like, you know, before the Kill Virus?"

"What do you want to know?"

"Well, did you have a boyfriend?"

"I did." She swallows. "His name was Riley."

"Riley, huh? Was it serious?"

She's hit with a memory of her and Riley, playing in his backyard when they were kids. Their parents sat near the BBQ, having drinks and laughing together. Riley had one of those playsets, a nice one with a slide and a jungle gym. They spent hours on it.

She nods.

"How serious? Like marriage serious?"

She laughs. "No, not like that. We were in high school, you know. But we were together for a long time until…" She trails off.

"Do you know what happened to him?"

She shakes her head. "I don't know what happened to him or any of my friends. My dad said there were these mass cremations. I don't know if that's where they are or somewhere else. They're just—gone."

The peaceful moment is broken. She doesn't like talking about this. It's another reminder of what she's lost. What she'll never have back.

"Can we talk about something else?"

"Yeah, of course," he says. "So what else did you do? Work? Do drama? Or were you one of those mathletes?"

"A mathlete?" She chuckles. "Um, no. I hated math."

"Then what did you do?"

"I don't know. Mostly, I went to school and played tennis a lot."

"Tennis? Impressive. I've tried it a few times. Never really any good at it, but it wasn't like they had a ton of tennis courts where I'm from. Lots of shooting ranges, but no tennis clubs."

She gets quiet for a moment. "I had a scholarship."

"Scholarship for tennis?"

"At Ohio State. I was going to play for the Buckeyes."

"Damn, the Buckeyes? They're my dad's favorite college football team. You must be good. Like Serena Williams good, huh?"

"Not even close. But I don't know, maybe one day I could've been." She rubs her bitten hand.

"Do you miss it?"

"Sometimes, I guess. It's still there, every time I leave the house, every time it rains. Every time—" She stops when she nearly says *every time I look at you.* "I don't know. Now it's like something I dreamed about once. That it was never me, but someone else. Someone I don't even recognize anymore."

Derrick leans toward her. "How did it happen to you? It's all anyone really can talk about. The guys on the crew. We all know each other's Infection stories, but I don't know yours."

She stares up at the sky. She knew he'd eventually ask. She's been waiting for it, but even though she knew it would come, she's still not ready.

"You know you can talk to me, right?"

She knows she can, but she doesn't know if she wants to.

Her stomach twists around the bit of cracker she ate. She should tell him the truth about what happened that night at Mason's, but now it feels like that window has closed.

Things will change between them. He won't be able to look at her, at least not in the way he looks at her right now.

Derrick has made her feel less lonely. With her dad getting married tomorrow, Derrick is all she has left. Maybe it's selfish, but she doesn't care. She's lost everything and she isn't ready to lose this too.

"Please," he says.

She looks at him. She has to tell him something. He was Infected. She was Infected. Everyone he knew was Infected. It's touched them all. She'll only become more of a curiosity if she continues to keep it to herself, and with that curiosity might come suspicion.

"It happened on my eighteenth birthday. I was bitten on my hand. Trying to help someone."

"Do you know who?"

"No." She shakes her head. "It was some guy. I, uh, didn't get a good look at him. It happened so fast."

Talking about it makes the memories come flooding back. Like it did when she first saw Derrick. Her friends screaming, Leyton calling 9-1-1, the blood. She closes her eyes, trying to push the memories away. She wants to be here under the stars with the candlelight. Not back at Mason's.

"It's not much of a story," she says.

"Is this where?" he asks and takes her gloved hand.

She nods.

He holds on to it. His touch is soft, gentle. He lifts her hand to his mouth. Her heart thumps against her chest. The urge to snatch her hand away from his grasp is unbearable. Her arm trembles as she watches him, feeling powerless as the memory of the searing pain of his teeth tears at her scarred flesh. She cries out when he places his lips on her glove.

He lets go and she yanks her hand away. She can sense his eyes on her and regrets her behavior for souring the mood.

Why did she have to freak out like that? This isn't Derrick outside Mason's. She knows that, and yet she couldn't swallow her fear.

She holds on to her hand as an uneasiness grows between them. She hates it. It only makes her feel more alone.

Derrick says, "I didn't mean—"

"No," she interrupts him. "It's me. I'm sorry. It's the memories. It got to me, that's all. It wasn't you."

He continues to stare at her.

"Let's forget about it, okay? I, uh…" She starts to get up. "I should probably be getting back. Tomorrow's kind of a big day. My dad decided to drop his wedding on me."

"It's tomorrow? That was fast."

"He asked me to be his best man. So I should, you know, not be a zombie or anything."

She cringes at the word. She hadn't meant to say it.

"True," he says.

She helps him put the crackers away and fold up the blanket. Things still feel a little weird. Or maybe it's her. She can't tell.

They blow out the candles and the overwhelming darkness returns.

Derrick keeps one lit as he takes hold of CeCe's hand, her unbitten one, as he leads her back to the ladder. She goes down first and waits for him while he fiddles with the trapdoor.

Once downstairs, he turns off the stereo. The record stopped playing a long time ago and it spins on its wobbled axis. He continues with the neon lights, one by one, until shadows coat every guitar and cassette in stillness, snuffing out the warmth.

"Ready?" he asks.

"Yeah." She pauses. "Thank you. For everything. This has been the best night I've had in, well, years."

"You mean it?"

"I do."

Derrick smiles. "It was the best night for me too."

He opens the door, and she steps out. As she gets onto the sidewalk, a sound startles her; it's like a gurgled howl that crawls up the back of her neck. A man staggers toward the shop. His clothes hang on his body from years of wear and his movements are unnatural, irregular. His mouth opens and shuts, clacking like a pair of dice.

He's Infected.

As if materializing from the walls, another Infected follows from behind. A woman wearing what remains of a suit with one heel still on her foot. Her hair hangs over her face. She screeches and the sound cuts through CeCe's flesh and buries deep into her marrow. She knows that sound. She remembers it.

The Infected lunge toward her.

She tries to scream but only a hiss rattles from her throat. She stands there, unable to move; she wants to, but her feet no longer feel part of her body.

"Damn," Derrick says. "They must've been drawn by the music."

He pulls her back inside, shutting the door as the Infected man slams into it.

CeCe starts shaking. Her arms, her legs, her jaw. She can't. She can't be here. She can't do this.

"It'll be okay," Derrick says, taking her by the shoulders. "I promise. I'm going to take care of this."

The woman screeches on the other side of the glass as she throws herself against it. One after another, they pound against the door, the only barrier between them and her. With each thud, she flinches. It's going to break. Any second now and they'll come in here. She backs up into one of the shelves. Vinyl records crash down at her feet. She covers her ears as she slides to the floor.

Derrick gets out his phone and dials a number. "Yeah, we got a couple of 557s on Maple Street. Okay. Yeah." He shuts the phone. "RRT is on their way. They're in the area, lucky for us."

He gets on the ground and puts his arms around her. She clings onto him, whimpering like when she was five years old. She can't help it. She couldn't stop even if she tried.

"It'll be okay," he says, trying to soothe her. "CeCe, I'm so sorry."

Car doors slam outside. She hears shouting. A floodlight burns against the glass door, outlining the Infected. There's a pop and the sound of fizzing. White smoke engulfs the man and woman and seeps through the door frame.

She breathes in the scent of rotting oranges. It's Nitrociptine. She instantly starts gagging.

Derrick takes off his shirt and holds it over her nose.

"Here," he says. "This'll make it better."

She presses it against her face.

"Breathe," Derrick tells her.

The Infected woman stumbles and falls onto the sidewalk. Then the man drops beside her. Four uniformed men materialize into the light. They surround the downed Infected, lift them by their legs and arms, and carry them away.

"They're gone," Derrick says. "They've got them. You're safe."

He gets up. CeCe grabs his hand and shakes her head.

"I'll be right back," he says. "Everything's fine now. I swear."

He opens the door. She tries to lower his shirt away from her face. Even though she knows the Infected aren't there, she wants to scream at him not to open it. Because there's always more of them. That's what her dad said. But she can't move the shirt without tasting the sickly gas in the back of her throat.

The floodlight is turned off and replaced with yellow and blue flashing lights. One of the uniformed men comes over to Derrick. She can't make out what they're saying, only they motion a lot toward her. The uniform radios something and the crackling noise of a response comes back. Derrick and the uniform stay like that, talking back and forth, crackling coming in and out of the radio. Finally, the uniform moves away.

Derrick comes over to CeCe. He leans down and takes her hand, the gloved one, the bitten one, and she shakes.

"The RRT are going to take you home. Okay? Just in case."

In case there's more Infected and the idea is so frightening that she's not sure if she can move.

"They've called your dad. He's waiting for you. It, uh, probably wasn't the best way for him to find out about me. I guess he had no idea who I am."

She looks at him. There's pain in his face, or is it disappointment? She isn't sure.

This time, it's her turn to tell him she's sorry.

Chapter Eight

Her dad is standing on the front lawn when RRT pulls into the driveway. He doesn't even wait for them to leave before he lays into her.

"What the hell were you thinking, CeCe?"

She's still shaken from the encounter with the Infected. She wants to talk to him about it, ask him if that's what she was like, those creatures, but instead her defenses shoot up and she digs a mental trench.

"I went out," she says, stepping around him and going inside. "I didn't realize I was a prisoner."

"No one said that."

She whirls on him. "Then would you have let me go?"

"No."

"Now you know why I didn't tell you."

Her dad follows her up to her room.

It's late, she's hoping he'd want to pass on the dad speech until morning, being it's his wedding and all, but he doesn't. She's tired and numb, and can't deal with him coming at her.

"Do you have any idea of what you've put me through? Any idea of what went through my mind when I got that call?"

She doesn't respond. It's not that she doesn't feel bad, she does. But it isn't like she would've left the house if she'd known what was going to happen.

"Who is this guy you were with?"

"Derrick."

"I know that already. The RRT gave me that much. What I want to know is how *you* know him and why you haven't told me about him. Does he go to your school?"

"No."

"No?" He crosses his arms. "Then how did you meet this Derrick?"

"When I walked home that first day. I met him passing Ed's. He's in the Sanitation Department. You saw him when you picked me up from school. It's not that big of a deal."

He waves his arm. "Oh sure. Like that makes it all right. Some guy I saw through the car window one time is fine to take my daughter out at night and wrangle with Infected. I see your logic."

"Stop it, okay? Derrick is used to it. He sees the Infected all the time."

"But you don't."

He isn't wrong. She thought she'd be so tough. That she could handle coming across the Infected, but she'd crumbled into nothing. Frozen. No wonder she'd gotten bit. If it hadn't been Derrick, it would have been someone else eventually. She's classic prey.

"From here on out," he says, "I'm driving you home from school."

"You can't do that. Walking home with Derrick is pretty much the only highlight of my boring existence."

"I don't even know who he is. Even if I did, how could I trust him after this? How can I trust you?"

"It doesn't matter if you trust me or not."

"Excuse me?"

She faces him, her cheeks turning hot with anger. "I don't have anyone. Not Riley. Not Leyton. Teddy. My mother. Not even you. You're with Lauren now. Who do I have? You've had two years to adapt. Me? I've had barely any time since I woke up to deal with everything."

"You're being unreasonable."

"*I'm* being unreasonable? Are you serious?"

"Enough," he shouts. "I'm not listening to this. This selfish, poor me, I'm so lonely narrative. It's all been for you, CeCe. Everything I've done. When I got that phone call, I thought you were dead. I thought that was it, she's gone. Just like—" He stops. "I can't. I can't lose you. All right? Do you understand?"

He looks at her, taking one deep, deep breath after another. He's never talked like that to her before. Never gotten this mad.

"Tell me you understand."

She nods.

"Okay," he says and repeats. "Okay." He puts his hand on the doorknob. "We'll discuss Derrick later, and we *are* going to discuss him."

She wants to tell him she's sorry, that she never meant to scare him. And tell him maybe he's right, maybe she *is* being selfish, but she can't bring herself to utter the words.

***

The next day, CeCe is in the main hub of the CAVE wearing her navy-blue gown and picking at a bulky seam. It's a size too big and the sleeve scrapes against her armpits. She sits at one of the tables as her dad's coworkers finish decorating for the wedding she doesn't want. The room buzzes with excitement, happiness, expectation. They talk amongst themselves, rearranging one item for another, adding more, taking away. They boast about having raided an abandoned event and rental store and using it to transform the space with tablecloths and runners, lanterns with flameless candles, and even managed an arbor that they brighten with fake flowers and twinkle lights. Every other available space erupts with bouquets of balloons, courtesy of leftover helium tanks. If it weren't for the occasion, she'd be impressed.

She watches all this from her lonely table. Most of these people have known each other since the beginning of the Infection. They've struggled together, survived together. She's an outsider. All that connects her here is her dad, and he hasn't spoken to her much today.

He crosses the room to her. She feels like she should be doing something. Help out or whatever, but everything's done, and it isn't like anyone asked her to do much other than fold the napkins.

"I think we're almost ready," he says, his face tight. "I wanted to let you know. Please try to act a little happy for me." He turns away.

"I'm sorry," she blurts out. "I'm sorry about what happened. I should've told you. About Derrick. He's really a nice guy. But it's no excuse for leaving last night."

His shoulders relax and he takes the seat next to her.

"You know I trust you, right?" he says. "But I need you to trust me too. It never was an issue between us before. I don't know why it is now."

"I do trust you."

"Then don't hide things from me. I'm on your side. Always and forever. You're not alone. You have me, and you might not think it, but you also have Lauren. She wants to be there for you. She's not your mother. She never will be. No one can replace your mom, and no one can replace you."

He puts his arms around her and in that moment, she feels small again. She's a little girl who wants to crawl into her dad's lap and stay there, protected from the world. He releases his embrace and gently pinches her chin.

"I love you," he says. "And I'll rethink this Derrick walking you home, but I'm going to need to meet this guy. No more secrets. We agreed, remember?"

"Yeah, I remember. I love you too. And thank you, about Derrick."

Her dad's attention turns as an older man enters the hub wearing a full military uniform with medals lining his chest. He's flanked by two other officers. This must be the infamous General MacGregor, six-star general.

He takes off his hat and tucks it under his left arm. His jaw is hard, his eyes serious and unflinching. He seems like the last person who'd have his officiant license or be near anything where people are happy.

Her dad squeezes her hand. "It's time."

CeCe follows him to the arbor and stands alongside him. Music plays on a portable speaker. It's something classical. Familiar in a vague way. She should probably know it, but doesn't. Lauren comes around a corner. She's in a simple white gown, hair upswept, and holding a bouquet of yellow roses. She's glowing, and CeCe can't help but think how beautiful Lauren looks right then. And that maybe if Lauren had that much love for her father, she could give her a chance. It feels like a betrayal to her mom for thinking so, when what's left of her mother is a bloodstain on a piece of pavement.

Lauren takes her place beside him, clearly happy, and he's happy too. CeCe feels something. Not quite happiness, but it's not sadness either. Ambivalence, maybe. She supposes that's progress. General MacGregor starts the ceremony. It's short and simple. Efficient and before long the "I do's" are over and her dad and Lauren kiss.

She looks down at her feet when they do. Almost like out of a knee-jerk reaction. She isn't ready to see that yet

Lauren hugs CeCe.

She stiffly accepts.

The celebration continues with music and champagne and a meal of scavenged food. Among the Cured, they'd found a famous chef named Sam Slater. He used to have his own television show, *Get Cooking with Sam*. CeCe has never seen him before, but she bet her mom would know who he is. For the wedding feast, Sam made a pasta alfredo from powdered milk and noodles. It's warm and creamy and feels nice in her stomach.

Her dad and Lauren have their first dance and cut a cake made from a box mixture and whatever they used to substitute for eggs.

But it had been done so nice it was hard to tell that it hadn't come from a bakery. Probably another one of Sam's contributions.

The whole while, Lauren and her dad look thrilled, and watching them this way reminds CeCe of her mom and how much she misses her and how much this seems a little like a nightmare she must smile through.

The afternoon turns into night and guests start leaving once the last of the wine is gone. CeCe yawns as she sits at the wedding table. She wants to go home, but can't. Her dad made plans for her to stay the night at the CAVE since he and Lauren are staying there too.

She'd packed her backpack that morning since her dad made it clear he didn't trust her on her own. She didn't like the feeling of being fourteen again, but then again, the thought of being by herself after a night of the Infected didn't seem ideal either.

After she helps clean up, her dad takes her to her room. It's not much of one. More like a prison cell with a twin bed and a standard-issue mattress. They had the same ones at the Costco. He says good night, and he'll see her in the morning, and then she's alone.

She drops her bag on the bed and unzips it, taking out a pair of sweats and a tee shirt, Riley's folded shirt, and Derrick's rock that she still carries with her.

So many times today she wanted to call him or send a text. If anything, only to tell him she's okay and to see if he's okay and if *they're* okay. But they confiscated her phone at the door. Security protocol and all that. No official CAVE badge, no phone. She won't get her hands back on it until tomorrow.

She looks at the rock and wonders if Derrick had tried to contact her and what he must be thinking when she hadn't responded. Probably that she doesn't want to talk to him, but she's never wanted to talk to him more.

Last night frightened her, sure, but she has other memories that aren't so unpleasant. The music, the lights, even the stale crackers. It was sweet and it meant something to her that he'd go through all that trouble. For her.

Setting the rock down, she changes out of her dress, balling it up and shoving it in her backpack. She stands at the mirror above the sink, washes her face, and brushes her teeth. When she's done, she crawls into the bed and stares up at the ceiling, rolling Derrick's rock over and over in her hand. It's quiet in the CAVE, a suffocating kind silence that presses against the temples.

She closes her eyes, tries to go to sleep, but sleep is difficult even on a good day. Now she's here in a new place on a hard mattress. She counts. It's worked before, but she gets to about two hundred before she realizes it's pointless.

It's not the unfamiliar room that's bothering her. It's that she's at the CAVE. Inside the facility that discovered the cure. Everything known about the Kill Virus is here. Everything she doesn't know, including P73-7, a secret bigger than her, is here too.

She gets up. She'll pretend to get something to drink. See what she sees. She opens the door, almost surprised that she wasn't locked in, and heads down the hallway to the commissary.

Soft white and green lighting emanates from the floor like she's in some kind of a spaceship. As soon as she enters the kitchen, motion-sensors flick on, reflecting incandescent light off the stainless-steel counters.

It's hard for her to imagine her dad living here all this time. Shuffling here in the morning in his worn-out slippers, robe tucked across his chest, and holding his #1 Dad coffee mug while she and her mother were zombies in the parking lot.

But this is where he ate his meals, socialized, where he fell in love with Lauren.

Rummaging through the cabinets, she makes enough noise to draw attention if anyone is up. She finds the glasses and holds one under the faucet until it's full. She drinks until the water is gone and looks around for a dishwasher. She doesn't find one and puts the glass in the sink. With her rock back in hand, she stands there, waiting, listening for footsteps, but hears none. There must be some kind of rule about bedtime, or the wine put everyone to sleep.

She wanders down the hallway. The CAVE is a series of corridors tucked underground with only one entrance in and out. Her dad told her it was once a top-secret location for surveillance.

Now instead of spying on other countries, they spy on the Infected. He's never given her any kind of a tour. He was always dragging her to the vet hospital where he worked before, but not here. The wedding was the first she'd spent any amount of time inside other than waiting by the entrance when he needed to pick something up.

The same mood lighting snakes along the bottom of the hallways as she passes more stainless-steel doors. They could be other rooms or broom closets for all she knows. She wonders if, in her drifting, she's gone by where General MacGregor is sleeping. She can't visualize him slumbering inside one of these cells like the rest of them. Maybe the CAVE has something of a penthouse suite somewhere.

Down one wing, she comes to an abrupt dead end facing a large door with a blinking keypad. It could be an observation deck or a lab—the place where her dad discovered the cure. She hopes it is. Otherwise, it's going to get really awkward if she walks into a team of people watching satellite images—if there's a team even in there.

She stares at the keypad and enters the passcode her dad has used for everything, including the one he had on his computer. As soon as she hits "Enter," the red blinking light flashes green and she hears the lock unclick. He's so predictable.

Slowly, she opens the door. Like the commissary, bright lights automatically switch on. She steps into a large hallway with floor-to-ceiling glass on either side. They're enclosures, like the cages in the backroom at her dad's vet practice, but larger.

A moan fills the space, deep and agony-ridden. Her body registers the sound before her mind does. Her legs shake and then her hands, the rock nearly fumbling from her grasp. More groans follow and then the high-pitched screech she heard the night outside the record store. There's a thump against the glass, and the shrill of fingers running along it.

Infected. There's Infected in here.

Her heart races in her chest, threatening to seize in her rib cage. This time there's no Derrick to pull her back. No one to call RRT. She's on her own. She thinks of what to do. Leave and make sure the door is shut before screaming there's Infected in the CAVE, but then they must already know. Her dad already knows. They had put them here.

She takes a trembling step forward and then another, though her brain doesn't want to. It's as if she's trudging through sand. Her legs strain with the force, the impact, but she keeps going. She approaches the first glass enclosure. Inside is an Infected woman with half her body missing. The woman looks up at her, dragging herself along the floor. CeCe stifles a cry. The noise only makes the Infected woman come faster. She smacks against the glass, pressing against it, her mouth contorting. Opening and shutting.

CeCe stands paralyzed. Every instinct tells her to sprint from the room, but she stares transfixed as the woman paws at the glass, trying to dig out, dig to her. Only she can't. They have her trapped. CeCe takes a deep breath and another like she would before a big match, and her nerves were spidering its way across her veins.

The woman's gaze locks on her, and she forces herself to look back—to really look. At her bloodshot eyes. Her ravaged face. Her body in threads. She was human once and no more than six months ago, she and CeCe were the same.

As she stands there, the woman stops her effort. She slumps down, sliding against the glass, quiet. Her jaw grinds together. Pity replaces CeCe's fear. She can't help it. She feels sorry for this woman. Sorry that she's being kept this way, and she wants to know why her dad would do this. Why would he allow her to linger in such a state? He wouldn't do the same to any of the animals who'd come to his hospital who were hurt and suffering and needing to be put out of their misery.

There's a number on her locked door.

P39-2.

Blood pushes through CeCe's veins as her heart rate accelerates. She looks down to the other enclosures. P73-7, the subject of her dad's emails, the big secret, is an Infected and whoever they are, man or woman, they're here.

She steps away from P39-2 and walks to the next cage where another Infected waits. It's an older man with a gaping hole in his chest from the remnants of a gunshot. Wisps of his hair hang limply around his ears as he presses his forehead against the glass. His rabid eyes fix onto CeCe. His need still present, still raw. This time, she doesn't react and neither does he. Only his mouth twitches, biting out of reflex.

She continues down the walkway, staring into the enclosures, at the Infected, severely wounded in one way or another. She studies each and every one and the numbers by their door handle. P42-7. P51-9, and on and on. Finally, she comes to P73-7. The infamous P73-7.

She stands before the glass, not sure what to expect, but expecting something. A young girl stares back at her, no more than six years old with her hair pulled back in a braid. Old bite-mark scars cover her arms and legs. She's sitting up in a bed, her arm around a familiar stuffed dinosaur.

Bowtie, Teddy's word for him because he couldn't say Brontosaurus. She doesn't know why the girl has it, but that's not the issue right then.

P73-7 is not Infected.

The girl gets to her feet. They gawk at each other.

To her right, a voice whispers, "Hey. Hey you."

CeCe jumps at the sound.

A man comes toward her. He's in scrubs with a name badge attached to his breast pocket. She recognizes him from the wedding. Her dad had introduced them, but she can't remember his name. Bill or Bobby.

"You're not supposed to be in here," he continues to whisper. "How did you? It doesn't matter." He motions to her. "Come on, you need to get out."

CeCe points to the girl. "She's not Infected."

Compared to his voice, hers sounds like a loudspeaker.

He shushes her.

"Not your concern," he whispers. "I mean it, let's go."

She looks back into the enclosure, at Bowtie dangling in the girl's hand.

"But she, she—"

The other Infected bang against the glass. Moans, turning into screeching that falls in a cacophony around her.

"That's it," he says, no longer trying to stay quiet. "You've upset them."

He comes over and grabs her by the arm, pulling her away from the girl. CeCe turns to look at her. She stands at the front of the glass where all the other Infected now are, watching them go.

Once they're back in the hall, Bill or Bobby shuts the door behind them, extinguishing the sound of the Infected.

"That girl," she says again.

"What girl?" he says. "I didn't see a girl."

CeCe rolls her eyes. She can't help it. Is that how he's really going to play this? She looks at his name badge. Steve. She was way off.

"I can't ignore what I saw, *Steve*," saying his name as if she's spitting out a piece of gum.

"You didn't see anything, you understand? You shouldn't have been in there. Do you have any idea what kind of security breach you've caused? And of all days when we have General MacGregor here. Jesus. Do you—" He stops talking. "Get back to your room and stay there, okay? Don't let me catch you out again."

He walks her back, making sure she's in and then she hears the click of a lock. Even if she'd wanted to go back out, there was no chance of that now.

She can't sleep. She's thinking about P73-7 in that glass cage with Teddy's stuffed animal. *What girl?* Steve had said, as if CeCe was so stupid. What is with all the secrecy surrounding that girl? Who is she? *What* is she?

The next morning, the doors are unlocked when she wakes. She doesn't even bother changing, not that she'd brought any clothes to change into, and goes into the commissary. Her dad is there with Lauren and some of the other CAVE employees, including Steve, who found her last night. He stands next to the coffeepot.

The moment she enters, all their eyes turn in her direction. She goes to the coffeepot. They watch her cross the room. It's like walking past the popular girls' table at school, knowing that the moment she's out of earshot, they're going to start talking crap about her.

"Hey," she says to Steve as she gets a mug.

He returns her greeting with a tight smile. "Hey."

She fills her cup and leans against the counter. No one speaks and an uncomfortable hum fills the room. The air's so thick she could use it for creamer. Her dad says something to Lauren. She nods and gets up. She motions to the others. They follow her out like chicks chasing after the mamma hen.

He turns to CeCe and says, "Have a seat."

She takes the place opposite from him. He stares at her. His eyes are tired. Like the sight of her makes him want to lay his head on the table and take a nap.

"Ask," he says.

"Ask what?"

"What is it you want to know? The reason why you went digging into my computer and now made your way into an unauthorized area of the CAVE. A breach that could have gotten me court-martialed and thrown in prison if it wasn't for my relationship with General MacGregor. Is that your goal here? To have me arrested?"

"No," she says. "Of course not."

"Then what is it? What are you looking for?"

He waits for her to speak.

"Answers, I guess," she says. "I want to know what you know."

"What is it you think I'm hiding from you?"

"Well, obviously, you're hiding the fact that there's a little girl with Bowtie in the Infected Zoo Exhibit you have going on. She's cured. What's she doing there?"

"She wasn't cured."

CeCe shakes her head. "What do you mean she wasn't cured? I saw her myself."

"P73-7 is immune."

"Immune?"

"We found her on a patrol. She was being attacked by a cluster of Infected and bitten, badly. I couldn't leave her, not like that, alone and scared. I told them to bring her back with us. We treated her bites the best we could, which wasn't really much. Mostly, we stopped the bleeding. We knew it was only a matter of time before the Infection took hold. Only it never did. It's because of her, because of P73-7, that we have the cure."

"Damn," CeCe says.

"Damn is right."

"Why do you have her caged?" she asks. "Like some prisoner. She should be treated like royalty, or at least have her own room, but she's in there with all those Infected."

"Not a prisoner." Her dad shakes his head.

"You don't call that a prison? She's in a locked box."

"Hers is not locked. Never has been. She refuses to leave. Believe me, we've tried. *I've* tried. She'll only go out a few feet before she starts getting upset. I know it feels wrong to have her there. It feels wrong to me too, but I can't force her to leave. I've always figured she'll come out when she's ready. She's been through a lot, I imagine. I can't tell you why, but she feels safe there."

"What do you think happened to her?"

"Before the cure, the Infected weren't the only problem. Some had their own personal heyday. Criminals, mostly. And if it wasn't them causing problems, looting, killing, and the like, then there were the zealots. The Infection was the perfect breeding ground for every fanatic everywhere to take up a pulpit in the absence of common sense. You knew what you were getting with the crooks, not so much with the other ones."

"Like the Revies?" she asks.

He sits back. "How do you know about them?"

She shrugs. "There's talk at the school."

"Well, yes, there's the Revies. Extremists. Every last one of them. We've heard some things. Abuse, mostly. They're extremely orthodox, distrustful of government even before the virus, and living off the grid. A lot of Survivors found their way to them."

"So, this girl, P73-7, you think she's a Revie?"

"I don't have to think. She has the mark. They brand all their people with the Mark of John on their foreheads. You probably couldn't see it from how far back you were standing, but without a doubt," he nods his head, "she's one of theirs."

A mark on the forehead. She thinks of Olivia and the scar she saw, hiding underneath her bangs. Maybe it wasn't a bite mark after all.

"They left P73-7 to die," her dad says. "The area where she was found, it was swarming with Infected even before. They had to have known that. My guess is maybe they suspected what she was and were trying to get rid of her, but I don't know."

"Even if they did know, how could they allow that to happen to a little girl?"

"Groupthink is a powerful thing."

"What about her parents? Have you asked her about them?"

"I've wanted to ask her a lot of things, but she hasn't uttered a word since she's come to us. We don't know if it's because of what she's experienced with the Revies or the trauma of the horde attack. Could be neither or both. We're working with her, but it's been a slow process and it's not like we have the manpower or the expertise. I was a veterinarian. I know chemical compounds, bacteria, and now viruses. I know nothing about psychology. I brought her Bowtie because I thought it might help in some way. Something that reminds her that she's still a child. That the world wasn't always scary."

CeCe lets out a long breath. She doesn't know what to think. The mysterious P73-7. The savior of them all. A little girl without a name, only a number, sitting in a glass cage with Infected as neighbors.

"Why are you keeping her a secret?" she asks.

Her dad says, "To keep her safe. Not everyone was happy a cure was found, the Revies included. We've had our dealings with them and none that have gone over well." He looks hard at her. "No one can know about P73-7. I'm very serious, CeCe. You have to promise me. We can't let anything happen to her. I'm trusting you on this."

"Of course, I promise. I'd never put her at risk. One thing though. You all can't keep calling her P73-7. She has to have a name."

He raises his eyebrows. "Any suggestions?"

She picks up her coffee. It's cold. She drinks it anyhow and they go back and forth for a while on what they should call her. Naming a person is hard. Eventually, they decide on Penny.

After a breakfast of leftover pasta alfredo, she asks if she can see Penny again and her dad takes her back to the room, punching in a new code. He's already changed the password and probably every other lingering password too. This will be the last of the secrets that he'll let her stumble upon.

The door opens and she walks past the Infected as they shuffle to the glass, but she's not here for them and pays them no attention. She goes to the end where Penny sits at a little table with paper and well-loved crayons. Bowtie sits on the table with her, along with a My Little Pony toy. Penny glances up and then goes back to what she's doing.

"Can I?" CeCe asks her dad as she puts her hand on the door.

He nods. "Sure."

She goes inside the room, slowly stepping toward Penny. The little girl watches her. Her eyes are so bright, like golden wheat. She sits down on the other side of the table. The gouges in Penny's arms are deeper than she realized. Chunks of her flesh are gone. It makes her insides squirm to see that, to see what had been intentionally done to her. CeCe leans closer and peeks at her forehead. A puckered scar shows a cross with three sharp spokes at the bottom, looking like something of a bird's foot. The Mark of John. The mark of the Revies. CeCe's whole body stiffens in the beginnings of rage for what has been done to Penny. But she doesn't want her first visit tainted with her anger. It needs to be something happy.

CeCe reaches out and picks up the My Little Pony toy with a pink mane and tail. Its yellow body has been scratched in places and worn down in others. Penny stops what she's doing and stares at CeCe's hand holding the toy. The girl's jawline clenches slightly, her nostrils flaring.

"Is this yours?" CeCe asks.

The little girl doesn't say anything.

"Is she your favorite?"

Penny nods.

CeCe hands it to Penny. She takes it and hugs the pony and Bowtie close. Then after a moment, she offers the pony back to CeCe.

"It's okay?" she asks before taking it.

The little girl nods again.

CeCe starts to jump the pony back and forth like it's galloping. Penny watches it and then slowly she joins in with Bowtie hopping along the table. CeCe stays like that, playing with Penny, long after her knees ache from pressing against the cold floor. Whenever Penny moves, she can see another scar, another set of teeth marks. Penny hadn't been attacked, she'd been mauled, and it makes CeCe's one bite mark on her hand insignificant in comparison.

She spends the rest of the day with Penny, hanging out in last night's clothes, but not really caring. Penny gets a lot of visitors.

Most of the staff at the CAVE come in and out at various points of the day, including Steve. They ask CeCe how Penny's doing, as if just by being there, she's turned into some kind of an expert when they've been living with her for upwards of seven to eight months. Even General MacGregor comes in. He stands at the glass for a long time, not saying a word, and then turns and walks away. The whole encounter bothers CeCe, but Penny doesn't act all that concerned.

On the drive home, CeCe checks her phone.

Savannah had texted.

S: *Hey, what are you doing? I'm bored.*

CeCe had given Savannah her number about a week ago. They've been texting on and off, nothing much.

Derrick had also texted a few times, even called once. That was new.

D: *How was the wedding?*

D: *Are you okay? Last night was intense.*

D: *Please say something.*

D: *Please, CeCe, say something.*

C: *Just got my phone back. I'm okay as long as you are. I'll text later. Promise.*

Her dad looks at her. "That Derrick?"

"Yeah."

"I meant what I said yesterday. I want to meet him before any more walks home."

"Or you can ambush him after he walks me home tomorrow. Deal?"

He thinks about it for a moment. "Fair enough."

They pass a checkpoint where guards stand with M16s. One of them waves at her dad and lets them through. The CAVE is only about ten minutes from the house, but it might as well be in another world. Large blockades stretch along the side of the road where fields shoot off in the distance. There are a few houses tucked far back with abandoned trucks in the driveways and broken-out windows.

She puts her phone back in her pocket. "What are you doing with those Infected in the cages? Why haven't you cured them?"

"You saw their injuries. None of them would survive if I did."

"Then why not put them out of their misery?"

"Because they can still be of use."

CeCe looks at her dad. "So, what, you're experimenting on them?"

"Would it surprise you if I told you we were?"

"Surprise wouldn't be the word."

"What we're doing is important research. The CC-L virus might turn out to be one of our greatest miracles."

"A miracle? You're joking, right?"

"If we can use it properly, I think it can end up saving people, not killing them. Imagine no one having to die because they need a new heart or a kidney or a liver. Or dying before a new cancer treatment is discovered. We can use the effect of CC-L to put them in a stasis."

"And what about that side effect of wanting to kill people? Are you just going to list that under the warning label?"

"It would be different. They'd be monitored by doctors, under constant care and supervision, until they're brought out. It'll be no different than waking from a deep sleep. The therapeutic implications of CC-L are mind-blowing."

"Yeah, until it blows up in your face."

"The only reason this happened was because we didn't have a method to combat it; now we have one. Thanks to Penny."

She understands what he's trying to do. Leyton's mom died of cancer when they were in middle school. She'd watched her friend crumble after her mom died. She knows her dad wants to help people like Leyton's mom, but it seems all wrong. Keeping those Infected like lab rats. Keeping the virus.

"And what if the cure stops working?" she asks. "What then?"

He looks at her. "That's not even something to kid about."

"I'm not. You know, what if? What if the parasite becomes resistant? Evolves like everything else on the planet?"

"Then we alter the cure. Science will win out, always."

Once they're home, CeCe takes a quick shower and gets her laundry going before she texts Derrick.

C: I'm fine. My phone was confiscated. That's why I was MIA.

She wants to tell him that she'd gotten a little desensitized over the Infected this weekend, but of course she can't without getting into Penny. That's two secrets now she's keeping from him.

C: Dad helped me work through the whole Infected encounter before the wedding.

D: And how was the wedding?

C: Okay. Food was good.

D: I'm jealous. I'd give anything for a decent meal.

D: I missed you.

C: I missed you too. See you tomorrow?

D: Yeah. See you then.

She takes Riley's shirt out of her backpack and picks up his gift. She goes to her closet and gently places them together on a shelf and closes the door.

Chapter Nine

At school they have a practice test in algebra. Not CeCe's best subject. When they're done, Ms. Dobson has them bring them up to her desk.

CeCe gets up; Olivia does too and stands right behind her. Close enough to make her want to push back. Instead, she turns and peers at Olivia's forehead, trying to find the scarred cross under her thick bangs.

Olivia raises her eyebrows. "Looking for something?"

"Are you? You're the one practically on my back."

They stare at each other, the tension growing between them, until CeCe hears Ms. Dobson say, "Girls, you mind moving the line along?"

CeCe hands over her test and goes back to her seat. She didn't see the full scar, the Mark of John, but her gut tells her it's there, that Olivia is one of them. And if she is, whatever she's trying to do, intimidate or frighten CeCe, it isn't going to work.

At the end of the school day, CeCe catches up to Derrick.

"Hey," he says like he's unsure of himself. Like he's waiting for her to say something bad. But then she smiles at him, and his shoulders relax.

"Hey yourself."

They head for home. She wonders if her dad has made good on the deal and is waiting for them. If he is, she should probably give Derrick a heads-up about what is coming. Or not and let her dad have his satisfactory "Dad moment." She can't really choose.

"So," Derrick says. "How are you really?"

"Do you mean the wedding or the record store?"

"Both, I guess, but mostly the record store."

"I told you, I'm okay."

"Are you?"

"Yeah," she says. "I wouldn't lie to you." She feels a hiccup after she says it. "Really," she continues, quickly. "I wasn't expecting that to happen. I should, I guess. There's still Infected out there. I shouldn't be so naïve. You've told me. My dad's told me, and I've been pretending like they're all gone. Everyone's cured. But we're not."

"I feel really bad though. I'd thought about it all weekend. I felt like such a jerk having put you in that situation."

"You didn't know there'd be Infected. It's not your fault." She takes his hand. It's the first time she's ever initiated physical contact and she can tell by the way he relaxes that the small act hasn't gone unnoticed. "I'm fine. Stop overthinking it. Please."

"Okay," he says and gives her a smile. "Okay."

She lets go and they keep walking. She tells him about General MacGregor and Sam, the celebrity chef. They're down the street from Ed's MiniMart when she hears something. An uneasiness sprinkles across her nerves. A prickle at first and then it gets stronger. Is it coming from an Infected? Could one of them be here? She glances at Derrick.

"You hear that?"

He stops. They both listen and then she recognizes it. The rumbling of a truck.

She turns. A red pickup idles at the last intersection they crossed a few blocks back. Her heart thumps. It's Olivia and her friend. They've been following her.

"Look," she says.

Derrick squints in the direction of the truck. "Is that the Revie girl?"

"The one and only. What should we do?"

Derrick lifts up his hand. She quickly pushes it down. "What are you doing?" she asks.

"I want them to know we see them."

"Awesome, now we invited them to come closer."

"Better now than have them tail you all the way back to your house."

"Good point."

He gets out his phone and starts typing in a number.

"Who are you calling?"

"RRT. They can't stand the Revies. They'll chase them off."

"No," CeCe says. "They'll tell my dad and he'll—"

She doesn't have to finish the statement because he already knows what she's going to say. Her dad won't let him walk her home anymore. He'd barely given Derrick a second chance already. She doubts he'll get another even though this is another situation that isn't his fault.

He shuts the phone and slips it back in his pocket.

"Okay," he says. "Now what?"

She turns back to the truck. It's still keeping its distance.

"We can't outrun them, obviously," she says, "but we can't wait them out either. My dad will know something's up if I'm not home."

"Then we'll find another way to get you there." Derrick nods to one of the houses. "Follow me."

He goes to the side of a gate, opens it, and hurries to the back. She stays on his heels, the gate clicking shut behind her. Weeds and vines strangle what's left of the backyard. There are hints of how it used to be. Remnants of a rock pathway. A cracked fountain. Patches of marbled pottery. It used to be someone's refuge in its day, but now only a haven for black widows and snakes.

Derrick looks around and heads over to a bench propped against the fence. He gets on top and hoists himself up to see what's on the other side. She moves to him and almost steps on the remains of a dead bulldog. Its tan and white fur is shriveled against its bones, eye sockets empty, with a blue collar still clamped around its neck. The

Infection hadn't killed it. Neglect had. She stares at it, feeling sorry for the poor thing. It had died here not knowing why it was abandoned.

"Come on," Derrick says, waving her over. "I'll boost you."

Crawling into another unknown backyard with other unknowns wasn't her idea of the best plan, but then she hears the truck. It's coming down the street. They must have seen them take off. She goes over to Derrick and stands on the bench. The wood planks creak underneath her and she expects them to snap at any moment. Before she has a chance to say so, Derrick is already grabbing her by the waist and hauling her over. It's awkward. The fence posts dig into her thighs, and she scrapes her arms and stomach on the boards before she drops on a border of pebble rock. A moment later, Derrick lands beside her with the finesse of a gymnast.

She gets to her feet, pulling her sleeve up to assess the damage. Three angry welts are already swelling around some scrape marks. She pushes her sleeve back into place and looks around. Compared to the other yard, this one's in much better shape. It had been laid with the same rock she'd fallen on with one overgrown patch where grass must have been at some point. In the middle is a towering play structure, one of those megaliths they sold at Costco before it was a makeshift hospital for ex-Infected. A pile of dried leaves hovers at the end of the slide as if waiting for two little legs to go barreling into it.

She turns as she hears the pickup. It's getting louder. She can't tell exactly where it's at, but it's close enough to make her jumpy. Derrick cocks his head toward the fence. He's listening too. Truck doors shut.

Derrick takes her hand, and they hurry to the backdoor of the house. A pink Barbie jeep sits nearby, the coloring long faded from years of sun exposure.

"We'll wait inside," he says.

"What about Infected?"

"There won't be any. This area's been swept."

"You said the record store was swept."

She sees him cringe. She wasn't trying to be mean, just practical.

"Yeah, I know," he says. "I'll go in first."

He goes to the door. It's unlocked.

"See?" he says. "Swept."

He inches the door open, slips inside, and motions for CeCe to follow. She steps into a kitchen. The air is thick and stale and has a tang to it like old lemons. On one side is a light blue wall with well-loved plates, carefully displayed in a cabinet. On the other, a countertop with a stainless-steel coffeepot and an electric mixer coated in a grimy film. Hanging on the refrigerator are a child's drawings, attached with alphabet magnets and the name "Charlotte Harding" written in crayon at the top.

A set of knives sit next to the stove. She grabs the butcher knife and holds it in her hand.

Derrick looks at her. "What are you going to do with that?"

"Use it if I have to."

He smiles. "Aren't you the tough girl."

"Yeah," she says, thinking about that night in the record store and how she crumbled at the first sight of danger. "Tough as nails."

Derrick pushes aside the dining room table where there's a window. He peeks out the blinds; glittery dust clings to his fingertips.

She comes beside him and looks out.

It's hard to tell anything from here and there's not much of a gap between the wood planks separating the yards. Every time she thinks she sees something her eyes adjust and it's nothing. She wouldn't know if Olivia and her friend had already driven off or if they were about to join them.

Derrick turns from the window. "I'm going out there."

"No," she says. "I don't want to be here by myself."

"I'll only be a minute. You can watch me from the window."

She opens her mouth to tell him to stay, but he's right. They can't tell anything from inside and she'd rather be in here than anywhere close to Olivia and whatever she and her friend plan to do if they catch up with them.

Derrick steps outside. She watches him, nearly pressing her face against the dirty blinds. He stands on the back porch, unmoving. Then he takes a few steps, stops, takes a few more, and stops again. Her heartbeat pounds in her throat as she waits for any kind of sign that he sees them. After a moment, he turns to her and lifts his hands up in an exaggerated shrug.

He comes back inside.

"I'm pretty sure I heard their truck take off. I can go back over the fence if you want me to be sure."

"No," she half-yells.

"Whoa," he says. "It was only a suggestion."

"Do you think they're gone, gone? Or are they circling?"

"Hard to say."

"Let's go to the front window," she says. "See if they drive by."

"Yeah, agreed."

With Derrick at her side and her hand still gripping the knife, she moves from the kitchen to the living room. The curtains are drawn, casting a dull shadow as the outside light presses against it. A beige sectional couch sits like a cushioned Stonehenge, crowding the space, making it seem small and cramped. She goes around the side of an end table toward a big pop-out window and stops. The knife drops from her hand, landing with a thud onto the carpet.

At her feet are three sleeping bags. One red, one blue, and in the middle, a pink Disney Princess bag where wisps of blond hair, flashes of skeletonized teeth, and leathered skin peek out of the top. A baby doll rests in the withered arm of a once living and breathing child. A strangled gasp erupts from CeCe's throat as she thinks of the drawings on the refrigerator. Charlotte Harding.

"Damn," Derrick whispers.

The other two bodies, who she assumes are Charlotte's mom and dad, lie facing the girl. Their heads bowed toward her, toward the child they loved with their sunken hands clasping each other's over the top of her body. Whatever this is, or was, it's a sadness so raw that it drums against the muscled chambers of her heart.

Her eyes sting with tears. She wants to mourn the loss of the Hardings, but it's more than that. It's CeCe's family too. All the lives lost. The lives taken. Her eyes ache and her lower lip trembles.

Derrick moves toward the top of the sleeping bags. She reaches out to take his arm to stop him from disrupting them, here in their tomb. It is sacred in a way she can't describe. But he slips away, and she realizes that she hasn't moved at all.

He says, "The little girl was Infected."

"How do you know?"

"She'd been shot in the head. The other two weren't."

"No," CeCe whimpers. "No."

She grips her bitten hand until it throbs.

"This is so wrong," she says. "I—" Her breath catches in her throat. A scream that's been lodged since she woke in the mall parking lot. Tears blur her vision as she steps back, bumping into the end table. It topples behind her. She jumps as it bangs against the floor.

Derrick takes her by the shoulders, getting so close that the only thing she can see is his face. The room is gone. It's only him. "Let's go to the window," he says. "If the truck is gone, we'll go. Okay?"

"What about them?" she asks. "What about the Hardings?"

"I'll call it in once I get you home. I'm not sure how the crews missed this, but I'll find out. I promise."

She nods, not knowing if it's the right thing, but knowing she can't be here anymore. Be here where the loss clings to the air like a leftover scent.

The Hardings chose this place, perhaps out of necessity, but this is where their memories were. She can't say what they'd want, but there was no one else to make that decision for them.

Derrick takes her hand. "Keep your eyes on me, okay?"

She nods, gripping onto Derrick's shirt as she carefully moves around the sleeping bags and toward the window. She stands next to him, trying not to think of the Hardings behind her and the color of their hair, the hollowness of their mouths.

She doesn't know how long they stay there. It could've been a minute or twenty before Derrick opens the door and moves down the walkway toward the sidewalk. He looks around, and then motions for her to come out.

She keeps her gaze in front of her as she goes to the door and shuts it. Leaving the Hardings once more at peace in their resting place. She moves toward Derrick.

There's no sound of the truck anywhere, so they continue down the street.

After a while, Derrick tries to speak to CeCe, but she doesn't offer anything more than a few words. She can't let go of the Hardings and the hopelessness of it all and what they must've been feeling when they made the decision to take their lives.

Her dad thinks the Kill Virus can save people.

It can't save anyone.

It only destroys.

Chapter Ten

They continue on to her house, listening, but it's quiet. Before they get there, she can see her dad outside, rustling around the front yard in his work hat. With the whole ordeal with Olivia and her friend, and then coming across the Hardings, she forgot he was going to be waiting for them.

Yesterday, she was sort of looking forward to her dad and Derrick meeting, but now it's one more thing she has to deal with.

"My dad's here."

Derrick lets out a long breath. "He's there for me, isn't he?"

"You got it."

"Good." Derrick nods. "That's good. I've been wanting to do this for a long time now."

As they get closer, her dad is hunched over, pulling weeds. Clearly this little chore was designed so that he wouldn't miss them. Derrick quickens his step, charging ahead. Her dad stands as he approaches with a typical Disapproving-Dad-Look. Before she can introduce them, Derrick is already apologizing for what happened at the record store.

"It was wrong of me," Derrick says. "I knew she was sneaking out. I should have asked her to talk to you, to have her introduce us properly. It's not how I was raised, I assure you of that, sir. If my mom were here, she'd be smacking the back of my head."

Her dad says, "A lot has changed with the Infection, but some things haven't. You've been walking my daughter home for a while now and I had no idea. I don't like that it was kept from me."

"You're right." Derrick nods. "And that wasn't my intention to be some kind of secret and I should've done better. Please know, I'd never let anything happen to your daughter and if you don't want me to see her anymore, I'll understand. It'll be hard, but I'll respect your wishes."

Her dad looks down at the weeds in his hands. She tries to read his expression, but she can't tell what he's thinking. After a moment, he sighs. "Listen, Derrick. I'm happy that CeCe has found someone. And what happened the other night, coming across an Infected, I suppose it's unavoidable until everyone's cured. To be honest, it sets my mind at ease knowing she's not out there on her own. But my gratitude is all I can give you. The rest you'll have to earn."

"Fair enough," Derrick says.

Her dad takes off his gardening gloves and offers them to him. "If you help me with these weeds, then you can stay for dinner."

Derrick glances back at CeCe and gives her a smile. "You got it."

She stays outside with Derrick, helping with the yard, yanking out the memory of Charlotte and Olivia with each weed. After a while the pulling starts to hurt her hand, so Derrick has her hold the trash bag and follow him around. When they're done with that, he breaks out the lawn mower and gives the patchy grass a trim. As they work, Mr. Luken comes outside and starts digging into the flower beds under his front window. CeCe doesn't know what it is about the ringing sound of a lawn mower that's like a school bell for a neighborhood.

Derrick puts the mower away and they go inside. Ice waters in hand, they sit at the kitchen barstools as her dad puts the final touches on another casserole. This one with tuna and pasta. He says that Sam had given him the recipe. It stinks up the house, but Derrick keeps saying how good it smells, and after working in the yard, she has to admit it does.

She stays quiet as she listens to her dad and Derrick talk. Derrick is easygoing, seemingly not at all haunted by what they'd seen in the Hardings' house. Maybe it's because Derrick's used to it, being in the Sanitation Department. Revies. Dead bodies. For him, it's just another Monday, while she's still working her way into this new existence.

"Did you go to school with CeCe?" her dad asks.

"No. I was in my second year at Chico State."

"Huh? I went there."

"Oh yeah?"

"A long time ago, but yes, I did. What were you majoring in?"

"Business."

"Business?" CeCe says. "You never told me that."

Derrick shrugs. "You never asked."

A prickle of guilt edges around her stomach.

Her dad says, "A business major? That's impressive. What were your plans to do with it?"

"As soon as I graduated, my dad was going to retire and sell me the surplus store, but, you know, that's all changed. Now I work for the Sanitation Crew."

"How's that?" her dad asks. "I know you have a tall order with the city being in the shape it is."

"It's been good," Derrick says. "I mean, there's a lot of not-so-nice things, but we've been making a lot of headway getting places cleaned up. You know the Safeway on Cypress? I was on that crew. It was a big job."

"You come across Infected then quite a bit, don't you?"

Derrick glances at CeCe. "Yeah, from time to time. But the RRT gave us these."

He pulls out a small cylindrical can from his back pocket.

"We all have them in case of an emergency."

CeCe looks at it. "Nitrociptine?"

"Yeah," Derrick says. "It's not enough for much, but it'll buy some time in a pinch."

"Why didn't you use it the other night?"

Derrick looks between CeCe and her dad. The question had made him uncomfortable. She couldn't help that, but she had to know. If he had Nitrociptine, why didn't he use it?

"I wanted to," he says, "but I would've had to open the door and I didn't want to make anything worse. I knew RRT would respond quickly. It seemed like the right thing to do at the time."

He's trying to be nice about it, but what he's saying without saying is that it's because she was freaking out. She thinks back to that night. The terror that coursed through her limbs, her inability to do anything but shake and crumble. She hadn't been in a good place, literally or figuratively. If he'd opened the door, even if it was for the Nitrociptine, she probably would've passed out.

Derrick puts the silver canister back in his pocket as the timer dings for the casserole.

Her dad pulls it out of the oven and sets it on the counter. The top bubbles. She gets up and opens the cupboard.

Derrick leans over the counter toward her and says, "You're not mad, are you, that I didn't say anything about the Nitrociptine?"

"Not mad," she says, grabbing three plates. "I wouldn't mind having one of those canisters though."

"Here." He digs it out of his back pocket. "Take it."

"Are you sure?" she asks. "What about you?"

"I can get another. See that little pin on top?"

She looks down at a metal loop.

"That's where you need to pull. Okay?"

"Okay," she says and wraps her hand around it. "Thank you."

They follow her dad into the dining room. She carries the plates, Derrick the silverware. As soon as they enter, Derrick looks up at the family picture above the dining room. She cringes. She's never told Derrick about Teddy. Not that she hasn't wanted to or that she was keeping it from him, but more because it's hard to talk about.

Knowing that he is out there somewhere and there's nothing she can do about it. Derrick has his sisters, and his hope that they are still running the fields of Montana, but Teddy isn't playing in some mythological park with unicorns and giant cheeseburgers. He's missing in a city where anything could have happened to him, and none of it is good.

"Who's that?" Derrick says, pointing to Teddy.

Her dad puts the casserole in the middle of the table.

"That's CeCe's little brother," her dad says. "Teddy."

"A brother?" Derrick raises his eyebrows and turns to her. "You never told me you had a brother."

CeCe gets quiet. She looks at her dad.

"Teddy's missing," her dad says. "It's a difficult thing for both of us, especially since we lost her mother. It's almost a little too much for any one of us to handle if you understand what I mean."

Derrick nods. "I do. There's a lot of people struggling, angry, sad. I wish I'd known is all." He motions to the picture. "But I see where CeCe gets her looks from."

"Yes," her dad says. "Her mom, she was beautiful."

"Her mom?" Derrick says. "I was talking about you, Dr. Campbell," and winks at him.

That gets a laugh from her dad, but CeCe's tense as she watches Derrick, wondering what he's thinking.

They sit at the table. Her dad serves portions of the casserole. Derrick first, being a guest and all that, then CeCe, then himself.

She takes a bite, tasting the tang of dill and something else. It's good, she has to hand it to Sam. She tries to catch Derrick's eye as they eat, wanting to gauge how he's feeling about her not telling him about her brother, but right then he only has eyes for the casserole.

"This is amazing," Derrick says, already halfway done.

"There's plenty more."

Her dad reaches over and shovels Derrick another generous helping. "So, Derrick," her dad says, settling back in his seat. "How were you Infected?"

Derrick gets animated as he goes into his Infection story. Her dad listens intently, asking questions, and digging into the specifics or as much as Derrick can remember of the specifics. CeCe can tell that

Derrick likes talking about it. It reminds her of the 9/11 conversations when people would ask, "Where were you when 9/11 happened?"

CeCe hadn't been born yet, but her parents could recount where they were in detail. Mom was in a substance abuse class in college, fifth row back, toward the left, when the second plane hit. Her dad never made it to class at all. Grandma had called him at five that morning in a panic, begging him not to go, telling him the US was under attack. He sat in his cramped apartment with his TV propped up on a used console and watched the news all day.

Now, instead of "Where were you when 9/11 happened?" it's "Where were you when you were Infected?"

Her dad asks Derrick, "What's the last thing you remember?"

"Pike Street," Derrick says. "The sign. I remember looking at it. It's all pretty much a blank after that."

Her dad looks at CeCe. "Weren't you also on Pike Street?"

CeCe freezes as Derrick's eyes widen with surprise, discovery, or confirmation that maybe he'd been right and did know her, he *had* seen her. She looks between them. She'd never told her dad the whole story. He knows it happened with her friends, and she was attacked by a guy on the street. Her dad is smart. He discovered the cure after all, but not even he could put Derrick and CeCe together in that way. It would be too much of a coincidence and he's far too pragmatic for that.

"No," she says. "I was downtown, but nowhere even close to Pike Street. We were at that Mexican restaurant on Nineteenth. My and Leyton's favorite place."

"Huh," her dad says. "I thought it was Mason's. For some reason that rings a bell to me."

Derrick stares at CeCe as the tuna casserole stirs inside her stomach.

"No, uh," she says. "Leyton had wanted to go there but we couldn't get a reservation."

Her dad nods. "Mason's was always a popular spot. I still dream about their cheesy potatoes."

"Me too," she says with a nervous laugh.

Derrick stares down at his plate. She continues to watch him. She can't help it. She's two for two in a matter of fifteen minutes.

What she wouldn't give to peer into his head like a jewelry box and see what's going on in there. After a moment, Derrick picks up his fork and starts working on his second helping of casserole. Maybe if he's eating, he's not thinking.

After dinner, CeCe and Derrick sit in the living room while her dad discreetly cleans in the kitchen and talks to Lauren on the phone. She was supposed to join them tonight but caught some kind of stomach bug—non-Kill-Virus-related—and didn't want anyone else to get sick. CeCe can't say she's disappointed that Lauren couldn't make it.

Derrick sits beside her, quiet. He's never quiet.

"Are you okay?" she asks him.

"I don't know." He shrugs. "It's weird you never told me about your brother. I told you about my sisters, my mom, dad, all of them. I mean, I get that you're not obligated to tell me everything. I guess I thought you'd share at least that part of your life with me."

CeCe swallows. "It wasn't intentional like I was keeping it from you."

"Then what was it?"

"I don't know. Talking about it makes me think about it, and then I have to imagine my brother out there, alone, frightened. What he might be going through, every worst-case scenario, and I'm not there. We're not there. After losing my mom, I can't deal knowing that he might be gone too, so I've shut him out like he doesn't exist. Like he was never there because it's easier than facing the truth." She holds her head in her hands. "That makes me sound incredibly selfish."

Derrick gently pulls her back. "I meant what I said earlier. I get it, CeCe. I really do. But if your brother's missing, I want to help you find him. You don't have to do this by yourself, not anymore, if you don't want to. If you'll let me, we can figure this out together."

He takes her unbitten hand and weaves his fingers around hers.

"I care about you," he says.

She looks into Derrick's eyes.

Derrick isn't Riley. She and Riley had fit together like two perfectly matched pieces. Derrick's different, but she's different now too.

"And I care about you," she says.

Gently, he squeezes her hand, and she squeezes it back. She leans into him, her gaze going down to his lips. It's an invitation. She wants him to kiss her. She wants to feel it, wants to know what a kiss from Derrick would be like.

Her heart speeds up as that short distance between them gets even shorter, but then she hears her dad's footsteps. They separate as if they've been caught doing something they shouldn't, even though they hadn't done anything.

Her dad wipes his hands on a dishtowel.

"Can I give you a ride home, Derrick?"

It is a not-so-subtle cue that it is time for him to go.

Derrick gets up. "That's okay, Dr. Campbell," he says. "I'm fine with walking."

"Nonsense. It's getting dark out."

CeCe sits on the couch as her dad and Derrick go back and forth. Derrick insists on walking, her dad on driving. Her dad wins in the end. She knew he would.

When they leave, she goes upstairs and gets ready for bed. As soon as she hears her dad pull back in the driveway, she's on the stairs before his keys even jiggle in the lock.

He shuts the door behind him, and she waits.

"I like him," he says.

She smiles.

"Me too."

Chapter Eleven

The next morning at school, CeCe goes into the classroom and makes a direct line to Olivia. She thought about what she was going to say to her all night and is eager to get to it. CeCe doesn't know what expression she's wearing, but for the first time, attention is focused on her as she crosses the room.

She plants her hands on Olivia's desk. Shock brushes over Olivia's face, but then it quickly dissolves.

CeCe says, "You and your friend have fun following me yesterday?"

Olivia sits back in her chair. "Following you? Wow. That's a stretch."

"Really? Is that how you're going to play it? Just a coincidence?"

"Yeah, we just so happened to be going the same way."

"Is that so? Then where were you going?"

"Not really any of your business, is it?"

"I think it is."

"You know what *I* think," Olivia says, leaning closer, her eyes glaring into CeCe. "I think you're being a tad paranoid."

"Paranoid my ass."

"Girls," Ms. Dobson says behind her, but CeCe doesn't turn around. Instead, she clenches her teeth.

"Stay away from me," she says to Olivia.

"Or what, you going to bite me, Infected?"

The way she says the word, *Infected*, it's meant to make CeCe feel dirty. Like she's something beneath her. She knew this is how Olivia feels, but to hear it come from her mouth with so much venom still knocks the wind out of her lungs. But like an opponent who'd hit a good shot, CeCe quickly recovers, ready to fire back.

"Or I'm going to drag you out of that truck."

"Oh." Olivia makes a shivering noise. "So scared."

"Girls," Ms. Dobson says again, louder this time.

CeCe pushes away from Olivia's desk and goes back to her own. The rest of the students watch her every step. She sits and faces the front of the room with a full adrenaline load pumping through her veins.

She's not sure what Ms. Dobson is thinking, but whatever it is, it's nothing good. She looks between CeCe and Olivia and says, "That better not happen again. Do you girls understand? The outside has no place here."

Ms. Dobson glares at them.

"Well?"

CeCe nods. Then after a moment, Olivia does too.

"Good."

Ms. Dobson looks down at her desk and takes a deep breath. "Now, I have the test results from yesterday, and we need to review. Everything on there is going to be on the GED. Before we move on, you must be able to master these equations."

CeCe glances at Olivia. She looks back. No matter what Ms. Dobson says, it's not over between them. Olivia isn't going to stop. And whatever she wants with CeCe, she's going to keep coming at her until she gets it. But it's not knowing what that is that puts CeCe on edge.

Ms. Dobson spends the rest of the morning going over the algebra test—CeCe had only missed two questions—before moving on to the next section of equations. It's hard to concentrate. Harder than usual. She senses Olivia like she's somehow connected to her, and she can't shake free.

At lunch, CeCe works on a drawing for Penny. She'd started it while Ms. Dobson was going over their tests, mostly to get her mind off Olivia, but also because she thought Penny might like it for her wall. It's a picture of her My Little Pony toy. CeCe's always been decent at art. She'd never been proficient, but she can do a half-decent sketch. She works on the three butterflies on the pony's flank. It would be easier if she could go on her phone and look it up, but it seems right. Later, when she gets home, she'll color in the pink hair and yellow body with some of Teddy's old colored pencils.

Savannah puts an apple on CeCe's desk. She brings her one every day. If Savannah stopped, she's pretty sure she'd miss them.

"So," Savannah says. "What was that all about?"

CeCe tells her about Olivia following her home yesterday, but left out the part about finding the Hardings. She focuses on the pony's mane, pushing away the image of Charlotte and her baby doll with each swipe of her pencil.

"Good thing you weren't alone," Savannah says. "Your boyfriend was with you."

"Derrick?" She shakes her head. "He's not my boyfriend."

"Stop it. You can't tell me he walks you home every day for the fun of it. Let's not even get started on the weird rock you carry in your backpack."

"Okay, I can see where you're going with this."

"I might've had worms in my brain, but I'm not brain-dead."

CeCe chuckles as she puts the final touches on the pony.

"Cute," Savannah says, looking at it. "I didn't take you for a My Little Pony fan."

"I'm not, it's for—" She stops herself.

"Please tell me it's not for Derrick," Savannah says. "I mean, I know there's not much to pick from out there, but a secret obsession with My Little Ponies would be a step too far."

"It's for no one," she says. "It's the only thing I could think of to draw."

Olivia comes back to their classroom after doing whatever she does at lunch, probably hanging out with her weirdo friend. CeCe's never gone outside during school. As far as she knows, he might be there in his truck the entire time. Olivia cuts down the first aisle, one over from CeCe. She never goes that way, obviously, she's doing anything to annoy CeCe, anything to make things uncomfortable. Olivia smirks as she comes closer and CeCe's hand clenches into a fist.

As Olivia passes, she glances at CeCe's drawing. The smirk falls from her face. There's something in Olivia's eyes, almost like disbelief, but not quite.

CeCe flips the picture over. "See something interesting?" she snaps at her.

"You can say that." Olivia slinks away toward her desk, dropping into her seat with a satisfied expression, probably gloating about CeCe's childlike drawing. If the roles were reversed, she might have done the same.

"God," Savannah says, "she's so odd."

The rest of the day, CeCe catches Olivia watching her. Every time she does, Olivia slowly turns her face away as if she doesn't care that she's been caught. CeCe grips onto her pencil until her throbbing scar goes numb. She's done with this. Done with Olivia trying to intimidate her. Whatever it is that needs to happen to get Olivia to back off, at this point, she'll welcome it.

After school, she walks out with Savannah. CeCe promises to text her later then she heads down to Derrick. He's leaning against the stair railing, watching Olivia's friend in the pickup, never breaking his gaze even as CeCe comes up to him.

"Hey," she says. "He say anything to you?"

"Nope. We're having a staring contest."

"Sounds like a blast."

"Can't tell for sure, but I think I'm in the lead."

Olivia bounces past them, giving Derrick and CeCe each her biggest smile yet before she jumps into the truck. She sticks her elbow out the window and watches them as they drive off, leaving behind the smell of exhaust.

Derrick and CeCe share a look as they walk home. They're quiet as they listen for the pickup, glancing over their shoulders. But so far, the only sounds CeCe hears are their footfalls on the pavement. Still, she can't shake the feeling that Olivia and her friend are behind them, but out of sight.

They come up to the house with the overgrown backyard that they'd disappeared into yesterday. From the street, she can see the top of the Hardings' roof.

"Did you call it in?" CeCe asks.

"Yeah." He nods. "They're processing it later today. Apparently, there was an overlap on the initial work order. I was supposed to go too, but they gave me the afternoon off. They know I have kind of a standing appointment."

CeCe smiles. "So they know about me?"

Derrick bumps her in the shoulder. "Everybody knows about you."

Her stomach warms, making it flutter, and it's a nice feeling. She likes that he's told people about her. As if she's special, and she likes being special to someone.

They make it to her house without any trucks shadowing them. Derrick comes in and has dinner with them again, and they spend the evening playing a board game like regular people.

On Friday, Derrick waits for her after school as usual. Olivia's been acting stranger than ever, but she's left CeCe alone. She doesn't trust it, but all she can do is wait for Olivia to make another move.

In the meantime, she and Derrick have taken precautions. They hang out on the steps, waiting until they can no longer hear the muffler of the pickup before they start heading home. As an added measure, they don't take the same route twice. It makes for a longer walk, but they don't mind. Sometimes they see other people. More often, there's no one.

Derrick reaches over and takes her hand. It's what they do now.

He says, "Me and the guys are getting together at the record store tonight. Nothing big or anything. Do you think your dad will let you come?"

CeCe exhales. "After what happened last time, I doubt it."

"What if you told him that we've been sweeping the area for Infected and it's officially gotten its clean bill of health from the SD? Plus," he says, "it won't be only us this time. You'll be with a group of people, all packing Nitrociptine."

He holds out the silver cannister RRT had given him.

"We're almost like a posse," he says.

"Posse?" she chuckles. "Your Montana is showing."

"Come on," he says. "Try to talk to him. Please? You'd have such an awesome time."

She thinks about it. A get-together? Like hanging out with actual people? It sounds fun and the more she thinks about it, the more she wants to go, and she bets she's not the only one.

Savannah complains all the time how bored she is on the weekends. CeCe wonders if Savannah's aunt would let her go, but she won't ask until she has her father's permission. He likes Derrick and seems to trust him, but maybe that only extends to him walking her home.

She says, "If I can go, can I invite someone?"

"Better not be another guy."

"Ha, ha. Funny."

CeCe waits for her dad to come home. She thinks of Penny at the CAVE with all those Infected. She hasn't seen the little girl since the wedding, and hasn't even given her the My Little Pony picture as she'd planned.

She wonders if Penny looks for her and if, in some way, she'd be happy to see her again. CeCe hopes so since her dad had promised to take her to the CAVE Saturday for a visit.

Her dad comes home and before he can even put his work bag down, she tells him about the party. His knee-jerk reaction is he's not a fan of the idea. But it's not a stern no, so she has some wiggle room. She uses the same explanations Derrick had given her.

"It won't be only us. It'll be Derrick and his friends in the Sanitation Department, and I was thinking of inviting a friend from school too."

He frowns.

"And we have Nitrociptine. Practically all of us. If I didn't feel comfortable with it, I wouldn't go. You know that, right? I was always the responsible one. Except for that one night. After twenty years, I deserve one free pass."

It was true. She'd never snuck out. She'd never lied to her parents about where she was going. She'd never had a reason to. All she did was go to school, practice, hang out with her friends, wash, rinse, and repeat. She always came home when she said she would and checked in when she needed to check in. She wasn't a rebellious teenager.

He pauses then says, "Fine. You can go but have your phone on you, and you need to send me a text every hour or so letting me know you're okay. You have to promise me this. If I don't hear from you, I'm coming down there."

She smiles. "Deal."

CeCe heads upstairs to change. She already has her phone out, texting Savannah about the get-together. Her reply comes back within seconds.

S: Yes, I'm in. I don't care what my aunt says. I've got to get out of this house.

Savannah gives CeCe her address, and she passes it on to Derrick. He tells her that one of his friends will make sure Savannah gets a ride. CeCe passes the information back and forth between Savannah and Derrick, playing intermediary until it's all arranged.

She takes her time getting dressed, going through her closet, brushing off the dust that gathered on the shoulders of her shirts. She opts for jeans and a light sweater. When she's done, she heads for the bathroom and puts on a little mascara. She still has to fight the urge to take it off, but she tells herself it's okay. She's allowed to look good.

Derrick's voice floats upstairs and she goes to meet him. He's standing by the door, talking to Dad. It's so normal-looking: a boy coming to pick up his date, and that it makes her cringe a little.

Derrick's eyes widen when he sees her. "Wow."

"Yeah, yeah," she says, playing it off, but secretly happy he's noticed.

They say goodbye to Dad, and head outside where Derrick's motorcycle sits by the curb.

"When are you going to get a real vehicle?"

His mouth drops like he's offended. "And I was just starting to like you."

CeCe gets on the back, taking her time with the helmet so it doesn't press her hair flat against her face, and then they take off to the record store.

When they arrive, there are two trucks parked along the curb. She takes off the helmet and looks up and down the street. It's empty. Despite her internal pep talks, and Derrick's confidence, the sight isn't exactly reassuring since it looked the same the first night they'd come. But there is safety in numbers. Unless the numbers are Infected.

She hears rock music and the low hum of voices coming from the roof. Derrick takes her hand.

"I can't wait to introduce you to everyone."

They head through the back of the store and to the ladder.

As soon as Derrick pops his head out the rooftop access, several voices call out to him. He scrambles up and then turns to offer her his hand. He pulls her up and she sees some people she doesn't know. She leans toward Derrick, suddenly feeling shy and unsure of being there.

"CeCe," Savannah cries.

She comes over and CeCe's grateful for a familiar face.

Savannah gives her a hug and then says, "Check it out."

She turns her head from side to side. She shaved her hair where her bald spot had been and then clipped the other side short and tapered it toward the back.

"What do you think?" Savannah asks. "Too edgy? My aunt did it." Her cheeks are flushed and her eyes are bright.

"It's perfect," CeCe says. "I absolutely love it."

"Really?" Savannah asks, running her hand along the side of her head.

"Really."

Savannah grins. "Thanks."

"So," CeCe says. "It sounds like your aunt was okay with you coming tonight?"

"She was surprisingly cool. It's the reason she did my hair. She used to be a hairstylist before everything." She turns to Derrick. "Thanks for arranging a ride. Your friends are nice."

Savannah waves at one of them. CeCe recognizes him as one of the guys with Derrick that day at Ed's MiniMart. He smiles at Savannah in a way that says he wants to be more than friends. The way she reacts, she does too.

"Yeah, they're good guys." Derrick turns to CeCe. "You up for some introductions?"

She nods. "Okay."

"I'll go get us some drinks first."

Derrick heads toward the corner of the rooftop, talking to people as he makes his way over. Savannah takes it as her cue to go back to Derrick's friend, leaving CeCe standing there like she's on stage about to perform, but has no idea what to do. That feeling was the main reason she quit dance class all those years ago.

Derrick comes back with two plastic cups. He hands one to CeCe.

"Thank you," she says. She looks inside at the red contents. She takes a small sip. It's cranberry juice mixed with something else. Vodka? Or it's old. Either is possible.

Derrick guides CeCe around and introduces her to the two friends she saw with him at Ed's. Conrad and Justin. They're from the city.

Born and raised. One got Infected at a nightclub, the other at a bus stop. Conrad's family didn't make it. Justin tells her all he had was his uncle and doesn't know what happened to him, but assumes he's dead.

"He wasn't in the greatest shape," Justin says. "Diabetes, heart failure. He probably would've done okay if he'd stayed on his medication. He had to have it and I wasn't there to make sure he did."

Savannah runs her hand against Justin's arm. "I'm so sorry."

"Yeah," Justin says. "Me too. He was like my dad. Took me in when my parents went off the rails, and they wanted to put me in foster care."

CeCe listens to everyone's stories. They're all similar. The more she hears, the more she realizes they are all in the same boat. She's not unique. She's not special in her grief or alone in it either. They share it together.

As requested, she texts her dad a few times, letting him know things are fine. She gets back, "Good to hear it" and "Hope you're having fun." After a while, she sends him another text, but he doesn't respond. She figures he probably went to bed.

Derrick and CeCe are on a couch his friends managed to hoist onto the roof. With the full moon hanging above them, the steady sounds of the music, and the drinks, the night is almost hypnotizing, luring her into something akin to tranquility.

Like it's okay, and they're all going to be okay. She stares up at the sky, watching the occasional shooting star as she hears Savannah and Justin giggling quietly nearby.

She leans closer to Derrick, breathing in his scent as he puts his arm around her. They stay like that, cuddled close.

As she closes her eyes, her mind wanders to Riley. She can't help feeling a little like she's been cheating on him. It doesn't make sense, but it's still there: a lingering guilt. Maybe if they'd ended things in a normal world, it would be different. But as it is, their relationship feels undone, as if a game stopped mid-point.

Someone puts on a slow song, broody and soft, a reminder of all the daily things that used to mean so much, but seem like a lifetime ago.

Derrick rubs her back to get her attention. "Care to dance?"

"What?" she says, lifting her head up. "Here?"

"You know a better place?"

There isn't. This is all there is, and might be for a long time.

Derrick stands and takes her by the hand, leading her to the middle of the rooftop. She puts her arms around his neck, and they sway in a circle.

She feels a little embarrassed dancing in front of everyone. Still, it's nice, comforting to be dancing again. Something so innocent, something she'd taken for granted, not realizing like everything else, it can disappear.

She lays her head against Derrick's chest and listens to his heartbeat.

They go around and around, entangled in each other's embrace. Others get up and join them, including Savannah and Justin, until everyone is dancing. Some in pairs, some not. They twirl like pinwheels in time, in this place that was never supposed to happen.

She looks up at Derrick. She wants him to kiss her, to seal this moment forever in their memories. She tilts up her chin and he tightens his arms around her waist, pulling her closer. He bends his head toward her, closing the short distance between them.

His lips find hers, bringing with it the sweetness she craved. His touch is so gentle, so tender, that it's hard to believe that these same lips had once been wrapped around her flesh. But it's like a nightmare she had once. Something that never was true.

Her stomach flutters with a lightness that tickles her insides, so foreign to the dread and anxiety she'd grown used to. She hadn't realized how much she's missed being touched in this way, and now that they're kissing, every cell of her body reacts.

She runs her hands along his back toward his chest, seeking more of him until they touch the top of his belt.

Derrick pulls her hand away. "Whoa," he says. "Not sure if I want an audience for that."

She smiles. "Are you shy?"

"Not shy." He looks around. "Okay, maybe a little."

He leans in to kiss her again when Savannah interrupts.

"Hey, guys. Sorry. I wanted to say bye. My aunt's been texting like crazy."

Texting.

Crap.

CeCe had left her phone on the couch. The last text she sent her dad was at least an hour ago. He could have gone to bed, or he could be on his way here.

"I'll walk you out," she says to Savannah. "I have to get my phone real quick."

CeCe goes back to the couch and picks it up. She's had two texts and four missed calls from her dad. All they say is "You there?" Her stomach, which had been filled with butterflies, is now full of wasps. She calls her dad, but it goes to voicemail.

"On my way home," she texts him.

Derrick comes over to her. "Everything okay?"

CeCe says, "I need to go."

She rushes through her goodbyes, and she follows Savannah and Justin back down the ladder and out through the record store. Her dad's car isn't there, so she takes it as a good sign that maybe he hasn't left the house yet to come after her.

She gives Savannah a hug before getting on the back of Derrick's motorcycle. When they pull up to the house, her dad's car is still in the driveway and the lights are on. Maybe she'd panicked for nothing, and he's gone to bed after all.

She gets off the bike and Derrick pulls her toward him, pressing his lips against her own. The kiss is long and makes the tickling in her stomach return.

She doesn't want it to end. If anything, she wants more.

A yearning for what's on the other side. But she'll have to wait. With effort, she pulls away from him.

"Can I see you tomorrow?" Derrick asks.

She glances back at the house. Tomorrow is her day to see Penny.

"I'm supposed to go with my dad to the CAVE, but I'll call you after. Okay?"

"Okay."

CeCe watches Derrick drive away before she goes inside. The lamps have been left on in the living room. Two oversize things that are mismatched and different colors her mom had found at an antiques swap market. She heads toward the kitchen, going to get a water before heading to bed. She finds her dad sitting at the dining room table.

She's about to say that she was sorry she'd missed his calls and texts. That she'd set her phone down and hadn't realized it, but her mouth opens and shuts. She stares at him. His head in his hands, a half-empty bottle of whiskey beside him.

A battered and stained red and yellow backpack lies in the middle of the table. A backpack that had once hung up on a hook next to the front door.

It's Teddy's.

Chapter Twelve

The RRT had found the backpack in a giant cluster of Infected stuck in Comer Ravine, a deep gouge in the Old Alturas hillside about fifteen minutes outside of the city. It was a popular hiking trail. CeCe and her family had gone up there many times over the years, especially when her mom was on a new exercise kick. Safety railings ran along the side in some places where its sheer drop could almost pull the breath from her lungs.

It was in Comer Ravine the Infected had fallen. Where Teddy had fallen.

And remained.

RRT speculated that the Infected must have followed the Survivors up into the hills toward the Revie settlement and were pushed in by their lifted trucks and commandeered bulldozers. It was a good strategy at the time, a natural holding pen when the cure was only a whisper around firepits, a dream shared with cans of fruit cocktail. No one expected that any of these Infected could be saved, and the fact that the fall would break nearly every bone in their bodies was not even a consideration.

Everyone knew about the ravine, her dad, the CAVE staff, the RRT, even General MacGregor, but no one had the manpower to address it.

And the Revies didn't want government interference for any reason, especially not to cure the Infected they already viewed as the devil's property.

But a horde of nearly a thousand outside the city had to be dealt with, and going in with medical personnel was impossible, suicidal at best. Instead, they gassed the entire area, as they had done with the first wave, dropping Nitrociptine canisters like bombs, and hoped for the best.

Only a handful of Infected had made it and those who did were so bad off they weren't expected to survive. Too many life-threatening injuries. It was only after they started clearing bodies that they came across Teddy's backpack, his name still on the upper tag where her mom had put it the first day of school.

Teddy's body hasn't been found. Not yet. They're still going through the dead, burning them in piles where they'd landed, but he's presumed to be among them.

CeCe listens to all this as she sits at the table, unable to take her eyes off his backpack. Her body is tight and rigid, and she feels it, the bowing, the splintering of bone.

"We shouldn't have gotten separated, I should have... I was his father." Tears sprinkle his cheeks. "He needed me, and I wasn't there."

She jumps when he throws his glass against the wall, shattering it into a hundred pieces. Whiskey leaks down the paint like old rainwater.

"I'm sorry," he says, holding his head in his hands. "You don't want to be around me right now. You really don't."

He pushes the backpack toward her.

"Please, take it. I can't look at it. It reminds me of him and I... I can't."

Her dad hunches over, folding into himself. Before the cure, if she'd seen her dad in this shape, it would've frightened her, but this is what broken looks like, and she knows that look well. She gets up from the table without saying a word because there's nothing that can be said.

He starts crying. Large, hacking sobs fill the room with his brutal grief. Grief so deep it pulls at the veins, at the very cells and chromosomes of something irreplaceably lost, never to return, and the world is worse off because of it.

She goes to him, wrapping her arms around his shoulders. Her eyes prickle. She hasn't cried, not really mourned, in all this time. Not even when she stood over the place her mom spent her last moments. But now the tears crest over her eyelashes in fat droplets for the family they used to have, and the abyss of what's left.

Her dad reaches up and clutches CeCe's arm. They're holding on to each other, holding on to what is left.

When they seem to run out of tears, she reaches for the backpack, feeling the strap against her fingers, as she slides it off the table and into her arms. She cradles it like a baby, as if it were Teddy when he was little, and takes it up to her room. It's heavier than she expects, or maybe it just seems that way. She places it on her bed.

She wipes at her swollen eyes as she slowly unzips the top. A half-empty Aquafina water bottle rolls out, its label faded and torn in places. Her mom bought the same kind and stocked them in the pantry. Is that where he got it? Had he carried it with him ever since her dad picked him up from school? Or is it a different one?

How long had he been using it before he'd gotten Infected? Her mind starts spiraling over something so insignificant but carries so much substance in this new world they find themselves in. The bottle had been touched—used—important enough to carry, and that matters.

She sets the water bottle aside and pulls out snack packs: two bags of Cheez-Its and a Chips Ahoy cookies. She holds them as if they are heirlooms. These were Teddy's go-to snacks. Every week her mom bought them from the grocery store, and every week he went through them like a buzzsaw.

If it was the end of the world, this is what Teddy would bring with him. Her hands shake as she presses her thumbs against the bags, their contents crumbled into bits. This is not a good sign. He would've needed food, and these wouldn't have been in his bag long unless he was Infected around the time he and her dad got separated.

But he could've gotten these snacks anywhere. A grocery store, a convenience store, someone else's house if he had to scavenge.

She places the snacks next to the water bottle and returns to the backpack. There's only a book left. She already knows what it is before she takes it out. *Harry Potter and the Goblet of Fire.*

Holding it in her hand is like a gut punch. A memory that smacks her straight in the heart. She was the reason Teddy had been reading the series. She'd encouraged him to give them a try when her parents were pushing him to read and he didn't like to.

They were the first books he'd ever gotten into, and he'd sit on the couch for hours with the TV on mute and then ask her questions about the plot, questions she refused to answer except with "just wait and see" answers.

To celebrate when he finished the first book, they watched the movie. Then the second and third. This would've been the fourth. She flips through the pages, touching what he'd touched.

A photograph falls out.

It's a picture they'd taken at the Grand Canyon, the trip CeCe had told Derrick about. It was their summer vacation before the Kill Virus. The last one she thought she'd be taking as a high school student, not the last one they'd share as a family.

Her dad had rented the motor home and they drove all over the Southwest, checking out universities and staying in parks where there were tennis courts and swimming pools. They'd completed their tour at the University of Arizona the day before and planned a stopover at the Grand Canyon before heading home.

She remembered standing with their legs against the railing, her mom, Teddy, and herself. Her dad was going to take the photo when someone offered to do it for them. With their arms linked, hair whipping around their faces, and the chasm at their backs, they smiled wide cheesy grins, half their shirts stained from the chili dogs they'd had earlier.

She stares at the photograph, holding it for a long time, imagining what Teddy had been thinking when he looked at it. Did he miss them? Did he wonder about them? She thought of how frightening it must have been. He was just a kid. He didn't even make his own lunches.

She picks up the backpack to put the items back inside when she feels something tossing around at the bottom. She reaches in and pulls out a switchblade with a polished wooden handle. She rolls it around in her palm.

Her dad didn't have anything like this. He dealt in scalpels and needles, not pocketknives. Her heart begins to race. Someone gave him this. Or he found it, but regardless, it meant Teddy hadn't been Infected right away. He'd survived the separation.

But for how long? How long had he been out there? She's so excited that she almost rushes out to tell her dad, but she thinks of him at the table with his bottle of whiskey and the shattered glass, and decides to wait.

Instead, she wraps her hands around the knife, feeling the blade's weight, feeling Teddy. He'd held this. He'd *had* this. She pulls the blade away from its handle until it locks in place. It's clean and still sharp.

She sets the knife down.

A water bottle. A book. A picture. Snacks. A knife.

Each one sacred. These are the things her brother took with him, and are all that's left. Tears crawl down her cheeks as she carefully puts each item back in the pack and zips it up.

She lays it beside her, clutching it to her chest as she remembers her brother when he was a goofy toddler with his fat cheeks and hands, and hair that flopped down over his eyes.

He had a way of making her laugh, even when she wasn't in the mood. They had their not-so-great moments. He could be annoying, so could she, but he made everything easy.

Loving him was easy.

The next day, Derrick texts her early.

D: Hey. I know you won't have your phone when you get to the CAVE so I wanted to make sure everything was okay last night and that I'm thinking about you. Text me when you get home.

CeCe's not going to the CAVE. Her dad had already left without her. She heard him that morning, rummaging around. The faucet turning on. The toilet flushing. Then the front door opening and shutting. He'd left without saying a word.

She's not angry about it. It's a relief, really. She couldn't have gone, carried a smile, and faked it even for Penny's sake. He did her a favor.

The phone hovers in her hand. She thinks about ignoring the text, letting Derrick think she'd actually gone with her dad, and she'd talk with him later. But she's so tired of feeling alone. If she wants something with him, truly, she can't keep shutting him out.

C: Didn't go. Can you come over?

D: Yeah. Be there in a few.

Within ten minutes, he's at the door. She comes down, carrying the backpack.

He takes one look at her face and asks, "What's happened?"

They sit in the living room. The blinds are drawn. The lamps still on from last night. Broken glass glitters on the dining room floor, and on the table is the empty whiskey bottle. Derrick turns to her as she clings to the backpack. She tries to form what she wants to say. Her eyes sting with tears.

"This is Teddy's," she whispers.

She tells him about the ravine, the Infected, and RRT.

He already knew about the gassing at Comer, but he didn't know about Teddy. Derrick listens quietly, asking questions when he can, when he must think it's okay.

She knows he's tiptoeing around her emotions, but she needs him to.

"They say it's a matter of time before they find his body." She sniffs. "But he's dead. My little brother is dead." She grips the backpack, digging her fingers into the straps. "It's so messed up," she cries. "It's not only us, or me, I know that. I'm just so tired of this. Tired that this thing, this parasite, something so infinitesimally small had the power to take everything away from us.

"Every time I turn around, every time I think things might be okay, it takes something else." She looks at him. "Nothing is going to fix this. Not a GED program. Not a stupid flip phone. They should've just left us alone. Left alone to rot or until a comet came to wipe us all out. At least then we wouldn't have to know. We wouldn't have to feel like this."

Derrick takes a breath like he has something to say, but then he seems to deflate. She knows all the things he could say. That if it weren't for the cure, they wouldn't be here right now, and she'd still be standing in the parking lot. Or that if it weren't for the cure, there would be no "them."

But he doesn't. He doesn't say any of those things. He simply stays still and lets her be, and she wants to love him for it but can't feel anything but anger.

He stays with her far into the evening. She wants him to spend the night, so she can feel his warmth, and hopes his heart isn't as broken as hers.

But Derrick leaves after her dad comes home. She hears them talk for a little while in the kitchen before Dad drives Derrick back to the Housing Center.

The following week is a blur. She goes to school. Derrick walks her home. He stays, then he leaves.

She spends a lot of time in Teddy's room with his hundreds of Legos, and sits on his bed.

Sometimes when she's there she thinks about her mom. She thinks about Leyton and Riley, and sometimes of Penny alone in that glass cage and the My Little Pony picture still in CeCe's bag.

But thinking of Penny always brings her back to Teddy. And when she thinks of him, she's reminded that he's somewhere in the bottom of Comer Ravine with hundreds of other dead Infected, decaying in the growing warmth of the spring sun, waiting to be found.

On Friday, they arrive home after school like usual and sit in her room. She gets a text from her dad that he's going to be home late. She shuts the phone.

"That your dad?" Derrick asks. "Any word yet?"

They've all been waiting for the news they expect any moment: confirmation of Teddy's body.

"No," she tells him.

"What if…" he starts to say. "What if they don't find him?"

"I'm sure they will eventually."

"No. I mean, what if he's not found because he's not there?"

She shakes her head, irritated. She knows what Derrick is trying to do, but all it will ever be is false hope.

"How would his backpack have gotten in the middle of a horde of Infected if he wasn't? I can't see him parting with it. And even if he did, of all places to end up, at the bottom of a ravine? There's unlikely."

"I don't know," he says. "It's odd, you know? That they found it right away, but not him. You'd think he would've been close to it."

She turns to him. "I know what you're trying to do, and you can stop now."

"What?" he says, looking surprised. "I'm not trying to do anything."

"You're trying to give me hope Teddy is still alive, and I don't want to hear it. The 'maybe this' and 'maybe that' doesn't exist anymore. There's dead, Infected, Infected and now dead and left behind, and that's it."

Derrick doesn't reply.

She feels bad for snapping at him. She hadn't meant to come off that way, but she can't help it. She hasn't been in a good place since they found Teddy's backpack.

At least before she'd been maintaining, but now she can't even do that. She doesn't know how Derrick does it, how he can stand to be around her while she wallows in her hatred and her bitterness.

But he stays, and he takes her hand, and keeps acting like, somehow, it's still all worth it.

Chapter Thirteen

Saturday morning CeCe gets a text from Derrick.

D: Get dressed. I have a surprise for you.

She's still in bed and planned to stay there until Monday when she's required to be at Franklin because her dad insists she go. Even though all she does is show up, sit at her desk, keep her face forward, ignore Olivia, and wait for the clock to tell her she can go back home. She doesn't open her book. She doesn't do a single ounce of work Ms. Dobson assigns.

Savannah has been supportive, texting, asking if she needs anything, or if she wants to talk.

CeCe hasn't replied to any of them.

Derrick texts.

D: Get dressed. I have a surprise for you.

C: No more surprises.

D: You're getting out of the house.

C: Nope.

D: Wear something comfortable. I'm on my way.

C: Nope.

He doesn't answer, and she throws her phone onto the bed. Why does he do this? Push things when they don't need to be pushed? She glances at Teddy's backpack by her bed. She's not going anywhere.

There's a knock on her bedroom door.

That's ridiculously fast. She sits up as her dad comes in. She's relieved and annoyed that it's him. They haven't talked much since she'd come home from the get-together. Somehow this last week, he's managed to have long days at work. She respected his need to deal in his own way, but now he's here when he's ready to talk and she's not.

"Hi," he says.

"Hey."

He glances at Teddy's backpack and stands there for a moment before coming over and reaching for it. She has to stop herself from snagging the pack away from his hand.

"You look inside?" he asks.

"Yeah."

He unzips the top and rummages through it. He stops suddenly and then pulls out the pocketknife.

She asks, "Is it yours?"

"No." He shakes his head. "He must've gotten it somewhere."

He stares at it for a long time, emotion playing over his face. Then he covers it with his hand. Tears leak through his fingers.

"He made it," he finally says. He brings his hand down and turns to her. "He didn't have this before. I would know. I packed his bag and it had much more than this inside. I must've shoved thirty of these snack bags in here and five waters."

She stares at the knife, her heart thrumming with pride. Pride that her little brother had been out there, and he'd been making his way until something changed, but that doesn't matter. What matters is that he had more survival skills than she did, and she smiles at that knowledge.

Her dad wipes his eyes.

"I'm sorry about the other night. I thought for so long and hoped your brother was okay. That maybe he would find his way back to us, and even if he couldn't, that he could be cured. I didn't take it well. I should've been here, and I haven't."

She doesn't need him to apologize. Not exactly. He hasn't been here for her, but she hasn't been there for him either.

"It's okay," she says.

He offers her the knife. "This was his. It should go with the rest of his things."

She takes it from him, and he gets up.

"I'm leaving to get Lauren. She's still not feeling well. I was going to try my hand at soup."

CeCe's annoyance taints their bonding moment. They've barely begun to grieve for Teddy, and she doesn't want Lauren here, doesn't want her to be part of it.

Married to her dad or not, it feels like a slap to even have her here among her mother's things. Her books on the shelves, her pictures hanging on the walls, the decorations she picked out. It's like they're having a romantic picnic over her grave.

"Derrick said he was coming to pick you up."

"That's what he says."

Although now that she knows that Lauren is coming over, going with Derrick sounds more appealing.

"You should go," Dad says. "It might do you some good to get out of the house a bit."

He turns to leave.

"When they find Teddy," she says, stopping him, "I don't want him thrown in a burn pit or going into a crematorium to be mixed in with a bunch of people he doesn't know. I want him buried. Have a funeral. He deserves that from us. Promise me."

Her dad nods. "I promise."

He shuts the door, and she listens to his footsteps going down the hallway. As she does, she holds on to the pocketknife.

She puts it away and shuffles to the window, cracking it open, letting fresh air flow into the stale room. Sunlight floods across her face and warms her cheeks. She goes to her dresser and throws on some shorts and a tank top before heading downstairs.

On the counter is her old water bottle. The stainless steel scratched from years of being dropped on asphalt. She picks it up. It's already filled with water. Whatever Derrick has planned, her dad's in on it.

She hears a knock on the front door, grabs her water bottle, and goes to open it.

Derrick's eyes widen. "You're dressed?"

"You told me to get dressed," she says, shutting the door behind her.

"Yeah, but I didn't know for sure if you would come. Check it out." He points to a white Dodge behind him. She recognizes it from outside the record store. "A *real vehicle* like you wanted. I borrowed it from Justin."

"It's an improvement."

He takes her over to the truck and opens the door for her. She gets in. The inside is remarkably clean and smells of lemon.

Derrick gets in on the other side and starts the engine.

"Where are we going?" she asks.

"I don't want to tell you."

"Is that your pitch? I'm not sure it's working."

"Wait until we get there, okay?"

"Why? Are you worried I'll refuse to go?"

"Something like that."

They drive down several residential streets until he turns into a familiar parking lot, the Drop Shot Tennis Club.

"What are we doing here?"

"Isn't it obvious?"

She sighs as she glances up at the sign with the tennis racquet and the palm tree. Even after all these years, even after the Infection, it looks exactly the same. It's where she first met Riley and then later Leyton when they both had missing teeth and would rather twirl on the tennis court instead of play. It's also where she learned to love the game.

Derrick puts the truck in park.

CeCe shakes her head. "I can't do it."

"You said you missed playing."

"I said I *sometimes* missed playing."

She grips her scarred hand.

"Come on," he says. "Give it a try."

"Even if I did, I don't have anyone to play with."

"Ouch."

"No offense."

"None taken," he says, shutting off the engine. "That's why I found you a ball machine."

"Of course, you did."

She gets out of the truck and follows Derrick inside the small tennis clubhouse. The clothes still hang on their racks, a layer of dust on the shoulders and bands of the skirts and shorts. In an apocalypse, tennis clothes are apparently not a go-to item.

They move around the racks toward a glass door that leads to the courts. He holds the door open for her and she steps outside. Stretching before her are the remnants of the blues and greens and white lines of a sport that consumed her whole life.

Dried leaves cover most of the asphalt, along with sagging nets from years of neglect, but the ghosts of what used to be are still there like a whisper only she can hear.

Hazy phantoms of lacing broken-in Nike shoes, orange balls being fed from a coach, laughter, cheers of shots well made, groans with points lost. It's all there replaying before her eyes, and it makes her so ridiculously miserable and sad, and left with a longing of what she wouldn't give to go back to that time.

"Over here," Derrick says.

She follows him to Court 3. He opens the gate. Its metal latch screeches as he lifts it. Here, the net is taut, and every scrap of debris and leaf has been brushed away. Her tennis racquet is propped against a ball machine. She hadn't even noticed that it'd been taken from the house.

"Your dad told me about this place," he says, shutting the gate behind them. "The guys helped me clean it up, and then we found this bad boy here in storage."

He taps his hand on the side of the machine.

"Still works. Had to give it a try to make sure, and gave the guys a good laugh. But anyway." He picks up her racquet and hands it to her. "I've been dying to see what you've got."

She looks at it and then slowly peels off her glove. Derrick glances down at the skin that's been puckered from months of wearing it, but then turns his eyes away, trying to be respectful.

She takes her racquet from his hand, her two-year-old grip tape dry and crinkled. The strings equally as bad. She stands there, holding it, feeling the weight of it again as her scars stretch and pull.

Derrick goes to the ball machine and turns it on. It purrs with life as the balls turn in the hopper, ready to drop into the shoot.

"I found a bunch of new balls in the clubhouse," he says. "So, they're all fresh. Your dad told me it's a thing."

"Yeah," she says, still staring at her racquet. "It is."

"You ready?"

She's not, but she goes to the other side of the net, walking backward to the baseline. Her thoughts gel together in a glob of pieces, each vying for space.

Part of her is irritated that Derrick pushed this on her. Another part curious. Can she hit after all this time? Does she even want to know?

And yet she stands there, facing the ball machine, her body taking over. Accustomed to the court, to the racquet, to the anticipation, and it knows exactly what it wants even if she doesn't.

A tennis ball shoots from the machine, giving off the familiar sound of the *thwack* when it hits the court and bounces up. Her body springs toward it. Her arm ready. She hits it, swinging all the way through, up and across her chest. The ball sails back across the court with so much topspin it practically skips like a rock until it smacks against the fence.

"Damn," Derrick says.

She has to agree. It went better than she thought.

She waits for the next one, tensing with so much expectation she's already split-stepping before she hears the whoosh of the ball from the machine. She sends it back across, faster than the last one. She waits on the other side, her eyes focused. She hits again and again. It's like no time has passed at all. Her hand aches, but she ignores the pain. She returns the last ball, and she stands there, out of breath and her heart drumming in her chest. She looks at Derrick and says, "Again."

They work together to fill the machine. When every ball has been collected, she goes to the speed dial and ups it a notch. She jogs to the other side of the court and nods to Derrick that she's ready. She's late to the first one and it launches up, still landing in the blue, but far from a flawless shot.

A sharp pain whips through her hand. She should stop, but instead grips her racquet even harder. When the next ball comes, she smacks it in the middle of the strings, firing it right in the far corner. Derrick claps.

She continues like that until the basket is empty. Sweat seeps through her tank top.

"Again."

Once more CeCe cranks up the speed. She nods to Derrick to start it and she hits one shot after another, and in what feels like less than a minute, the machine is out of balls.

"Again."

"You sure?" Derrick asks. "Don't you want a break?"

She shakes her head. "No."

This time she takes the ball machine as high as it can go. Derrick looks at her, concern tainting his earlier smile. She ignores it and goes to the other side of the net, racquet ready. She nods to him to push the start button. The first ball erupts from the machine so fast that if she blinked it'd be gone, but she doesn't. She sends it back, equaling it with so much force it rockets off the court and lodges itself in the chain link fence.

The sun burns down on her shoulders, marching slowly toward the west as she hits, they refill, over and over. Her arms and legs shake from exhaustion, but she doesn't want to stop. Can't stop.

"Again," she says, staggering.

"CeCe," Derrick says. "It's okay. We can come back. It's not going anywhere."

"Again," she shouts at him.

Derrick stares at her before picking up a tennis tube and stabbing at the first ball he comes across. She didn't mean to shout, but she needs him to listen. It takes a long time for them to refill the machine, but they finally do. She gets back to the other side and waits.

A ball streaks across the net in a green blur. She swings at it, making contact, feeling it bow against her strings. Her hand finally gives out and her racquet jerks out of her grip and into the air before skidding on the asphalt.

Derrick turns off the machine.

She opens and shuts her hand, wincing. The pain is so deep it grates against her bones and taps the sticky ligaments of her tendons, but she savors it, enjoying each pulse of adrenaline, tasting it like it's ice cream at the bottom of the bowl.

He comes over to her.

Her chest heaves. Everything feels like it's on fire.

"Take off your pants," she tells him.

"What?"

"Take off your pants."

"Are you serious? CeCe, I—"

"Take them off. Please."

"Okay," he says, nodding his head, as if he's as unsure of himself as he is of her.

Derrick unzips his jeans and pulls them down, finagling a bit to get his ankles out. Once they're off, he throws them to the side and stands before her in a pair of navy-blue boxers. He watches her, his gaze uncertain. Her hair's sticky with sweat, her skin too. But her appearance is the least of her concerns at the moment.

"Your shirt," she says.

He pulls it over his head, and it joins his jeans.

She glances down.

"Your underwear."

He hesitates for a moment and then slides them over his legs. He stands before her naked with goosebumps rising on his arms despite the heat.

She steps to him and kisses him, her lips pressed hard against his. Slowly, she pushes him onto the court, yanking at her sweats and kicking them off. She tugs at her underwear, hearing them rip. She pulls off her tank top and goes to remove her sports bra and cringes at the sudden rush of agony.

"You don't have to," he says.

"I'm fine."

She grips onto her sports bra, clenches her teeth, and pulls it over her head in one swift motion. Her body screams at her, but she ignores it. She drops the bra. The cool air presses against the sweat on her body. She puts her hands on Derrick's face, bringing him closer to her.

"Are you sure?" he asks, pulling away a little. "This isn't exactly how I imagined it."

"Shut up."

She straddles him. His body is already responding to her touch. She feels a moment of pain. Of unfamiliarity. Riley was her first, but this is new. This she needs.

His hands run up her waist, careful of the bruises and of the knots forming over her ribs, as her yearning becomes almost unbearable. She grips onto him, throwing her head back. It doesn't take long before pleasure washes over her, and after a long while, her heartbeat slows.

She's gasping as she stares down at him, and he up at her. She rolls to the side and onto her back. He takes her hand, and she tilts her head toward his, feeling him next to her, and they stay like that, looking up at the sky, naked, together.

After a while, the once-warm breeze turns chill. She's the first to sit up. Every part of her aches, but it's a good sore. One that she earned. She reaches for her glove, putting that on first, before her underwear and her sweats. She takes her time with each article of clothing. She rolls up her sports bra and puts it in her pocket. The effort of wiggling it back on isn't worth it.

"You going to get dressed?" she asks him.

"Yeah." He moves his hand for his shirt. "Yeah," he says again.

Derrick puts his pants back on, covering the trail of brown hair that goes down under his belly button. A part of her wants to make him take them off again, but now that she's been sitting, her body has stiffened and she's not sure she can get to her feet, let alone anything else.

"Help me up?" she asks him.

Derrick stands and reaches out his hand. She pulls against it, hoisting herself up and onto her feet. She moves around the court, trying to loosen up her tendons that feel coated in superglue. She makes her way to the nearest ball and bends over. She grimaces, hissing through clenched teeth.

"I got it," Derrick says.

"You sure?"

"Yeah, of course."

She hobbles around, forcing the blood through her muscles, forcing them to work. She'll need to take some painkillers when she gets home. She doesn't want to. This is a feeling she enjoys, but she also wants to be able to go to the bathroom.

She watches Derrick gather all the tennis balls and rolls up the cord to the ball machine. He holds on to her tennis racquet, the grip tape dark from sweat.

She follows him as he pushes the ball machine back into the clubhouse and then out the door to the truck. On the ride back, gingerly, she massages her muscles around her triceps and forearms, feeling the throbbing greet her in return. Derrick drives back slowly, creeping along the streets, and she's grateful for it.

When they pull up, her dad's car is in the driveway. He's home, which means Lauren's here too. She sighs at the thought of it.

Maybe she can bypass them both without being seen and limp to her bathroom where she can soak in the tub with half a bag of Epsom salt.

Derrick pulls up along the curb. He jumps out and opens her door.

"You going to be okay?" he asks.

"Give me a few days and I'll be ready for the court again." She winks at him. "And other things too."

"Are we going to talk about what happened back there?"

They should, but the longer she stands outside the twinge in her sore muscles turns into a nagging burn. Being on her feet any longer is turning into less and less of an option.

"Can we later?"

He nods. "Yeah, okay."

She leans against him and he against her like they're two splintering oaks ready to collapse until her body threatens to do it for real. She pulls away from him.

"See you tomorrow?"

He grins. "I do have to check my schedule. I'm a busy guy."

She punches him lightly in the arm. "Stop it."

"Of course, tomorrow," he says. "Wouldn't miss it."

He takes her hand, the bitten one, and kisses it gently on top. It doesn't make her want to cringe anymore. She accepts his kiss as if it were any other, as if it was only meant in love, and never in anything else.

"See you then," he says.

As he gets back into the truck and pulls away, she goes inside and finds her dad and Lauren in the living room. They're hugging with smiles that stretch across their faces. Seeing them this way stops her. The pain in her body no longer a concern. It's the strangeness that gets to her. The oddity of this happiness. It seems wrong and out of place.

Her dad turns to her. Tears in his eyes.

Teddy? She thinks. *This is about Teddy.*

But it can't be about her brother. Her dad's too happy and Teddy's dead in a ravine. Even if he was found, he wouldn't act like this, unless… She can't even form the words in her mind, but she wants to.

Unless Teddy is alive. Maybe Infected. Maybe beat up a little, but alive.

By the time her dad speaks, she's already convinced herself this is why they're holding each other with such blissful faces and that maybe, just maybe, good things can still happen. That it isn't all blackness and nightmares.

"What's going on?" she asks.

"We have news," he says.

She braces herself to hear that RRT has Teddy. That her little brother is waiting for them, and he's excited to come home. She only needs him to say it. Say that Teddy's okay.

"We know why Lauren's been so sick lately," he says. "She's pregnant."

CeCe wobbles as if the floor has jerked beneath her. "What?"

"It's a miracle."

He takes Lauren's hand.

"A miracle," he says again. "You're going to have a little brother or sister. Isn't that incredible? Isn't that the most amazing news?"

A crack opens inside her, splintering across her body and burying deep inside her spine, something so deep that she's not sure where it even came from. Her disappointment foams in her mouth and spills out. "Are you kidding me?"

Her dad stares at her. "What do you mean? I thought you'd be happy."

"Happy?" She breathes hard, staring at each in turn, all the pain and tenderness from the tennis court pulsing against her. "Why would this make me *happy*? Finding Teddy would make me happy. Having my mother here, my life back would make me happy. But this?" She shakes her head. "No, this does not make me happy."

"CeCe." Her dad says her name as if he's not sure it belongs to her.

She holds her hands up. "I cannot deal with this right now. I can't. We've just found out about Teddy. They haven't even found his body yet and you're already celebrating your replacement kid. It's such complete bullshit. And bullshit that you actually thought I'd be happy for you."

She leaves them in the living room, knowing she's messed up their perfect family moment, knowing that she probably hurt her dad, and hurt Lauren too, but she doesn't care. She doesn't care what they think of her.

This is who they made when they brought her back.

The monster to his Frankenstein.

Chapter Fourteen

The next day, her dad tries talking to her, telling her how she isn't getting replaced, that no one could replace her, her brother, and mother, but she heard it all before at his wedding.

"You can say it all you want," she says, "but there's nothing more obvious than the obvious."

He puffs out his cheeks and exhales. She can tell he thinks she's being selfish, playing the typical "don't want a brother or sister" game like a three-year-old would do. It's probably what he wants to say but doesn't. If he did, she would tell him it's not about Lauren or the new baby. It's about what it all represents. She's still mourning for the family she used to have and, as its last survivor, she deserves to.

She stays in bed, nursing her strained muscles, and breaks out the smelly cream that she rubs into them. Coupled with some painkillers, she sleeps most of the morning. Derrick texts her in the afternoon.

D: You want company?

C: Ugh. Dealing with angry muscles.

D: I have heating pads I can bring over. Interested?

C: Totally.

He comes over and plugs in the pads and lays one on her chest where, surprisingly, it hurts the most. The heat feels so good.

"How are you feeling?" he asks.

"Like crap. I think I pulled every muscle in my body."

She grimaces as she reaches for her water bottle. He hands it to her and sits on the edge of her bed.

"And how are you feeling about, you know, the other thing?"

"You mean, what happened after?"

"Yeah, that."

She doesn't regret it. She'd craved it. Craved that closeness with him. Still does.

"Did you not want to?" she asks.

"No, of course I did. But I want to make sure you're okay."

She takes his hand. "I'm more than okay."

He smiles and leans down and gives her a kiss. "Good."

When he pulls away, she says, "I could use some more Advil though."

He hands her the bottle. "Your dad seems different today."

"Lauren's pregnant."

"Pregnant?"

"So it appears."

"And I take it that it's not good news?"

"It's not the *best* news. A little time would've been nice. A breather to figure things out, to let go, but it's been like—bam— here's a new stepmom, here's a new baby brother or sister. My mom's dead and Teddy's still out there somewhere, waiting to be found, and it's like he's on to his next life."

"I don't think it's exactly like that."

"It feels that way." She looks at him. "Why are we talking about this? You should get in here with me."

She pulls back the covers. Derrick takes his shoes off and slides in next to her. He breathes into her neck. "Hmmm, Aspercreme. So sexy."

She laughs and tries to jab him, but the movement hurts too much. Instead, she lets him hold her even though it aches. But if she lays really still, it doesn't feel so bad.

Memories of them on the court pulse through her mind like heart beats. She presses against him and keeps pressing until he starts to respond. She reaches behind her and starts pulling down the back of her pants.

His voice is deep and throaty. "Your dad is downstairs."

"Then we should be quiet."

She feels him hesitate, but then his hand is on her waistband, helping her shimmy out of her shorts until they are bunched up around her knees.

Derrick pulls the blanket over him as he unbuttons his pants and slides them down. Her body is as eager as her heart. She arches her back, leaning into him, opening herself to him.

She keeps her moans quiet and soft. It's different than yesterday. Softer, less rushed, but equally intoxicating. She grips onto his thigh as she climaxes, stifling her moans as much as she can. He groans into her neck, his hot breath sending chills down her back.

They lie together, both spent, both released. He kisses her before he pulls his pants back up. She follows suit, wincing as she moves them over her hips.

"Can you stay the night?" she asks him.

He redoes his belt.

"I don't think your dad would like that."

"I'm not really concerned about what he thinks right now."

"But I am," he says.

She pats his cheek. "Such a good boy."

They stay in her room, touching each other, kissing, holding, and exploring their bodies. She's never had this kind of closeness and it's a revelation. It soothes and stimulates, and it makes her want to get even closer to Derrick.

When they don't hear any noise in the house, CeCe goes downstairs and scavenges for food, which consists mostly of her dad's homemade bread and peanut butter. At the same time, Derrick hauls up the old DVD player out of the living room.

Night creeps in as they watch old movies. Midway through the third one, she falls asleep.

Her dad knocks on the door. Her eyes blink open to a glaze of sunshine coming through the blinds. She glances over to the side of the bed where Derrick had been. It's empty.

"You awake?" her dad asks cracking open the door.

She jerks up, setting off a deep throbbing in her chest. She's in a tee-shirt but no underwear. She pulls the blankets over her and grabs her old iPhone off the bedside table. It's dead. Crap, her alarm didn't go off.

She tucks the blankets around her as her dad comes in. Frustration ebbs across his face when he sees her.

"Why aren't you up?"

"My alarm didn't go off."

He sighs. "I have a meeting. I can't be late."

"Then leave me here."

"No," he says. "That's not an option. You're going to school."

"Have you forgotten that I'm twenty-one? If I don't want to go, I won't."

"Technically, you're an adult, but if we're going to get technical, you're also an adult without a high school diploma. As your father, and yes, I'm still your father, I can't allow that. Now get up."

He shuts the door behind him. CeCe moves out of bed. She wants to jump in the shower, get the sweat off her, get the smell of great sex off her skin, but she doubts her dad will give her the time. She goes to the bathroom and wets a cloth and does the best she can before she starts throwing on some clothes. Shorts are the easiest, a bra another issue. She grits her teeth as she struggles to get it hooked in the back.

"CeCe," she hears her dad shout from down the stairs. "Let's GOOOOOO."

"I'm coming," she shouts back.

She gets her bra and a shirt on and then shoves her feet into sneakers without bothering to tie the laces. She grabs her bag and it feels too light. She looks inside and finds the demon picture, Derrick's rock, a few pencils, her notebook, and the can of Nitrociptine. But no GED book. When did she take it out? It's not like she did any of the work.

"Crap," she says again as she rummages around her room, looking on the sides of her bed, on her desk, under her desk. She gets on her hands and knees when she hears her dad holler, "CECE."

Screw the book. She's not going to need it anyway.

"I'm COMING!!!"

She goes down the stairs and darts pass her dad.

"You're too old for this," he says, following her out to the front. "I know everything is terrible for you, but you need to be respectful of my time."

"I am respectful. I told you. My alarm didn't go off."

"And who's fault is that?"

"Lemme guess. Mine?" she smarts back. She gets into the car and slams the door.

"Really?" Her dad shakes his head. "What are you, five?"

They're not fighting about her being late. Deep down, she knows that this is about everything else.

About what they've lost, about what has changed, and why they can't see eye to eye on what they need to do to move on, and how they can't talk about it.

They always talk about other things like casserole recipes, what's been restored, cured rates, Infection numbers, when a coffee shop will be up and running, or the fact that she hates the stupid GED program.

They'll talk about anything and everything that has nothing to do with their pain. That's something both of them stay away from as far as possible.

He starts the car and then checks his watch.

"Ridiculous. They're going to be waiting on me."

"Oh shoot. Not the discourse on Zapping Infected to See How High They Can Jump? Man, they're all going to be so disappointed."

She wishes Sirius was still up and running so she could lean over and turn the music on as loud as possible.

"That's not what I do."

"Could've fooled me."

"What is your problem? Why are you treating me like I'm some kind of bad guy?"

She doesn't answer his question. Instead, she says, "Is there a reason we're still sitting here? I thought you're going to be *late*?"

"Unreal," he says, punching the car in reverse and stepping on it.

Something slams into the back, and he brakes hard.

She looks at her dad. He's staring at the rearview mirror, the anger wiped from his face.

"What was that?" she asks.

"I don't know." He unbuckles his seat belt. "Stay in the car."

She doesn't listen and gets out with him, her untied shoelaces whipping around her feet. The moment she steps out, she can hear the screeching, but it's not the normal kind. It's the "I got hit by your car" kind.

It's an Infected kind.

Sprawled on the ground behind the bumper is a girl. Not quite a girl, but not quite a teen either. Bone sticks out of her left leg where it's shattered. She snarls at them, her mouth opening and shutting, as she scoots herself toward them despite her injury.

"Get back," her dad says.

The girl whirls at the sound of his voice and snaps at him, using her hands to drag herself toward him. He moves in a wide arc. Her head follows him like a dog tracking a command.

"Jesus," he says. "Where'd she come from?"

CeCe can't help but wonder the same. It's like having a fox or a bear trapped in the backyard. The girl shouldn't be outside next to the sidewalk where she and Derrick had pulled weeds not that long ago, and yet she is. CeCe wonders if the Lukens are watching, or the Morgans from the slits in their blinds, and if they are, what they must be thinking.

"I thought this area was cleared?" she says.

"Cleared isn't always one hundred percent. You of all people should know that."

She thinks of the night outside the record store and the Infected man and woman. How many more of the wild Infected will wander in? Where are they coming from and where else will they show up? At her school? Outside the living room windows?

The girl tries to get up, pulling her crushed leg underneath her, but collapses. She scoots herself close enough to her dad to lunge at him. A whimper escapes from CeCe's throat, but all he does is step away from her. To her dad, she's a sick girl on the ground with a crushed leg. But he's never been bitten by one.

She unzips her bag and gets out the canister of Nitrociptine.

"No," her dad says. "Don't."

"Why not? You said there's never only one. We have to gas her before more show up."

The girl turns from her dad, to CeCe, to her dad again, following their voices like a tennis match, mouth opening and closing. She starts heaving herself toward CeCe, perhaps deciding she's a better target.

He looks down the street. "You're not wrong, but they would've been here by now. It's possible she's solitary and if you cure her with that leg, she'll die. She'll bleed out long before we can get her on a table. It has to be reset before we do it."

CeCe looks at her dad, at the determination on his face. She sees the man she used to know. The guy with the Band-Aids and the antibiotic ointment, and a rub on the back to let you know it'll be okay.

The one who'd rush down to the vet office at night to calm down worried owners as he treated their pets.

She puts the canister in her pocket.

"What then? Do we call RRT?"

"No. Their orders are to gas on sight. We need to get her to the CAVE."

"How?"

He nods to the car.

"Have you lost your mind?"

He gets out his keys and pops the trunk.

"Okay," she says. "You have." She looks at him. "How are we supposed to get her in there?"

"We'll lift her. She can't be more than a hundred pounds, maybe not even that."

CeCe stares down at the girl. Her shirt is loose, her pants even looser. She's surprised they've even stayed around her waist. Lifting her isn't the problem. She's Infected. They might as well be trying to kennel a rabid dog.

She shakes her head. "No way. No way. Even if we can get her in there, we can't leave not knowing for sure she's the only Infected in the neighborhood. What about the Lukens? The Morgans?"

He makes a hissing sound and looks down the street. "I forgot about him. We should hurry."

"Forgot about who?"

"Mr. Morgan. If he sees her, he'll shoot her. Did you know he's an ex-Marine? A sniper, apparently. Funny how you live next to people for years and still learn new things about them."

Great, she mumbles and turns to the Morgans' house. Not only does she have to worry about getting an Infected into the trunk of the car without being bitten, there's also Mr. Morgan, who might start firing shots at them.

"We'll call RRT on the way and have them do a sweep," her dad says, "but we have to get her out of here first." He turns and heads to the house.

"Where are you going? You can't leave me here alone with her."

As if on cue, the Infected snaps her jaws.

"I'll be right back," he says while walking. "Stay clear. A bite will feel like the worst stomach flu you've ever had."

"Noted," she says, taking a few steps away.

Her dad opens the garage and runs inside. The girl leans onto her thin arms, moving one after the other. CeCe sidesteps her and keeps sidestepping, watching in fascination that someone so tiny, so fragile-looking, can be so dangerous.

Her dad comes back with a blanket and drops it over the girl. Her head jerks around like a cat does when it's been covered. It would be almost laughable if it weren't so dangerous.

Her dad leans over to grab her. "I'll take her shoulders. You get her legs."

"No," she says. "It's too close. You've never been Infected. It'll be better if you stay that way, considering Lauren and pretty much everyone. I'll take her shoulders."

He looks at her. An understanding passes between them. In her way, she's trying to make amends for the fight, for her behavior. It isn't much of an apology, but it's all they have time for.

"Okay," he says and moves to her feet. "Be careful."

"Got it."

She doesn't know if she can do it, but then, as if she's watching herself, she claps her hands around the girl's shoulders. Her muscles want to resist, but adrenaline pulses through them. Now she wishes she'd taken the time to tie her shoes.

"On my signal," her dad says.

Even under the blanket, the Infected girl's mouth presses against the cloth, opening and shutting, as she thrashes around, desperate to work her way out. CeCe's losing her nerve with each passing second.

"Now," he says.

They lift and the girl starts screeching and bucking against them, snapping her arms and her good leg. If Mr. Morgan didn't know she was here, he must by now.

They crab-walk her over to the trunk. Under any other circumstances, this would look like they're abducting some innocent kid fighting for her life, but these aren't ordinary circumstances.

Finally, they get to the car. They toss her in and slam the trunk down. The rear tires bounce as the girl beats against the trunk's lid.

"Let's go," her dad says.

CeCe slides into the passenger seat. They're both out of breath as he pulls out of the driveway. As they head down the road, she stares behind her at the bulging backseat, half expecting the girl to chew her way through the cushions and the coils and to lunge at them like a bobcat.

The hammering is relentless and seems to only get louder the farther they get from the house. It's not a long drive to the CAVE, but it's a drive. If somehow that girl gets out, they'll crash in some fiery car-flipping type of explosion, and she'll still be gnawing on them long after.

Her dad is on the phone. "This is Dr. Campbell," he says. "I'm enroute with a 557 secured in the trunk of my car. My team should be in the Miller Conference Room. Please advise RRT to do an immediate sweep of Sector Twelve."

She hears a voice reply back and her dad's responses turn into a morse code of yeses and noes. He hangs up.

"Well?"

"It's covered."

She grips the door handle, her gaze moving from her dad to the back of the car. Everything is taking too long.

Every turn, every stretch of road. It's like he's deliberately going slow, but when she glances at the dash, the odometer says eighty mph. The security gate looms ahead. It's already open and the guards are waving them through. He speeds past them and brakes along the front of the building, where three people are waiting in hazmat suits. She hears a thump as the Infected girl slams against the seat.

One of the hazmat people is Steve, the tech she'd met when she snuck into the Infected Zoo. The other is a guy she recognizes from the wedding and the awkward morning after when she felt like she was slithering into the commissary.

Beside them is Lauren.

CeCe and her dad get out of the car, and Steve motions to the trunk. "Damn, Shawn. That's a first."

"Yes, well, I wouldn't recommend it."

Lauren's eyes are wide as she stares at the trunk, the Infected girl screeching at full volume. Lauren's face is pale, but it's hard to tell if it's from the situation, morning sickness, or the plastic shield.

Her dad says to Lauren, "You shouldn't be here, not with the baby."

"I can help. You need my help."

"You might be right," he says. "But I can't do this while worrying about you. Please. Go back inside."

Lauren looks at CeCe, who's not sure if Lauren wants her support, but she doesn't offer it. Her dad's right. She still might not be on board with a new brother or sister, but she doesn't want anything to happen to him or her either. Lauren's lips thin, but she turns and goes back inside.

"Steve, Mike," her dad says. "Come with me."

They move to the back of the car.

Her dad holds the key fob. "The R45 is a female, roughly eleven to thirteen years of age. She has a compound fracture in her left femur. If she's cured, her survival rate drops to ten percent at best."

Steve says, "So, we're going to do this before she's gassed?"

"That's the plan."

"Huh. I suppose there's a first time for everything."

CeCe stares at her dad. *First time?* This is the first time he's doing something like this? Her heart thuds in her chest as she stands beside them, her shoelaces still dangling around her feet. She should tie them, but can't bring herself to bend down to do it. She can hear the girl thrashing around inside. A bobcat ready to spring from her cage.

Her dad says, "We have to get her restrained as quickly as possible and in the OR. Ready?"

Steve and Mike both nod while CeCe holds her breath.

Her dad pops the trunk.

The girl pushes out and drops onto the pavement. She twists her body toward them, snarling and biting at the air. She slides herself along the smooth concrete like an eel and reaches for Steve's foot.

Steve reaches down and latches on to her like he's picking up a snake by the head. Her dad and Mike go for her feet. Despite her thrashing, they lift her without effort like she's nothing but a squirming toddler. It's such a huge difference from when it was only CeCe and her dad.

She turns to him. "What do you want me to do?"

"Stay in front and get the door. We have to take the access elevator. It's at the end of the corridor."

She nods and runs down to the end of the hallway, punching the elevator button. It takes an excruciatingly long time before the doors finally open. She hears the girl struggling and the guys getting closer. Nausea seeps into her mouth, but her dad, Steve, and Mike are calm and seem unfazed.

They've done this before. Of course, they have. Otherwise, where did the zoo come from? Only this is the first time they've ever tried to fix them.

They bring the girl inside the elevator, and her shrieks ricochet off the steel walls like tiny pins stabbing CeCe's eardrums. She presses herself flat, staying as far away from the girl's mouth that keeps jerking at each of them. All CeCe can think about is the girl getting loose while they're stuck in this box.

CeCe's freaking out. Her breathing accelerates and she tells herself if she doesn't stop panicking, she's going to pass out.

The doors slide open, and she's the first one out. She speed-walks to the lab, her gaze going from the girl to the door.

As soon as she gets close, her dad shouts, a bunch of numbers that means nothing to her. It doesn't match any birthdays or her mom and dad's anniversary.

"Okay." Her finger shakes as she punches it in. "Okay."

The light turns from red to green and she holds open the door as they haul the girl through.

The other Infected start reacting. They bang against the glass, frenzying within their prisons. It's like they know an Infected is on the other side, near prey, and the nature of the horde calls to them, along with the need to infect, to spread, to consume.

CeCe thinks of Penny, who must be frightened, wondering what's happening. Or maybe she's seen this all before.

Penny is standing at the front of the glass, her face impassive as they approach, but her eyes are wide with curiosity. CeCe tries to get her attention, if only to give her a nod, some kind of reassurance that it's going to be okay, probably more for herself than Penny, but she's watching the Infected being held fast by her dad, Mike, and Steve. As they pass, Penny's eyes change. Curiosity morphs into surprise, and then into alarm.

She bangs on the glass so hard that it reverberates under her little fists. For a moment, CeCe can't tell the difference between Penny and the other Infected. Seeing Penny this way makes her insides want to recoil. But it's not fear or rage or anger on the little girl's face. It's concern. Like over someone she cares about. Someone she loves. And she realizes that Penny knows this Infected.

"Hey," CeCe says to her dad as she keeps staring at Penny. "Hey. Wait a minute."

Neither her dad, Mike, nor Steve pay her any attention. The girl rears against them, twisting her body, her mouth cracking as they get her on a table. They hold her down, or try to, as they strap down her wrists.

Penny comes out, and CeCe reaches over to her.

"Wait," she says, taking her by the arm. "You can't. You can get hurt."

Penny looks at the girl on the table. She wants to go over to her. It's all over Penny's face, but she, more so than all of them, should know what an Infected is capable of doing.

"You recognize her, don't you?"

Penny turns to CeCe and nods.

"My dad is trying to help her. She's been in an accident."

CeCe isn't sure how much to say and decides it best to leave it at that. Whoever this girl is to Penny, she doesn't need to know how serious the injury is, or what would happen if they can't fix her.

Penny's shoulders go up and down with her breaths as they stand together, watching as the men work to fix the straps. Steve holds down the girl's arm as they get one wrapped, but in one quick moment, her hand is out, and she's reaching for Steve.

"CeCe," her dad shouts. "We need your help."

"Stay here," she says to Penny before hurrying over.

The girl twists on the table and manages to slide off. She's yanking on her bound leg and all CeCe can think is that the girl will rip it in two, right in front of Penny, just to get to them. The parasite has no mercy, none at all.

Mike and Steve try to pick her up, but their hazmat suits make it impossible to get a good grip on her.

"Hold her down, CeCe," her dad orders.

She presses all her weight on the girl's other thigh as they hoist her back up. Steve fiddles with the leather strap to secure her arm. Now that CeCe's so close, she glances up at the girl's forehead. Under her matted hair is the Revie symbol. The same as Penny's. This Infected was one of them too.

She glances over at Penny and then hears Steve say, "Damn. I have to take these off."

He pulls at his gloves.

"Come on, man," her dad says.

"I'm trying."

The girl bucks underneath, lifting up off the table. She gets out from under Mike, and she rears up like something out of *The Exorcist* toward CeCe. Her dad puts his arm in front of her to push her away. Anyone would've done it out of instinct, but as he does, CeCe watches in one slow agonizing moment as the girl's mouth wraps around his forearm and clamps down.

Her dad roars as blood bubbles up around the girl's lips.

CeCe stares helplessly at the look on her dad's face, the reaction to the pain. The surprise. It hits her squarely between her eyes like her brain has been given an electric jolt, tearing open memories that'd been hiding behind a brick wall.

She's seen this before. Not only the night it happened to her, but to someone else, and the blood was on her lips, and she can still taste it. Almost as if it'd be there if she ran her tongue across them. The blood she drew from her teeth. Her gaping mouth. Her Infected need.

Her hands drop, the strength fading from her muscles. The girl writhes underneath her, frenzying with the taste of blood. Her dad's blood, but she feels like she's watching it all from the depths of a tunnel.

CeCe's somewhere else.

Someplace she'd forgotten but has returned to with such force that it squeezes her insides, smothering her under the weight of the past.

Chapter Fifteen

Infection

Phase One

She's in the backseat of the Uber, driving home from Mason's the night she was bit. Leyton's in the car, freaking out, and not freaking out. CeCe's cardigan is wrapped around her hand, blood seeping through the fabric. It's only the two of them. Where her other friends went, if they got their own Ubers, she doesn't know.

The driver keeps looking back at them.

"Do you want me to take her to the hospital?" he asks Leyton.

"No," CeCe says. "My dad can fix it."

"He a doctor?"

"Sort of."

Leyton unwraps the sweater from her hand.

"Shit," she says.

CeCe glances down. Her skin hangs in shreds in some places, and she can see flashes of bone in others. *It's over*, she thinks. *It's all over.*

Her head's pounding, a headache that starts in the back of her skull and works its way around to her temples. Sweat beads on her skin as the temperature inside the car goes from comfortable to a hundred degrees. *Fever.* Not only had some fiend ripped her hand almost in two, but he gave her something.

Whatever it is, she can fix it. She can fix this, but she knows deep down it's a lie. Something isn't right, but she won't acknowledge it. The idea's too frightening.

A wave of nausea rolls down her throat and into her stomach. She needs to throw up, but she refuses to allow it. She isn't going to lose control.

"Is the heater on?" she asks, unrolling the window with her good hand.

She leans her head out, and as she closes her eyes, the cool air presses against her face.

Somehow she's in her bathroom upstairs. Vomit skims the toilet and runs down the sides. A whooshing noise roars in her ears so loud that it wakes her. She gets up. Pain shoots up her arm. She looks down at her hand. Clotted blood fills the deep gouges.

She pulls herself up to her feet, searching for the source of the noise that seems to grow louder and scratches against her brain. Is there a helicopter above her house? What else can sound like that? She turns to the sink.

Water runs out of the faucet with blood smearing its white porcelain. She must've left it on. She reaches over and turns it off, and it's like she cut off all sound everywhere. She glances overhead. There's no helicopter. It was the water. How's that possible?

She opens the door, her head spinning, her knees want to buckle underneath her. The Uber driver was right. She needs to go to the hospital, but where's her mom? Her dad? How did she make it to her room with her hand in shreds, and they didn't see her? Then she remembers Teddy's thing at his school. A performance or game. Something stupid. She must've made it home before them.

She leans against the wall and inches her way into her room. Her limbs feel heavy, the sickness still turning in her stomach, and the pounding in her head is unbearable.

She hasn't felt this horrible since the night she and Riley went to a party where they took round after round of Fireball shots and swore never to drink again. But that seems like nothing in comparison.

Advil. She needs Advil. Like twenty of them, but she'll have to go downstairs to the kitchen and the idea of it is overwhelming. Impossible.

She calls out for her mom, but the sound of her voice is like a hammer against her skull. She'll have to go to them, but the longer she stands, the more her gut twists in on itself like tiny knives carving along her abdominals, only deep enough to hurt in the worst possible way. She'll rest a minute and then she'll go.

Leaning against the side of her wall, then her dresser, then her nightstand, she manages to get onto her bed and curl up on her side.

I'm dying. This is what it must feel like.

Advil won't fix this. She needs a hospital where there's IVs and medicines and doctors. Where's her phone? She'll call for an ambulance. She lifts her head to look for it and then sets it back down.

Next thing she knows, she's on her bedroom floor, the ceiling looming above her. She doesn't know how long she's been there or how she got there, only that doesn't matter. Her headache and the gnawing in her stomach are gone, but her throat burns with an overwhelming thirst. She's thirsty. So, so thirsty.

She grips the edge of the mattress with her bitten hand, no longer feeling any pain even though flaps of her skin bunch together, pinching out a dribble of blood. She can't feel anything. Not in her legs, her arms, her fingers.

Everything's numb.

All that's left is the incredible thirst. She stands, swaying. A baby ready to take a first step.

Stumbling a little, she makes her way out of her bedroom and toward the stairs. The light grows brighter as she creeps to the first floor. There's a noise coming from the living room. Voices. Her ears ring from the pitch, but something about it makes her thirst stronger and it digs at her throat like tiny claws prickling her esophagus, and all she wants in that moment is to make it stop.

She follows the sound to the living room. The voices are coming from the TV. It's a news broadcast with pictures of people running, and there's fire and gunshots. Her mother is on the couch, watching it.

The burning in her throat grows hotter, the ache deeper.

Her mom turns toward her.

"CeCe, honey, why aren't you at school?"

Her words are so loud that they're fists against her temples, but her throat convulses in so much need that her mouth opens and closes in anticipation. She springs onto the back of her mom, biting hard into the side of her neck. Her blood flows into her mouth, the warmth coating her tongue and throat, quenching the burning in sudden relief.

Her mother presses her hands against her. Pushing her off, but CeCe doesn't want to be pushed. She clings on, needing more of her blood that calmed her insides. The sudden crack of her mother's elbow against her cheek stuns her enough to let go. Her mom moves around the couch with her hand against her neck, her face twisting in agony and fear and confusion. Blood runs over her fingers and onto the floor. CeCe needs that blood. Why is her mom letting it go to waste?

She leaps over the couch as her mother sprints toward the downstairs bathroom. She lunges after her, her early-morning stumbling footsteps finding easy balance and agility. She chases her, but her mom makes it to the bathroom and slams the door shut. CeCe bangs against it, ramming her body against the wood, shouting at her mom to let her in, but it isn't words.

She thought it was words, but it wasn't.

It's screeching.

Chapter Sixteen

Now

The Truth

CeCe gasps for breath as the pain rips open a hole in her chest. It was her fault. She'd given her mother the fatal bite. She's the reason her mom is dead and wouldn't come back. Deep in her bones, she knows it and, perhaps in some way, always had.

She stands there by the table as her dad pushes the Infected girl away.

Mike and Steve hold her down and, in one swift moment, they strap the girl's other arm to the table and then another around her chest and forehead. They stand away from her, breathing hard as she squirms under the restraints, grunting and snarling and clicking her jaw, her lips still red from her dad's blood.

He goes over to a sink. She watches as he rinses the blood away, douses the bite in some watery solution, and then presses a gauze to it.

"Dad?" she whispers.

"It's okay," he says to her. "I'll be okay."

"Dad?" she says again.

"I'm fine. It stings a bit, that's all." He turns to Steve and Mike. "Prepare her leg for surgery."

"Dad." Her voice is so quiet that she's not sure if she said it or thought it. She starts backing away, gripping her hands together.

"Damn," her dad says, bringing his hand to his brow. "I have a headache. I'm already in Phase One. We're going to have to move fast."

Steve maneuvers a stainless-steel tray and Mike pushes a portable X-ray machine out from the corner. Her dad puts on some gloves, as if it makes a difference now. All this happens around her—life moving on to the next emergency—while she suffocates under the weight of what she's done.

She can't be there anymore and runs out of the room, past the Infected slamming themselves against the glass, and out the door. No one calls for her, but she doesn't expect them to. Even if they did, she wouldn't stop. She bolts down the hall. She doesn't know where she's going, only that she has to get out, has to get as far away as possible. She turns a corner and almost barrels right into Lauren. She's dressed out of the hazmat suit.

"CeCe," she says, her eyes widening from being startled. "CeCe, are you all right?"

"No." She shakes her head. "No, I'm not. Can you please take me home?"

"Yes, of course." She reaches out as if to touch her on the shoulder, but then brings her hand back. "Let me get my keys. Everything going okay in there?"

"No." Her lips tremble. "Dad's been bitten."

Lauren's eyes widen.

"They'll gas him, right?" CeCe asks. "Now, I mean."

"Not without curing that girl and every other Infected in that room. I should check on him. See if he needs me. I'll be right back."

Lauren moves past her. CeCe watches her disappear down the hallway and into the lab. She leans against the wall, her body caving in, every ligament and cell, as the memories course through her of that night. Of that morning. Of her mother.

Lauren comes back. She's flustered, presumably kicked out again.

"Well, he says he's fine. Let's get you home."

CeCe follows Lauren out to her car, and she gets in the passenger seat. They drive past the security guards and onto the highway toward the city. CeCe stares out the window, looking at everything. Looking at nothing.

Now that she's remembered, her mind is playing over each detail, examining every moment, and what she could've done but didn't.

She killed her mother.

And now that she knows, how can she take another breath, share another smile, eat another meal? She rubs her arm, hating her own skin. Wishing she could pull it off.

It'll never go away. The dread and horror. She'll never unknow what she's done.

There'll never be a time where it'll be okay.

There'll never be a time she won't despise herself.

Her eyes brim with tears that have been waiting to come for so long, and now that they're here, they boil over and course down her cheeks. She's unable to wipe them away fast enough.

Lauren pulls up to the house. Without even saying thank you or goodbye, CeCe jumps out of the car and sprints to the front door.

The tears turn into choking sobs as she stumbles inside.

Moving to the living room, she stands behind the back of the couch where her mom had been sitting, as if somehow by being there she could go back in time.

The fabric is clean. Impossibly clean. She rubs her eyes.

Could she have been wrong? Is it a real memory or something she made up in her fevered brain?

She runs her hands along the fabric. There had been so much blood. This should be stained with it, but it's not. Relief spools through her body, unwinding the vise around her chest.

She's about to move away, go to the kitchen or maybe her room, when she glances over at the matching loveseat pushed against the wall. It hasn't moved since the day her mom and dad brought the set home. That was its place with the "Home" pillow in its center.

Nothing is different, except the back cushions look a little too broken in for a couch no one really used, and a blanket drapes the front of it. A blanket that was always rolled up with four others in a wicker basket by the fireplace.

The vise that had loosened retightens as she goes to the loveseat. She draws the blanket off slowly, as if she's pulling a single thread. Her vision narrows as her heartbeat pounds in her ears. Underneath is a large dark stain. It's been cleaned, but it's there. Her mother's blood.

No. No. No.

She drops to her knees before it. Tears blurring her vision, her stomach turning. It can't be real, but it is.

She presses her face against the cushion and sobs until there's nothing left for her body to offer other than the guilt that courses through her blood like the Infection had.

She has no idea how long she stays like that. Her muscles stiffen and ache, but she refuses to move, refuses to do anything.

Her phone buzzes with a text. She ignores it.

She gets a few more and ignores them too. Then the phone calls start. One after another that she lets go to voicemail. Finally, she hears a knocking on the door and Derrick on the other side calling her name.

She listens to him, her grief morphing into an insatiable rage.

Derrick.

This is his fault. He did this to her. He turned her into a monster. Her mother would still be alive if it weren't for him.

If she hadn't come home with her hand half mangled and the Infection blowing a hole through her brain, she would've never walked down those stairs with the burning in her throat. She would have never, never, never hurt her mother.

But she had.

Because of him.

And she'd let him get close to her. To touch her.

It makes her so sick she wants to throw up.

"CeCe," she hears him call. "Are you here? Are you okay?"

She stays quiet.

The handle jiggles and the door cracks open. Crap. She hadn't locked it.

"CeCe?"

She doesn't want him here. Not in this house where her mother had lived and died, thanks to him, thanks to what he did to her. She won't let him invade this space, and the crumbled remains of her family, any longer.

Despite the resistance in her legs, she gets up and goes to the front door. When Derrick sees her, his face clears with relief.

He'd been worried.

Good.

She wants him to suffer, but more than that, she wants him to feel what she's feeling right now. To know that the pain he caused can never be fixed, and never be forgiven.

He sighs. "I thought something happened to you. You weren't at school and after what happened the other day with that Revie girl, I didn't know what to think. Are you okay?"

She wants to laugh and is surprised when she hears the sound of a chuckle escape her throat. "No, Derrick. I'm definitely not."

"Have you—" He reaches out to her face, but she pulls away. "Have you been crying? Did something happen?"

She glares at him; as her anger rises, saliva gathers in her mouth. She clenches her fists to stop herself from lashing out at him.

"I remember," she says. "I remember everything that happened the night I was turned. You want to hear it? You want to know? Want me to *share*?" She spits out the word. "Well, here it is.

"I remember celebrating my eighteenth birthday at Mason's with my friends and getting bitten by a guy who I was trying to help, who I thought was drunk. By a guy wearing a gray Chico State Sweatshirt. Sound familiar?"

Derrick's eyes widen. He takes a step back.

"And then I remember coming home, running my mangled hand under the water in the bathroom. Waking up the next morning with a thirst, a thirst that took me downstairs to find my mother sitting on the couch where I bit a hole in her neck. I…" Tears stream down her cheeks as she struggles to say, "I killed my mother. I made it impossible for her to be cured. I did that to her. And you want to know what?" She smears her tears. "It wouldn't've happened if I hadn't met you."

She takes her off her glove and holds it up to him.

"You did this to me."

"No," he says. "No." He's shaking his head, but he's remembering. She can see it in his eyes. The shock of it, the guilt of what he'd done, and she likes it. She likes seeing him this way. Revels in his pain.

"Why didn't you tell me?" he asks. "Why would you keep this from me?"

She looks at him, her insides drenched in venom.

"Because I don't owe you anything. Not a damn thing. And I never did."

"CeCe."

"Don't come back here again," she says as she pushes him over the entryway. "We're done."

She shuts the door and turns the deadbolt.

He doesn't knock. Doesn't call after her.

She wouldn't have cared if he had.

In her mind, he was another Infected.

Another monster.

Just like her.

Chapter Seventeen

Now What?

The next morning, she hears a jingle of keys in the door. She jumps up. It's her dad. He's home.

Instantly, guilt stabs through her. She hadn't thought much of him all night. Hadn't even bothered to call Lauren and ask how he was doing.

Her depression had been so deep she couldn't think beyond her mother and the role she'd played in her death. She relived the memory over and over, teasing out all the images, freezing them like photographs.

She has one parent left and she doesn't deserve to have him. She's been selfish, a terrible daughter in every way. In the worst possible way.

CeCe rushes to the door and instead of seeing her dad, it's Lauren. After yesterday, all the feelings of animosity she had toward her stepmother have vanished, along with her self-righteousness.

She has no room to judge Lauren or her dad when she's the reason her mom isn't in this world anymore. She's the one who changed their lives. Not him. Not her. It was CeCe.

Lauren steps inside, holding CeCe's backpack and a rolled-up paper bag. CeCe had forgotten she'd left her bag in her dad's car.

"I hope you don't mind," she says, "but your dad wanted me to check in on you. Was everything okay last night? He didn't like that you were alone."

"Yeah," she says. "I was fine. Thank you."

"Are you sure?" Lauren asks, frowning. "You look like you've had one hell of a night."

CeCe hasn't seen herself in a mirror, hasn't bothered to really care, but she can only imagine what crying for hours has done to her face.

"I, uh," she says, running her hands under her eyes. "I must've slept wrong or something. How is he?"

"He's fine," she says. "And going to be fine, I promise."

CeCe sniffs. "And the girl? Did they get her leg patched up?"

"They did. She might not receive full use of it, but she'll make a full recovery and that's something."

"That's good," she says, feeling vacant. "I'm happy for her."

"You sure you're doing all right?" Lauren asks again.

She thinks of the cushions. Her dad had to have done that. He'd known this whole time that she'd killed her mother, and yet he still wanted to save her. He still wanted to bring her back. To have her in his life.

She remembers the horrible things she's said to him, the things she's accused him of doing. There are no words for how she feels, but mostly she doesn't know how he can ever possibly forgive her. For any of it.

"Yeah," she says. "Do you know when he'll be home? I was hoping to talk to him."

"It's going to be a few days. I'd be happy to take you to him if you like. I'm sure he'd love to see you. He's been asking for you."

She wants to go, but now that she's remembered what happened, she can't without that hanging between them. Knowing what she knows. Knowing that they might all know this about her, and still smile and nod like everything's okay. That she's a good daughter coming to visit her dad when it's all a lie.

She has to tell them they don't have to pretend anymore. But she can't. Not there.

She runs her hands along her scalp. Her hair is stiff. She needs a shower, but it's the effort stopping her. "You're right. I didn't have the best night. Would it be okay if I see him tomorrow?" She swallows. "What happened with my dad brought back bad memories."

Lauren looks at her with genuine compassion, compassion CeCe doesn't deserve, especially not from her.

She treated Lauren like a dog no one wanted. But she must know too. Of course, she does. Her dad would've told her a long time ago what happened to his wife and daughter way before he even discovered the cure.

Shame coats CeCe's insides as the realization glides down her stomach. How can Lauren even look at her knowing what she did? How can she stand to be in the same room with a girl who'd killed her own mother?

Unrolling the paper bag, Lauren pulls out a Tupperware container.

"Sam made this for you. I'm not sure what it is, but it smells decent."

CeCe takes it from her hand. "Thanks."

"I'll come back to check on you tomorrow if that's okay. And then if you're ready, we can go see your dad."

"Yeah, that sounds good."

"Call me if you need anything. I mean it. I don't care what time it is."

"I will," she says, knowing that if anything did happen, if a horde of Infected came into the house, she wouldn't stop them. Wouldn't raise a finger to save herself. She isn't worth saving.

She walks Lauren out and shuts the door behind her. Once she knows Lauren is gone, she turns back to the living room. Her dad doesn't have to worry about her being alone. She isn't, not really.

She has her tortured thoughts for company.

Like the night before, she spends the evening in the dark. No lamps. No sound. She leaves the food on the counter, untouched. She barely drinks any water. She sits on the floor of the living room, next to the bloodstained cushion, with her head between her knees in the same clothes she wore yesterday and no desire to change or do anything.

Her phone buzzes from time to time. A few are from Lauren saying she's "checking in." And one is from Derrick.

"We should talk," he texts. "I'd like to talk."

She thinks of replying, "Leave me alone," but instead, she puts the phone down.

Sometime in the night, she falls asleep and wakes to the sound of knocking. She knows it can't be Lauren. She has the key and would come in like she did yesterday.

It must be Derrick, not giving up when she needs him to.

Whatever had been between them isn't happening anymore.

She huddles in the living room, waiting for him to go away. When the knocking gets louder until he's banging, irritation burns down her throat, searing a hole in her stomach.

She gets up to confront him. To tell him in a way that he'll understand that she wants nothing to do with him. She doesn't want to talk. She doesn't want to hash things out. It's over.

She flings the door open, ready to scream this at him, but the scream dies in her throat.

It's not Derrick standing there, but Olivia and her friend, the red pickup parked along the curb.

Her head jerks back in surprise. Them. Here. How do they know where she lives? And anyway, d, where do they get the nerve Ito show up? But here they are with Olivia standing on her doorstep like she owns it.

Olivia smiles at her, but there's nothing friendly about it. "Wasn't sure if you were going to answer. You look like shit."

CeCe ignores the comment. "What are you doing here?"

Olivia's friend shifts on his feet. His baseball cap is low on his head, but she can still see his dark eyes glowering into her. She doesn't like it. It's like he's mentally peeling back her skin to make a roast.

Olivia keeps her smile on her face. "You weren't at school these last two days. Rob and I wanted to make sure you're okay and all."

CeCe looks at Rob.

"Sure you did."

Olivia squints past her and into the house. "Your dad home?"

CeCe doesn't answer and instead moves her body to block Olivia's view.

"That's a no then, huh?"

"We're done here. Thanks for stopping by. Don't come back."

She goes to shut the door, but Olivia puts her foot in the jam.

"No reason to be rude."

"I have plenty of reason."

Olivia puckers her lips. "And here we were coming over to cheer you up. Had something to show you too. Bet it'll make you happy."

"I highly doubt that."

"And I bet if we showed you, you'd want to come with us."

"Come with you? You're weirder than I thought."

She goes to shut the door again, but Olivia keeps her foot firmly planted. It crosses her mind then that if Olivia wanted, she could push her way inside, both her and Rob. She thinks of that day they'd followed her and Derrick after school, and now they're here. If they get inside, what would they do? In her condition, she's not sure if she could stop them even if she tried.

Olivia removes her foot, and she takes the opportunity and quickly shuts the door, sliding the deadbolt in place. She takes a step away as if the knob will burn her.

"I guess you don't want to see your brother then," Olivia shouts from the other side. "Your loss."

Her heartbeat gallops into a sprint at the mention of Teddy. She shouldn't open the door. Every nerve in her body is begging her not to. But Teddy? How does Olivia know about her brother?

She cracks the door open. Olivia and Rob are already down the walkway near the truck.

"Teddy's dead," she says.

"Huh?" Olivia turns toward her. "That's funny. You see, I spoke to him this morning. I'm not sure a dead kid can talk. Can a dead kid talk, Rob?"

Rob shakes his head. "Nope."

"You're lying," she says. "Both of you."

Olivia pulls out a phone and flips it open. She brings it over to CeCe, holding it up. The photo's grainy, but without any doubt, it's him. It's Teddy.

Her breath stills as she gawks at it. He's older, but it's her brother. A close-up of his face against a blue background. He's staring into the camera, expressionless, but she knows better. He's scared and trying really hard not to show it. The time stamp in the corner is dated for this morning. Her heart drops.

He's alive.

Olivia snaps the phone shut and puts it in her pocket.

CeCe grips onto the door, igniting with a surge of energy, despite being depleted in every way over the last twenty-four hours. She wants to smile, hug something, someone. She'd even hug Olivia. But...

"Take me to Teddy," she says. "I want to see him."

"See, I told you." Olivia grins. "Come on then."

CeCe shuts the door behind her, not bothering to lock it or care that she hadn't. She trails behind Olivia and Rob, ignoring the hollering voice in the back of her head telling her this has been way too easy.

Why would Olivia want to help her? She wouldn't. She has no reason to give one iota about her or her brother. But here she is, offering CeCe the one thing she wants most and CeCe going right along with it.

She should be asking more questions. She should be wondering why Teddy is with them in the first place. Are they holding him against his will? Or turned him into a Revie like themselves?

But she doesn't care about the circumstances. She wants to see him too much to care she's going blindly down the sidewalk when she should run inside, lock the door, and call her dad.

He'd tear this city upside down to find Teddy. And while she knows this, she's worried that if she hesitates, if she tries to call for help, she'll never see Teddy again.

That this might be her only chance to get him back, even if it does smack of a textbook trap.

But she won't leave her brother alone with them. Not for another second. She has to do it for her dad, her mom, for herself.

There's nothing else left.

She gets to the truck. Right as Olivia opens the passenger door, Derrick comes up the road on his bike.

"Look who it is," Olivia says to Rob. "Your knight in shining armor." She turns a dark gaze onto CeCe. "Get rid of him or you won't be seeing your brother anytime soon or ever. The RRT aren't the worst things around. I've seen Infected chew a person to the bone. You understand?"

CeCe nods, not having to wonder if she's telling the truth. She believes her. Olivia will make certain Teddy is never found again, no matter what her dad does. No matter how many people he'll have out looking for him.

The world is not the same anymore. If she wants to get Teddy back, this is her one shot, and Derrick won't ruin this for her too.

Derrick stops his bike right behind the truck. He rips his helmet off, his eyes on Rob and Olivia. "You guys lost?"

He's ready to fight. She can see it on his face, but she is too.

"I told you to stay away," she snarls, moving toward him.

His surprised gaze lands on her. "What? Are you with them? You can't be serious."

"I need you to leave. Now."

He shakes his head. "No. Hate me all you want, but I'm not leaving you alone with Revie One and Revie Two." He gets out his phone. "I'm calling RRT."

She knocks it out of his hand.

"Leave," she says, her voice cracking. "Please, Derrick."

He looks at her, his dismay turning into a staunch resolution. "No."

Rob shuts the truck door. "I'm over this," he says and pulls a gun out from the back of his jeans. He points it at Derrick.

"You not hearing her? She told you to leave, man."

Derrick doesn't flinch, doesn't move. He turns toward Rob. The muscles in his neck tighten against his skin. "If you want me to leave, then I guess you're going to have to shoot me."

"Not a problem." He cocks the gun.

"No." CeCe stands between them. "No."

She might despise Derrick, want nothing to do with him, but she doesn't want this. She won't watch him die. Maybe when she first saw him, she would've gladly witnessed him crumble to the ground, his blood soaking the concrete around him. It might've made her smile a bit when nothing made her feel anything.

But that was then. And as much as she hates him, part of her still cares despite herself, despite her rage, and that part will not allow Rob to shoot him.

"Go," she says to Derrick, her voice trembling. "Do this one thing for me. Please."

Derrick looks from her to Rob and says, "What do you want with her?"

Olivia sighs. "Please shoot him already."

Rob levels the gun toward CeCe. "Move or I'll put a bullet in both of you."

Her heart speeds up as she stares at the end of the revolver. Rob's capable of doing it. Probably has done it many times before.

"Okay," Derrick says from behind her. "I get it. I'm going."

Rob doesn't lower the gun. Not even when Derrick starts his bike, and its hum fills the space between them. She hears every scrape of his shoe as he moves it backward, and then the squeal of the tires as they speed away.

It's only then that Rob uncocks the gun and puts it back in the waist of his jeans.

CeCe exhales, trying to quiet the thundering in her chest.

Olivia comes over and crushes Derrick's phone under her foot, smearing the plastic and the outdated innards into the asphalt. "Time's a-wastin'," she says.

CeCe goes with her to the truck and Olivia motions her inside, where it smells like grease and stale cigarette smoke. The seat is a patchwork of holes.

A jagged piece of synthetic leather digs into the back of her thigh as Rob puts the truck into gear and slams on the gas. They lurch down the street, gears grinding underneath them.

"If it makes you feel any better," Olivia says to her, "I wouldn't've let Rob shoot you. Your boyfriend, yes, but not you. I mean, that guy's stupid, but good thing that he's not that stupid."

Rob looks up at the rearview mirror. He slows down.

"Actually, he's pretty stupid."

CeCe turns and looks out the back window. Derrick's trailing behind them.

"Can't have a tagalong," Rob says and hands the gun over to Olivia.

"No," CeCe cries.

She grapples for the gun, not knowing what she'd do if she did manage to get ahold of it, but Olivia doesn't give her the chance to find out. She elbows her hard in the chest, setting off a wave of pain from her overworked muscles. She sucks in a breath at the shock of it.

"Careful," Olivia says to her. "We don't want to blow off half that pretty face, do we?" She cocks the gun. "Hold her down, Rob."

Rob's arm goes around CeCe's shoulder, and he yanks her so hard that she feels the sting of the seat ripping into her thigh. She struggles against him, and he digs his fingers into the back of her neck until she cries out.

"Sit still," he growls at her.

"All right," Olivia says. "Let's flush him out."

Rob swerves the truck hard from right to left.

"That did it." She chuckles. "He's coming now."

Olivia slides the back window open and then a loud BANG, BANG, BANG reverberates through the cab. CeCe's whole body jumps with each pull of the trigger.

Olivia laughs, but it sounds like it's coming from underwater. "Got him."

CeCe's heart hiccups in her chest. *Got him?* Her nerves prickle down her spine, fanning through her skin and out to her fingertips in a surge of electricity. Derrick's okay. He has to be okay.

"Let me go," she screams and bites down on Rob's arm.

He cries out and releases his grip, long enough for her to wiggle away and turn to the window.

Down the street, Derrick's bike lies on its side, wheels spinning in the air. For one satisfying moment, she believes Olivia's wrong. She'd missed him, but then he's there, as if materializing before her, his body sprawled out on the pavement. She waits for him to move, to get up, to do *anything* other than to lie still, but he doesn't. *No,* she wants to cry. *No.*

"You bitch," she hears Rob say. "You Infected bitch."

His fist cracks against her skull.

Pain shoots through the side of her face and down her jaw. She's never been hit like that before, not even by accident, and the force of the blow is jolting, making her stomach twist with sickening nausea.

Black crowds into her periphery. She's going to pass out. She feels it coming like a blanket being drawn over her. But she can't. She blinks and blinks again.

"Now, Rob," Olivia coos. "That wasn't nice."

"The bitch bit me."

He slams on the gas, pressing her against the seat.

"Relax," Olivia tells him. "She's had the doctor's snake oil. You'll be fine."

Tears sting CeCe's eyes. She tries to move her jaw, focusing on the throbbing to keep her awake. She touches the side of her face.

It's already swelling, making it hard to see from her right eye. She tries to turn her head, but the muscles in her neck spasm and the darkness threatens to return. She wants one last look out the window, one last look at Derrick, but Rob is already turning down another street, and that time is gone.

Her lips tremble. She doesn't want to cry in front of them, *especially* not in front of them, but everything in her is rupturing.

This was a mistake. She should've waited. She should've called RRT or Lauren, anyone, despite what she'd felt earlier and what she'd believed. Because of her, Derrick is dead or shot and dying, and there's nothing she can do for him.

She can't get help, can't do anything, and regret over what she'd said to him sours her throat.

She wants to take it back. All of it.

She was wrong, blind to her grief and needing someone to blame other than herself.

It wasn't his fault for what had happened to her mom. Maybe her mom might be alive if she hadn't been bitten that night, maybe she would've died from something else. There's no way to know.

The only thing she does know is that Derrick didn't mean for that to happen anymore than she meant for that to happen to her mom. That's the truth.

That's the reality of this messed-up world they'd found themselves in. But there's no unwinding the past and he'll die with her blame coating his final thoughts.

And all this is swimming in her head as she sits between Olivia and Rob going to who-knows-where to probably die, and she'll never have the chance to tell Derrick she's sorry.

"Oh." Olivia makes a pouty face. "Are you sad?"

"Go to hell."

Olivia laughs and sits back, her elbow hanging outside the truck's window, enjoying this. Enjoying every moment.

Chapter Eighteen

Game, Set, Match

New Balls

CeCe folds into herself, trying to think of what to do. No one knows where she is and the only person who could guess is already far behind them, most likely dying.

Foolish. She'd been so quick to leave, so enticed by the dangle of her brother as a carrot, she hadn't even thought to grab her phone. Her only hope is Lauren. Maybe she'll come to check on her and see her backpack still there. Maybe that'll make her suspicious, but even if it does, she doubts Lauren would come up with this scenario.

She's on her own and needs to escape with Teddy somehow. Only Rob has a gun and fists and Olivia's scrutiny, which will catch whatever CeCe tries to do.

Still, she has to do something. She can't let Olivia win. She's been down before, playing sets that were love-5, and still managed to come back for the win.

If I could do that then, I can do this now.

They pass through a part of the city she doesn't remember. It's run-down and gets more decrepit the farther they get. They go through an old industrial park with mechanic business names on the outside or signs that mean nothing now. They pull into the parking lot of one of the metal buildings. Rob turns off the truck.

Time's up and she's no closer to a plan.

CeCe crawls out of the truck, her face aching with the movement. She steps away from Rob and Olivia, the thought crossing her mind that she could make a run for it, but the area is too flat with no places to duck bullets, and she has no idea how far she is from home.

And her brother. She'd be leaving him behind, if he's even here. She doesn't know what to believe anymore.

"Where's Teddy?" she asks.

Olivia motions to the building. "In there."

She looks over at a glass office door that leads inside a warehouse, and she has an idea. It's a crapshoot, but it's better than nothing. She races over to the door. If she can get in, she can lock it, find Teddy, and then scramble for another place to hide before Rob uses the gun to blow it open. They'll have to wait it out, but someone will come. Maybe. It's not brilliant, but it's workable.

CeCe gets to the door and yanks on it, but it remains fixed in place. She tugs again and again in desperation, her last shred of hope ebbing away.

Olivia comes up behind her, holding a key. "Aren't we eager?"

CeCe sighs before moving out of the way.

Olivia slides the key in the lock and opens the door. "After you."

The darkness beckoning from within. If she goes in with them, she's not coming back out. And she supposes she always knew that, from the moment she saw Olivia outside her front door, this is how it would end. It wasn't hope she'd brought with her, only delusion. A whisper of the past that things would work out, but how many times does she have to be reminded that world is not here anymore?

"Do you really have him?" she asks.

"What's the matter?" Olivia says. "Don't trust me?"

CeCe glances over at Rob, one hand still over the bite on his arm. He already struck her without hesitation. What else would he be willing to do without thinking twice? A whole lot, she imagines, because she isn't human in his eyes. Only an Infected.

Olivia says, "Seems to me you don't really have a choice, do you?"

Rob stares at CeCe, ready to do whatever Olivia says, ready to be Olivia's loyal dog, but Olivia's right. She doesn't have a choice. If there is one small chance her brother is actually here, she'll have to take it.

She steps inside. It's a reception area of what used to be an office, long converted into a living space. Opened cans and used water bottles fill the trash. Kerosene lamps sit on one desk with a stack of clothes neatly folded on the other. Shirts and jeans that she recognizes as Olivia's. Along one side of the wall are two rolled-up sleeping bags. This is where they've been staying and, by the looks of things, for a while.

She realizes with sickening dread that their plan, the one she so eagerly jumped into, had been thought out a while ago and she played into it perfectly.

But what is Teddy's role in all of this? Bait? Alleged or real? She thinks of her brother alone all these years. He must've found the Revies, needed them to survive, and then what? Became one of them? Had he carried a burning hatred all these years for getting left behind? She imagines him with them, his love for his family splintering away.

They left you, Teddy. They left you like you were nothing.

Olivia and Rob follow her inside. Rob shuts the door and turns the lock.

"I know it isn't much," Olivia says as she comes beside her. "But it's home."

"Where's my brother?"

"We *are* eager, aren't we?" she says with a wink. "To tell you the truth, I am too. I'm a sucker for family reunions. This way."

Olivia heads past the reception and down a long hallway to another room. Automatic lights turn on, reminding CeCe of the CAVE, and then she is hit with the thought of her dad and how she might not see him again. And already she misses him as if she really were gone because in a way, that's how it feels.

They come to another door. It's pitch-black inside. She has no idea what's in there, but it's not Teddy. It's too quiet. Too still.

Olivia nods for CeCe to go in. Rob hovers behind her. This is where it'll happen. She tenses in expectation. Would it be the sting of a knife? Or the searing pain of a bullet splintering her skull? All these thoughts rush through her mind as she takes a step and then another into the oily darkness.

She jumps when Olivia flicks a light switch behind her. The room brightens with artificial light. It's empty save for one desk, some filing cabinets, and a floor-to-ceiling window across from her. No Teddy. She turns to Olivia.

"Now for the grand finale," she says and turns on more switches.

Outside the glass, floodlights fill a large warehouse. Forklifts and other large equipment are neatly parked along the metal walls with stacks of pallets covered in gossamer wrap. In the middle of it is her brother, strapped to a chair with a piece of duct tape over his mouth.

"Teddy." She runs to the glass. "Teddy."

He looks up at her. One of his eyes is a deep black with more bruising going down his jaw. When he sees her, his gaze widens and he rocks back and forth in the chair, trying to free his binds. Even from where she stands, she can see the Revie symbol burned on his forehead. If he was one of them, he isn't anymore.

She whirls on Olivia, balling her fists. "What have you done to him?"

Rob pulls out the gun.

"I'd take a step back if I were you," he says.

She stares at Rob, breathing hard, anger flowing through her arms and down to her hands. He'd done that to her brother. "So tough, aren't you, to do that to a kid? You're such a coward."

He cocks his gun. "Say that again."

"Now now, children," Olivia says. "Rob, you were told."

Rob glances over at Olivia. After a minute he uncocks the gun, but he doesn't put it away. He holds it in his hand as he leans against the wall.

Every part of her wants to charge at him, try to wrestle the gun from his hand, or bite him until she tastes nothing but blood. Anything to make Rob feel an ounce of what he'd done to her brother and probably countless others. But all she'd accomplish is Teddy watching her get shot.

"Let me go to him," she says to Olivia.

"That's why we brought you here, isn't it? We're in the business of reuniting loved ones."

"What a joke," she says.

"You might think so, but it's true." Olivia steps toward her. "Just one thing though."

Here it is. It's what CeCe has been waiting for. The reason they came to her house, the reason they've been holding her brother.

"You have her, don't you?" Olivia asks.

"Have who?" She shakes her head. "What are you talking about?"

"Don't tell me you haven't seen a little girl who happens to like My Little Ponies?"

Her stomach turns. "Penny?"

"You named it?" Olivia laughs. "You hear that, Rob? They named it."

Rob chuckles along with her.

Olivia turns back to CeCe, a smile still on her face. "I knew that's where they got the cure from. *Knew it.* Theo owes me his stash of Pop-Tarts. Don't he, Rob?"

"He won't be too happy about that."

"Well, you're my witness. I mean, come on, six months later," she snaps her fingers, "and poof. A cure. Magic." She says to CeCe, "You know, I gave her that toy. The one you were drawing. I gave it to her when she first came to us, but that was before we found out what she was."

CeCe stares at Olivia, hope filling the emptiness. "Is that what this is about? You want her back? My brother for Penny?"

It's almost a relief in a way. An exchange means everyone has to stay alive. She glances over at Teddy as she waits for confirmation.

He's exhausted himself struggling; he stares at them, his cheeks puffing out with his breaths.

"Uh, no," Olivia says. "We don't want her. Why would we want an abomination? We tried to do what was necessary, but the devil plays his games too. We'll get her back. Eventually. Then we'll finish what we started."

CeCe's putting it all together. Penny hadn't run away. Olivia had done that to her. Had placed her in the horde. Olivia could do that. She's capable of that.

"You tried to kill her."

"She's not some innocent *child*. She's an instrument of the devil, just like," she smiles, a twisted, sinister grin full of malice and anger and evil, "your father."

Any kind of hope CeCe had of surviving this leaves her body. She didn't have much anyway, but even that is gone. This isn't about her or Teddy. It's about her dad. Payback for discovering the cure. They're going to kill her along with her brother, to hurt her dad. That's why they brought her here. It's so obvious she can't believe she'd been so naive.

Olivia opens the door to Teddy.

CeCe stands there. Her legs shaking. She doesn't want her brother or her to die. No matter how messed up this world is, she still wants to be part of it. She wants them both to be.

Olivia nods to the door. "Well?"

She looks at Teddy. Fear washes over his face.

"I don't know if—"

"What's the matter?" Olivia says, frowning. "You were all gung ho this entire time. You don't want him out there all alone, do you? I mean, what kind of sister would you be? I suppose though, what can we really expect from an Infected?"

She motions to Rob, who pushes himself off the wall.

"No," CeCe says, glancing back at him. "I'll go. Okay. I'll go."

"That's a smart girl. Now come on. We don't have all day."

CeCe keeps her eyes on Teddy, focusing on him and trying to quiet every thought in her mind. It's like being in a match with a better player, but she can do this. She can find a way to win some points, to adjust, to change the game.

Move, she thinks. Her body reacts and she races past Olivia and through the door. It slams shut behind her.

"Teddy," she says as she gets close. "Teddy. Oh my god."

She gets her fingernails under the edge of the duct tape and pulls it off.

"Infected," he says, gulping breaths. "They have Infected."

"What? Where?"

"Behind the bay door."

She follows his gaze toward a giant rollup. Then she can hear them, the moaning and the occasional screeching on the other side and the thuds of their bodies as they bang against the metal. That's how they'll do it. That's how they'll kill them, but unlike Penny there will be no one to save them. She yanks on Teddy's bindings.

"We have to get out," she says. "There's got to be another exit somewhere."

Her hands tremble as she tries to undo the ropes around his wrists, but they're tight and her fingers won't stop trembling. Olivia thumps on the glass.

"I wouldn't bother," Olivia says. "You won't have time. You could try to save yourself. You can't, of course, but it's always worth a go. Either way, it's about to get crowded in there."

"Why are you doing this to us?" CeCe screams at her, the noise only infuriating the Infected in their holding pen.

Olivia shrugs. "This is war."

The room fills with a loud buzzing sound and the creaking of the bay door moving upward on its hinges. Legs sway underneath, some hidden behind tattered jeans and trousers, some bare with deep gouges.

They're coming and there's nothing she can do about it. She has no phone. No can of Nitrociptine.

No can of Nitrociptine.

She thinks back to the Infected girl they'd hit with the car. She'd taken the can out of her pack, but then had put it in her pocket. She hadn't changed her clothes.

"Please. Please. Please," she says to herself as she runs her hands along her front and feels the familiar bulge. She quickly yanks it out and turns.

An Infected man squirms under, ahead of the others. Pieces of his bottom lip dangle around his chin, exposing his teeth like the peeled skin of an apple. He moves toward them on all fours, his mouth clacking.

"Go," Teddy shouts. "You have to run."

She shakes her head. "I'm not leaving you here."

More of the Infected pour out, moving like a hive, their screeches echoing off the metal walls. Men, women, children. It's the children who nearly paralyze her in place as their jaws open and shut in anticipation.

She wants to pull the pin, only she has no idea how many are in there and she has to get as many of them as possible. But the man gallops toward them, already closing the gap, and waiting might not be an option. She steps between the man and Teddy, bracing her legs as if she's about to get hit by a fast serve. The Infected rams into her, harder than she expects, and it knocks her off her feet. The canister spirals out of her hand and clanks against the concrete floor.

He's on her, his white teeth clacking open and shut. She gets her knees under him and pushes him off, but he's unfazed and springs right back. His fingernails scrape along her skin, drawing blood, as she scoots backward.

Teddy howls, drawing her attention. An Infected woman has latched onto his arm and jerks her head back and forth, ripping into his flesh. More Infected are already surrounding him. Without the Nitrociptine, he'll be dead in seconds.

She scrambles for the canister. Just as she reaches for it, the Infected man clamps down on her calf. A stinging pain erupts up her leg. She cries out and kicks him hard in the face with her free leg and snatches the canister off the floor. She turns on her back and pulls the pin.

Nitrociptine fizzes into the air in a blinding white cloud that scratches at the back of her throat. She rolls over to her knees. The back of her leg is sticky with blood. The Infected man makes a grab for her, but his hand only paws at the air, as if he's not sure where she's gone.

CeCe's eyes water from the gas and her stomach turns from the scent, but she gets to her feet. She goes to Teddy, shoving the woman off him, who staggers away and then collapses. CeCe crouches before her brother, running her fingers over his bindings, looking for any give, any loose spots, as if reading a complicated piece of braille.

Teddy gags above her and it immediately makes her want to gag too. Her stomach spasms, but she forces it to still.

"Hold on," she says.

The gas hovers around them. It isn't much. It wasn't meant to be. It was only to buy some time, like Derrick had said, but it holds like a protective mushroom cloud in the enclosed space. The Infected stagger in and stall, collapsing under themselves. Those behind the gas screech and moan like wolves denied a meal.

She gets her fingers around one of Teddy's binds and finds some give. She yanks on it, and he shimmies his hand out. Quickly, she focuses on his other hand. This one is easier, and she's unwinding the rope when she's hit hard from behind.

She turns to face whatever Infected had done it, whatever Infected had managed to get through, but it's Olivia. Her face twists in rage.

"You've ruined all my fun."

Olivia straddles over her and swings her fist down, hitting her squarely on the jaw. CeCe's teeth clack together, and the acidic tinge of blood fills her mouth. Olivia pulls her fist back to do it again, but CeCe blocks it and wiggles out from underneath her. As she does, Olivia stomps down on her bitten thigh with her boot, sending a wave of agony up her leg and into her chest. She grits her teeth and forces herself upward.

Olivia rushes toward her, ready to deliver another blow, but this time, CeCe's ready. She pivots and connects her elbow to Olivia's nose. A gush of blood erupts from her nostrils. She wipes it away with the back of her hand and flings it to the ground.

"Nice shot," Olivia says. "I owe you one," and she charges.

CeCe goes to dodge her, but Olivia plants her hands on her shoulders, digging her nails into her flesh and forcing her toward the edge of the Nitrociptine cloud where a cluster of Infected hover. Their screeches ratchet upward, the clicking of their jaws beating into every one of her nerve endings. CeCe pushes back, but Olivia has the advantage, controlling the point while she's scrambling to keep up. Teeth clamp down on CeCe's triceps, her calves, her obliques. She wants to scream, but the pain is so intense that her mouth refuses to open.

"Infected eating the Infected." Olivia grins. "How poetic."

CeCe rams Olivia hard with her knee, breaking her grasp. She rushes past her, sprinting toward the safety of the Nitrociptine, but she stumbles and lands hard on the concrete with a thud that knocks the wind out of her lungs. Before she can even register a breath, Olivia's already on her, pinning her down, hands wrapped around her neck. She slaps at Olivia's hands, trying to make herself fight, but all the adrenaline has leaked away from her body and her muscles fail. She has nothing left to give because she's already given it all. Her breaths come in shallow spurts. Blackness fills the periphery of her vision.

Suddenly, Olivia flies off her and CeCe grasps for breath.

"You okay?" Teddy asks, bending down and offering his hand. Blood coats his arms like he'd dipped them in paint.

"Yeah, I think so."

Olivia screams. CeCe looks over. He's pushed her into the Infected. They've already swarmed, frenzying like dogs fighting for scraps as they tear into her skin. A part of CeCe wants to let the

Infected have her, but she knows she can't. She won't watch Olivia die. She won't be a monster. CeCe takes Teddy's hand and staggers to her feet.

"Help me get her out of there," CeCe says, moving toward Olivia, but Teddy stops her.

"No," he says. "She deserves this. Trust me."

"You're probably right, but we're not like her."

Even though she sees Teddy hesitating, he finally nods. They go over to the Infected that cling onto Olivia like flies, scurrying over her, feeding wherever they can. CeCe makes a quick grab for her arm and manages to get a good hold. They pull her into the safety of the gas, smears of Olivia's blood trailing behind. Her wounds are deep, peppered with glimpses of bone. Just as CeCe lets go, a gun cocks behind her. She turns to find Rob, his gun at her face.

"Do it," Olivia says, her mouth tinged in crimson. "Shoot her."

Rob's dark eyes drill into CeCe.

A loud bang guts the space. CeCe jerks back, expecting the searing burn, the inevitable nothing that is to come, but as she stands there, a red dot blossoms on Rob's chest. Confusion warps his features as he stares at CeCe. The gun drops from his hand and then he drops too, a halo of red spreading from his torso.

RRT circle toward them. Some with guns, some with black cylinders that they fire toward the back of the warehouse at the Infected. A flood of Nitrociptine engulfs the room. The gas is so overwhelming that she can't even be happy or relieved or grateful. Her stomach twists in on itself, and she collapses onto her knees, vomiting.

"Teddy?" she says into the fog.

A man in a black uniform and a gas mask lifts her away as if he were picking up an envelope. "Medics are outside," he says, hurrying through the warehouse and away from the gas. "They'll take care of you and your brother."

Her mind goes to Derrick lying on the asphalt, the wheels of his bike spinning.

"There's someone else," she says, struggling in his grasp. "Derrick. They shot him, a few streets down from my house."

"Try not to move," the man says. "Your bites are deep."

"What? I don't care about that. Are you listening to me? You have to help him. He could still be alive."

The RRT takes her outside where the brightness of the sun blinds her, and in her periphery are flashing lights. She's laid face-down in a gurney, still begging for someone to help Derrick, to find him, but they hoist her into the back of an ambulance. Scissors cut through her shirt and cool air rushes against her skin.

A woman's voice says, "This will help with the pain."

If she's given a shot, she doesn't feel it. All she feels is the gnawing in her stomach and the burning on the back of her legs.

She says Derrick's name and says it again, repeating it like it's a code or a password she's trying to remember, but already her eyes feel heavy, and she can't keep them open. He's going to die when she could have gotten him help.

A hand wraps around her own.

"I'm here," Derrick says. "I'm here."

Chapter Nineteen

CeCe wakes in a hospital room. Not the Costco where she was first cured, but in an actual room with a window and a curtain. But the comfort fades with the memory of everything that happened in the warehouse. The Infected on her and Teddy, their teeth burying into her skin. Olivia's blood-soaked body. Derrick's voice in the ambulance. *His voice.* He'd been there. Her heart speeds up. But was it really him? Or the gas messing with her mind? She doesn't know. She might've wanted it to be him so badly that she hallucinated it.

She tries to sit up, gritting her teeth as she presses her hands into the mattress. Her body awakens in a symphony of aching bruises and stinging bite marks and a rolling in her stomach. She lifts up one arm. A dressing completely encloses it from shoulder to wrist with an IV peeking out.

"CeCe," her dad says from somewhere nearby.

She turns to his voice. He's sitting with a book in his lap.

"Dad?" she says, her voice croaking.

A bandage is wrapped around his forearm. He's pale and looks like he's lost weight, but he's smiling.

"Where's Teddy?" she asks. "Is he okay?"

"He's right next door and anxious to see you."

Her dad comes over to the side of her bed. He puts his hand into her own and squeezes it gently.

"And Derrick?" she starts to ask, but is frightened of what she'll hear. "Did he make it? They shot him and I saw him lying there—"

"He's alive," her dad says. "He has a nasty case of road rash, but he's upright and breathing. He crashed the bike on purpose. I'm sure he didn't mean to scare you. But if he hadn't, he wouldn't have been able to follow you to the warehouse."

"He's the reason the RRT came."

Her dad nods.

Tears coat her eyes, turning the room into a watery blur.

Her monster. Her hero.

"Is he still here?"

Her dad shakes his head. "No, he got bandaged up and left. Honestly, I'm a little surprised. I thought he'd be here with you."

Derrick didn't tell her dad what happened between them before Olivia showed up at her door. How she'd blamed him for her mother's death. He saved her life, but he can't be around her, and she can't blame him for it either.

She says, "There's something I have to tell you."

She starts with the night at Mason's and how she and Derrick had really met and then seeing him again at Ed's MiniMart, and everything that happened after that right up to cutting him out of her life.

"Why, CeCe?" her dad asks.

"Because," she says, tears streaming down her cheeks, "because I remembered what I did to Mom after I was Infected. I—" her voice cracks, "I killed her. It's all my fault."

The confession tears at her insides. Everything shatters all over again. There's no coming back from this. There'll never be another moment in her life when she won't be reminded of what she'd taken from all of them and what can never return.

"No," her dad says, shaking his head. "No, it's not. CeCe, honey. It wasn't your fault. I don't blame you, and you shouldn't blame yourself either."

"How can you say that after what I've done?"

"Because under no circumstances would you have hurt your mother, and I know that like I know every square inch of your face. If she were here, she'd tell you the same. We'd never, ever blame you for what happened. The Infection was to blame. It was never you. Not the real you. The strong, determined daughter I know. The type of daughter who goes into a warehouse full of Infected to save her brother."

She shakes her head. Rob would've shot them. No matter what she'd done, they'd still be dead. "I was reckless and stupid. I shouldn't've gone with them. Derrick is the one you should thank."

"It wasn't only Derrick, it was also you. RRT would've never made it in time. *You* saved him, and my god, CeCe, your mother would be so proud." He smiles at her with tears in his eyes.

"And I am too. You brought your brother back to us, and I've never been more grateful in my life to have a daughter like you. A champion."

Her heart cracks open. He holds her as she sobs, releasing every moment of trauma, every pain, every bit of sorrow.

Grieving for what they've lost and forgiving the wounds that might never heal, but they're there, open and exposed, no longer hiding.

For the first time since the cure, she feels something more than despair, but possibility. And that as long as they're together, they can carve out a life in this new reality.

When every tear is spent, her dad stays with her for a long time. She asks to see Teddy, but he tells her she needs to wait for her antibiotic drip to finish.

"Soon," he says.

***

She wakes to a bowl of oatmeal and a few slices of oranges. It's been days since she last ate, and she shovels it down her throat, barely taking a breath between mouthfuls. She's licking the citrus off her fingers when Lauren comes into the room.

"Feeling better?" she asks.

"I'm starving."

Lauren sets down a tray full of gauzes and ointments. She removes CeCe's IV and begins to unwrap her bandages. Stitches run down her arms like barbed wire. She recoils at her red and puckered flesh. She thought she was ready to see it, but she isn't.

"I'm a chew toy."

"Not quite, but almost," Lauren says. "This is the worst of it. You'll see a big difference once the healing process sets in. Most of these will barely scar, and those that do, well, there's options."

Lauren's light fingers go through each wound, carefully inspecting, cleaning, rewrapping. When she's done, she has CeCe roll over on her stomach to treat the ones on her shoulders and legs. Lauren does all this in a methodical, practiced way.

"You're good at this," CeCe says. "Were you a nurse?"

"Plastic surgeon."

"Oh."

"Surprised?"

"Yeah, a little."

Lauren applies a cool liquid on the bite from the crawling man in the warehouse. It stings, and she hisses between her teeth.

"Now that the hospital is open," she says, "we can look at some skin grafts and other treatments for the worst ones. I already corrected most of the deeper bites, readying them, and those are starting to heal nicely."

CeCe clenches her scarred hand. She remembers seeing bone and the deep feathers of muscle that night, but it had healed. And not just healed, she could use it. Swing a racquet again when even in her delirious mind she didn't think it'd be possible. It had been Lauren.

"You fixed my hand all those months ago."

"Your dad told me how good you were at tennis. I wanted to make sure you could still play if you wanted."

Lauren tears a piece of tape and places it gently against CeCe's skin. She thinks of when Lauren had come to the house that night for dinner, and they announced they were getting married. CeCe had been so cold to her, and has been ever since.

"I'm sorry," she says, turning on her side so Lauren can see her, see that she means it. "Sorry about how I've treated you."

"I get it." Lauren shrugs. "I had a stepmom and a stepdad too, you know."

"Still, it wasn't fair."

"I never held that against you. All I wanted was to be your friend, and I know friendship takes time. You don't need to apologize for how you felt. It was a lot. The wedding and then the baby. I told Shawn it was too much, all at once. I understood where you were coming from, since sometimes I'm overwhelmed with it too."

Lauren places her hand over her stomach.

CeCe asks, "Have you told Teddy?"

"We did," she says, grinning. "His first words were, *Finally, I'm not the little brother anymore.*"

CeCe chuckles. "That sounds like him."

"Are you up for seeing Teddy?"

"One hundred percent."

"Let me get the rest of these and I'll take you over to him."

Lauren finishes replacing her bandages and gives her some medicine for the nausea that prickles at her stomach. It's not as bad as it had been in the warehouse. If anything, the nagging churning is more of an annoyance than anything.

Lauren rolls over a wheelchair.

"I think I'm okay to walk."

"No straining those stitches," she says. "Doctor's orders."

"Right."

Lauren helps her get in the chair and then guides her out into the hallway, where two nurses sit at the station. It looks so ordinary that for a moment, it's almost like the Kill Virus was just a dream and she'd been in some kind of coma.

One of the nurses turns toward her, half her face a swirl of scars.

Lauren rolls CeCe past them and into Teddy's room. He's lying on his bed, his shoulders covered with white gauze like her arms. In his hand is a Nintendo DS, pinging and making swooping noises.

His face isn't as swollen as when she'd seen him in the warehouse, but the bruising is there, along with his black eye that is now a swirl of yellows and greens instead of a deep blue. She touches the side of her face where Rob had punched her. She still has a lump and probably sports a black eye of her own.

Teddy pauses his game and quickly covers the Revie symbol on his forehead with his hair. He's embarrassed by it. Maybe Lauren can take care of that too. "Hey," he says.

"Hey yourself."

Lauren tells CeCe she'll be back in a little while and then quietly leaves.

Once she's gone, CeCe asks Teddy, "How are you feeling?"

"A little like I'd been thrown in a pit with angry boars, but other than that, awesome."

"Same." She pauses. "I've missed you."

He looks at her. His boyish grin still there after all this time, after everything he's gone through, but missing are those rounded cheeks she remembers, and in its place the angled jawline of a new teen.

"Don't be weird," he says. "But yeah, I've missed you too."

He reaches his hand to her, grimacing a little, knowing the stitches must be bugging him as much as they bug her. She takes it, holding his hand tight, trying not to squeeze even though she wants to, wanting to feel every pad of his fingertips, so she knows he's really there.

They hear a light tapping on the door.

CeCe turns and sees the Infected girl her dad had hit with his car. She's on crutches, her leg wrapped in a cast. Penny stands next to her. They both gaze at Teddy, faces beaming with joy.

"Harper?" Teddy says to the ex-Infected girl. "Isabelle? What? How are you guys here? I thought—"

"We were dead? Me too," the girl with the crutches says and looks over at CeCe. Her eyes widen. "Your sister?"

"Yeah." Teddy smiles.

"She looks just like her picture." She turns to CeCe. "Teddy showed it to us all the time."

She realizes the girl must be talking about the Grand Canyon photograph, the one she found in the Harry Potter book in Teddy's backpack. Penny nods with a grin. So, Penny knew who she was the whole time. And her dad too. That's why she felt safe in the lab, even with Infected, because she'd be with their dad, someone Penny could trust. Because of Teddy.

The girl says, "I'm Harper and," she turns to Penny, "this is Isabelle."

"Isabelle?" she says. "Well, I was way off now, wasn't I? I've been calling her Penny."

"Penny?" Harper laughs and Penny/Isabelle blushes a little.

Teddy glances down at Harper's cast. "What happened?"

"Got hit by a car while Infected. What happened to you?"

"Attacked by Infected in a warehouse while strapped to a chair."

"You win."

CeCe says, "I, uh, I was in that car. How are you feeling?"

"Now, *that's* embarrassing," Harper says, a red blooming over her cheeks. "I imagined I'd meet you one day, but not like that. I'm sorry if I—"

"No," CeCe says. "Don't even worry about it. But how are you already walking and talking? I was in a bed for weeks, and then in rehab."

"I hadn't been Infected long. Six, seven months? That's what Dr. Campbell, er, your dad said. It sounds about right though." She looks over at Teddy, sharing something unspoken between them. "Who put you in the warehouse?" Harper asks. "Is it who I think it was?"

He nods. "Olivia and Rob. Rob's dead though."

"Good. Where's Olivia?"

"Dad says she's being treated at his facility in a secure ward. I pushed her into Infected."

Harper reaches out and gives Teddy a high five. They slap their hands together and Teddy sits back, shooting CeCe a guilty look.

Harper asks, "Where will she go after that?"

He shrugs. "I don't know. She might stay there."

"She deserves way worse. We both know that."

CeCe listens to all this. She shouldn't be surprised they knew Olivia and Rob and probably knew them better than she ever did, but it still stuns her in the same way a random acquaintance isn't one at all.

"Okay." She finally jumps in. "How do you all know Olivia and Rob?"

Harper says, "We met them at the Revie camp. They were basically like prison guards, but worse. How did you know them?"

"From school. Olivia was in my GED program."

Harper's jaw drops. "Olivia was going to school? Like in a classroom?"

"Yeah."

Olivia must've started the program to keep tabs on CeCe. That's her only guess, but Olivia couldn't have known she was there. Not the first day. Could she? Unless Olivia and Rob had been watching her and her dad longer than she thought, only she doesn't like to think about that.

Harper laughs. "I can't even imagine her sitting at a desk, doing fractions and writing sentences. Not the girl who'd go around beating us for the fun of it."

"How did you get Infected?" CeCe asks her.

She motions toward Teddy. "When we ran away to look for Isabelle, Teddy and I. Olivia and Rob took her on a scavenging run. They liked the little kids because they could get into spots they couldn't. But Isabelle never came back, and they wouldn't tell us what happened to her. If she'd been Infected, they'd have said so, but they'd look at each other all weird.

"We knew they'd done something, and we went after her, but Olivia and Rob caught up with us. That's when I got bit. Last thing I saw was them taking Teddy and driving away. It's all pretty much a blur after that because, you know."

Isabelle snuggles into Harper. It's sweet. Isabelle was probably always sweet and Olivia and Rob left her in a horde. Maybe Teddy was right. She should have let Olivia die, but at least this way, she'll have to suffer.

"It's okay," Harper says to her. "I'm okay now."

"Has Penny, er, Isabelle ever talked?"

Harper shakes her head.

"We were teaching her how to read and write so she could talk to us. When we first met, the only thing she could write was the first few letters of her name. Then we had to keep guessing until we figured it out."

CeCe sits back. That's brilliant. Did her dad think of that too? Teaching Isabelle to read and write? CeCe didn't. The idea never crossed her mind, but it is so simple she wants to kick herself for not coming up with it like Teddy and Harper did.

Harper looks at Teddy. "How'd you end up in the warehouse?"

"After you, they took me back to the camp," he says. "Kept me locked up for a really long time. When they let me out, I ran when I got the chance. They grabbed me and said that if I didn't want to stay, they had a place for me in the ravine. They went through my stuff, seeing if I took anything. I had. A knife. And they found that picture at the Grand Canyon.

"All I can figure is that they recognized Dad. I had no idea about anything. I didn't even know there was a cure or that my dad had discovered it. It was all news to me. Shoot, I didn't even know he was alive.

"They locked me up and next thing I know I'm at the warehouse and CeCe's there, and no longer Infected. Honestly, at first I thought I was looking at a ghost."

"Well," Harper says, "I don't want to say it was a good thing you both were there but, hey, look at us. We're back together and away from the Revies. Beaten up, but together."

"Yeah," Teddy says with a smile as he looks at CeCe. "We are."

***

CeCe stays in the room. She listens as they talk about good memories, funny things that happened, and she learns more about pre-Cure life in thirty minutes than she ever did in the months following the Costco. How they broke in everywhere for supplies and shelter, hid from passing hordes. The way they talk, it's like watching Teddy with two more sisters at his side. They share a bond she'll never be able to have with him, and that's okay. They'd protected each other, survived together, and she loves Harper and Isabelle for it.

It's not until several hours later, when Lauren wheels CeCe back into her room, that she realizes she's filled with a lightness she hasn't felt in a long time. The bites don't even ache as much as they had that morning, but there is still an ache, one she can't ignore.

One thing still mars the happiness she feels at having Teddy back.

Now that she's alone, she thinks about Derrick, and there's a pit in her chest that won't close.

Chapter Twenty

After a week, Teddy and CeCe are released home with antibiotic ointment, and Lauren's daily visits. The moment they get through the door, Teddy hurries upstairs to his room and flops on his bed with a sigh that can be heard all the way downstairs.

Lauren turns to CeCe. "Someone's glad to be back."

"Clearly."

Since being in the hospital, CeCe's now able to move around better. The stitches hurt less; most of them have been taken out and are covered by large bandages. She has appointments for skin grafts. In the meantime, she wears long-sleeve shirts and sweatpants, and in those moments, she can pretend it never happened.

One morning, a moving van pulls up outside. Her dad comes downstairs, dressed in his work-around-the-house clothes.

"What's going on?" she asks him.

"I'm getting rid of the couches. It's time. Don't you think?"

She doesn't say anything as Steve and Mike come in. They help him lift the couches and haul them away, gutting the living room in the process. She watches each one go, her heart getting pulled right along with them out the door. But once they're gone, a weight lifts. One she hasn't realized had been there.

Teddy stands next to her. He brushes her with his shoulder.

"I'm sorry," she says.

She's said it so many times that it's almost like a reflex. He knows what she's done. She told him and he doesn't hate her. Even now, she can't understand why her brother and her dad can forgive her so easily.

He shrugs. "I never liked those couches anyway."

Her dad comes back in with an armful of folded-up boxes and duct tape. He looks at them.

"You two ready?"

"Ready," Teddy says and reaches for a box.

They pack her mother's things. First the dining room pictures next to the kitchen. Then her books, next her knickknacks. It's all carefully wrapped and labeled. With each box taken away, it's like a pallbearer carrying little coffins. They cry, they remember, and they miss her.

And while CeCe still carries the wound of what she'd done, a wound that will never fully heal, she feels a softness too, a calm presence as if her mother is with her, telling her that it'll be all right.

A few days later, Teddy and CeCe get a handful of roses and her mother's favorite lantern from the backyard. They go to where her body was found in the parking lot. Since CeCe had last been there, several places have been covered with candles, pictures of loved ones, and flowers, some fresh, some wilted.

They stand over the asphalt where their mother had been. The bloodstain is fainter, gradually getting washed away by rain and time. They place the lantern down and the flowers and talk to her, as if this is where she's been, waiting for them to visit.

Before they leave, Teddy says, "We miss you, Mom, but we're good. We love you. We'll be back again soon."

They go again the next day, and the next, bringing flat stones, pictures, and candles to cover where her mother had been. This is her grave, the place where they grieve, where they talk to her, and sometimes, CeCe swears, her mom answers in whispers she hears with her heart.

At home, they stay in. Play games. Watch movies on the new couches. Harper and Isabelle come over to visit so often that Dad and Lauren clear out Mom's old craft room downstairs and turn it into a spare bedroom. One night turns into two, then three, until they stop going back to the CAVE altogether. It happens so naturally it's like they were always here and haven't been home in a while.

"What about the Revies?" CeCe asks her dad. "Is Isabelle safe here?"

"They're gone," he says, "and their so-called Shepherd is in custody. Isabelle has nothing to worry about from them anymore. And she's in better spirits after she's been here. Even General MacGregor has observed that."

But Harper and Isabelle aren't the only changes in their lives. Lauren gradually stops leaving for the CAVE at night, and instead greets them in the morning with a smile and coffee and a ready-made breakfast.

Sometimes pancakes, courtesy of eggs from the chickens at the Revie encampment, and maple syrup that has a longer shelf life than the Infection. It's not the same as her mom's, but that's okay too.

Things begin to click into place. There's a sort of happiness again, the seeds of it, and it's enough to see that it'll be a regular thing, and if she thinks about it, CeCe's happy. Almost, except for Derrick. She misses him and is sorry for what she'd said.

So much time has passed. He hasn't texted, hasn't stopped by, and she's too much of a coward to reach out.

Her guilt still eats at her, festering around the edges and sore to touch. Somedays she almost calls him, but she can't bring herself to do it. Instead, she falls into a trap of checking her phone relentlessly, even to the point that Teddy and Harper make fun of her. But the only calls or texts she gets are from Savannah, asking when she's coming back to school.

"Soon," she tells her. "Soon."

Nothing is stopping her from going back to Franklin, except knowing that Derrick won't be there, waiting outside to walk her home. She'd ruined that. Stomped that relationship into the ground. And while she sits in her full house with laughter and voices that drown the quiet, there's threads of loneliness too.

It's Teddy and Harper who convince her to go back to Franklin. They'll all be together, and they're anxious to go, even Isabelle. When she sees their excited faces and chatter, the thought of school, the thought of being around other kids their age, she gives in.

The first day, they all pile out of Lauren's car. Teddy and Harper are ecstatic to be in high school since both of them were in middle school when the Infection started. The caseworkers guide them inside and they walk Isabelle to her class. CeCe parts ways with Teddy and Harper as they disappear down the hall to their assigned room. Their future in front of them. It's such a stark difference than when she'd returned that first day.

She makes it to Room 114 and takes a breath before she goes in.

The moment she opens the door, Savannah jumps up and gives her a hug. She even gets a few "Heys" from some of the other students who hadn't talked to her until now.

"I freaking missed your face," Savannah says.

"I missed you too." She looks around at the other students and lowers her voice. "Has, uh, anyone asked why I wasn't here?"

Savannah already knows the truth. She'd filled her in on what happened through a series of texts that came with responses of "OMG!" "WHAT?!?!" and "Are you KIDDING me???"

In those conversations, CeCe had casually asked, as best as she could, if Justin had mentioned anything about Derrick. Savannah told her that she and Justin didn't work out, and she hasn't spoken to him since.

"Yeah," Savannah says. "Ms. Dobson said you had a family emergency and would be out for a bit."

"And what did she say about Olivia?"

She shrugs. "That she dropped out and won't be back. Have you heard from Derrick?"

"Nope."

"He might still come around."

"If he was going to, he would have by now."

Ms. Dobson comes in, no longer struggling so much with her crutches. She smiles at CeCe. "Good to see you," she says. "Ready to get back to work?"

She holds up her GED book. "Ready."

"You've got some catching up to do."

"I'm looking forward to it."

CeCe works harder in class than she ever has and gets a list of assignments from Ms. Dobson to finish at home, along with a date for the GED test. It feels good to be productive, to have a goal again. She supposes her dad had been right about that.

After school, Teddy, Harper, and Isabelle wait for her in the hall. Along with Savannah, they walk out together in a group, like she'd used to do with Leyton and Riley. The memory smacks her across the chest and she has to suck in a breath. Only it's getting easier to breathe these days, and the memories don't paralyze her as much.

As they approach the doors, she knows Derrick won't be there, but her heart still races at the idea that maybe she might be wrong. But when they go through, his usual spot is empty, and she deflates from the disappointment. Savannah puts her hand on her shoulder.

"I'm sorry," she whispers.

Lauren gets out of her car and gives them a wave, her other hand brushing over her growing stomach. She has a bona fide bump now, and she has to use a rubber band to button her pants.

They stop and talk to Savannah and her aunt, Melissa. Lauren invites her and Savannah over Friday for dinner and game night. Melissa accepts and offers to cut everyone's hair as a thank-you gift.

"Honestly," Lauren says, running her hand over her long ponytail, "I don't think I'll be able to pass you up on that."

"It's the least I can do for Dr. Campbell and his family."

CeCe looks over at Teddy, Harper, Isabelle, and Lauren. She smiles.

Their family.

They pile into Lauren's car and drive home. CeCe does her homework downstairs with everyone else. All the while having her phone on her, checking for messages that never come, and thinking about Derrick. The first day is always the hardest, she tells herself. It'll get better.

Days then weeks roll by. She's undergone several skin grafts. Most of her scars aren't scars at all, thanks to Lauren. When she's not religiously putting on ointment, she steadily makes headway on her work to prep for the GED.

One morning, Ms. Dobson tells them that the public library is open again and they all get to go on something of a field trip. They get a school bus with one of the caseworkers offering to drive.

CeCe walks inside the three-story building. A woman sits behind the main desk with a stack of books and a few others move around, stocking and organizing. It smells like lemons and pine and bleach. She gazes at the ordered shelves. Derrick had been here. She feels him so strongly that with every corner she turns, she expects to run into him. But even though she doesn't, his ghost trails her everywhere.

They stay at the library for a few hours, looking for books to check out. They all get library cards and dates to return their books, and it feels so normal that it aches a little.

The day of the GED test comes. She's nervous, but she goes through the booklet and answers each question the best she can. There are equations she can't quite remember, and some she does. She finishes the last one and hopes for the best. She gives her test to Ms. Dobson, who has to grade them all by hand until someone can get the Scantron machine up and running again.

"I'm rooting for you," Ms. Dobson says before she leaves.

They won't get the results back until Wednesday and they get to stay home until then. CeCe and the others spend the extra time organizing, tidying. Teddy, Harper, and Isabelle clean up the backyard. Her dad found a trampoline tucked away at the Costco and they're all excited to get it up.

CeCe stays upstairs with Lauren in the utility room that had been an office-slash-storage for so long, she'd forgotten it was even there.

It's going to be the baby's nursery. They talk paint colors, something neutral since they don't know if it's a boy or a girl.

"I hope it's a girl," CeCe says.

Lauren smiles. "Me too."

CeCe picks up a box and sets it on the stack as Lauren finishes taping another.

"I saw Derrick the other day," Lauren says.

CeCe stomach twists at the mention of his name.

"He was at the police station on Oak Street. They're going to have four officers running it. Actual police, emergency services, crazy to think. But they had a little celebration for its grand reopening, and he was there. He asked about you."

She swallows. "What did you say?"

"That you were good. Healed up, back at Franklin."

"Oh." She focuses on folding a blanket, although her heart thumps between her ribs. "Did he say anything else?"

"No, but I could tell that you're a hard subject for him." Lauren takes a dusty trophy off a bookshelf. "He got permission to move out of the Housing Center. I guess most of them have left, since so many are getting cured, and they need the space. It was only ever meant to be transitional anyhow."

"He's not there anymore?"

"I guess not."

CeCe places the folded blanket in a box. Hearing her say Derrick's name, hearing what he's been doing, and that he'd asked about her, picks open a scab.

It all comes back. Despite how good things are, she's only this way because Derrick had started her down this road when she didn't even know one existed. She thinks of that night on the rooftop with the candles and the stars and the music. If she is to make a life for herself here, she wants him in it.

She turns to Lauren. "Can I borrow your car?"

"Do you know how to drive?"

"More or less."

CeCe doesn't bother to change. She has dust and fuzz on her leggings and tank top. Her hair is pulled up in a bun that's falling to one side, but she grabs Lauren's keys and gets in the car. She puts it in reverse and slowly backs out.

The last time she was behind the wheel was when her mom sent her to the grocery store for taco shells and that was, what? Three years ago? She gets onto the road, puts it in drive, and heads toward the one place she knows Derrick will be.

With no other traffic, she makes her way quickly to Old District. His bike's parked along the front of the record store. She slides in behind it and turns off the car. Now that she's here, she's scared to go in.

What if he doesn't feel the same about her anymore? Things change. People change. But if living in this post-apocalyptic world has shown her anything, it's that she cannot wait until a better time because there won't always be one.

She gets out of the car and locks it out of habit. She goes past his bike. Long scratch marks etch the paint where it'd slid along the asphalt. She's instantly hit with the memory of seeing him lying there and how afraid it made her feel, how it felt to think she'd lost him. It's the memory that empowers her to go through the front door.

Music thrums from behind the glass, something low and broody.

Bells rattle as she pushes the door open. She takes a few steps inside, steeling herself, as she waits for Derrick to react to their sound. She stands there for a few moments. The music is coming from the second-floor apartment. A thought occurs to her that he might not be alone. That he's moved on and he's upstairs with another girl. And the more she thinks it, the more it comes true in her mind, and the more she wants to leave.

But if he has moved on, she has to know that too. She can't go home with all these unanswered questions she'll only torture herself with later.

She goes up the stairs, taking them as quietly as she can, listening, but all she hears is the creaking of steps along the floorboards. She gets to the top. The door is cracked open like he'd meant to close it and it didn't catch.

She tries to peek through, feeling stalkerish, and recognizing the irony of having such a feeling since she'd accused Derrick of the same in the beginning. There's only a blur of movement on the other side, but she doesn't hear any voices, either his or another girl's. She lifts her hand to tap on the door, but she's so nervous that her hand stays hovering there.

The door suddenly whips open. Derrick's head is down, in his own world, on his own mission. He jerks backward with a cry when he realizes someone's in front of him, his eyes widening. Then he sees that it's her and he puts his hand on his chest.

"Holy crap, CeCe. You almost gave me a heart attack."

"Sorry. I was about to knock."

She looks past him into the room. Moving boxes sit on the floor. He's packing the old owner's things, alone.

"What are you doing here?" he asks.

"I, um, I wanted to see you. I thought." She clears her throat. "I thought I'd hear from you. That you'd call."

"I didn't have your number. That girl destroyed my phone."

"Right," she says, her cheeks getting hot. She'd forgotten all about Olivia grinding his phone into parts. And all this time, if she'd just texted him, maybe he'd have texted back. She felt so foolish, she almost wanted to get back into the car and go home.

"Besides," he says, "you made it pretty clear you didn't want me around anymore."

"I know." She looks at her stained sneakers. "I remember."

"It's good to see you though."

She moves her gaze back up to him. Sweat clings to his chest, dampening the front of his shirt. She wants so badly to reach out and touch him. To pull the shirt off his body. The desire is so strong that she has to clasp her hands together to stop herself from doing it.

"It's really good to see you too, but it's not the only reason why I'm here." She stops, gathering her courage. "I came because I wanted you to know how sorry I am for what I said. For blaming you for my mom. I know it wasn't you. It," she takes a breath as a tear glides down her cheek, "it was me. I bit her and I couldn't deal with it. It was so horrible and terrible, and still is, but I put it on you. I made you take that guilt from me, and that was wrong."

He doesn't say anything. She waits for him to, but he doesn't. Maybe this time it'll be Derrick who tells her to go away, to never come back. And if he does, she doesn't know if she'll be able to handle it.

"Since we, I guess, officially met," she says, "I know all you've been trying to do is make me happy. That night here on the rooftop with the candles, then tennis. Being there when I needed someone to listen. I didn't make it easy for you, I know that, but if this is the last time we talk, I want you to know how much I've appreciated everything you did for me, and how much I regret taking it for granted."

She looks at him, the pressure inside her building as he stares back at her.

"Can you say something?" Her voice cracks. "Please?"

He rubs his hand across his face.

"Honestly, CeCe, I don't know what to say. All I've been doing is thinking and I've had a lot of time to do it. I infected you. I made you become that thing. I don't blame you for not telling me. When you said you didn't owe me anything, you're right. You don't, but it's really messed me up. To know that I did that to you. To your family. God, your dad must hate me. I hate me."

"No." She shakes her head. "He doesn't. He knows it wasn't your fault, and I know that too. The truth is I forgave you a long time ago and I took my forgiveness back when it was the easiest thing to do. The easiest for me."

Tears fall down her cheeks.

"If you don't want to see me after this, I get it. I deserve it. Trust me, I know. I just wanted to thank you for saving my life and my brother's life at the warehouse." She pauses, not sure if she should say what her heart wants her to say, but she can't fight it. She doesn't want to fight it any longer. "Except you saved me long before that, and I can't stand being away from you. I can't. I love you with whatever that's left of me."

He gazes back at her, every second like an eternity spreading between them.

In one swift motion, he pulls her into his arms and says, "I'll take whatever that is."

She melts into his embrace and then she feels his lips on her cheeks, kissing her tears away, and then they're on hers, Finally, blissfully, she kisses him, drinking in the warmth of his lips, drinking him into her.

His voice in her ear is a bare whisper. "I missed you. I've missed you so damn much."

He lifts her up and she wraps her legs around his waist. He walks her over to the bed and sets her down. She pulls off her leggings and rips her tank top over her head. Her skin prickles with goosebumps in anticipation. Then his clothes are off, and he's pressed against her, and she craves his touch. She holds on to him, bringing him closer, opening herself to him completely. There are no more secrets.

They lie together, gasping for breath, but neither of them want to move. Derrick runs his fingers over her arms, tracing the bite marks. He stops at the one on her hand, the one he'd given her. He takes it and puts it on his chest, over his beating heart.

"I think of my roommate sometimes," he says. "If I saw that guy, I'd punch him."

She grins. "Don't think I hadn't thought the same about you. At least in the beginning."

"You know," he threads his fingers through hers, "I thought I would be the first."

"The first what?"

"The first to tell you I love you."

She lays her head on his chest. "You love me?"

"From the moment I saw you. I mean, the second time I saw you."

Playfully, she jabs him.

He taps his finger on her hand. "I do have one stipulation though before we move forward."

She turns her face up to him. "Oh yeah? And what's that?"

"You have to teach me how to play tennis."

She smiles and she knows it's big and ridiculous. "Okay."

"Okay?"

"Yeah, okay, I'll teach you."

Gently, he squeezes her hand.

"I love you," he says.

"I love you too."

He kisses her again, slow and sweet. Her chest explodes with love and hope. Actual hope.

Despite the world imploding, everything really will be okay, and they will move on from it. It won't look the same. It'll never be the same, but she's good with that. It's enough.

They spend hours together in bed. Sometimes they're slow and thoughtful, other times eager and full of want for each other.

It's only after their arms shake from the need for food that they get up. Derrick heats some cans of Dinty Moore beef stew that he pulls from the cupboard. It's a first for her and it tastes better than she expects.

She's about to take another bite when they hear a loud banging noise.

Derrick gets up. She does too, her stomach already replacing the comfort of the food with a dose of anxiety.

"An Infected?" she asks.

"I don't know, maybe."

He opens the door to the stairs and looks down.

"You stay here," he says, grabbing his phone and a canister of Nitrociptine.

"We're together, remember? New rule."

"We have rules?"

"We do."

She stays behind him as they creep to the first floor. When they get to the bottom, they hear it again, a clinking like the dropping of a stainless-steel bowl. They both look toward the back of the store. It's coming from the alley.

They move down a narrow hallway, past a bathroom with a sign on top that says, "Employees Only," and then to the door.

Derrick unbolts the lock and cracks it open. She leans against him, listening. They hear the noise again. A low scraping and a shuffling that's not quite footsteps. It's coming from a dumpster, overflowing with cardboard boxes and garbage that has been sitting out for years. The smell is tart. Whatever has rotted has long decomposed into a sludge.

Derrick steps outside. She leans against the door, keeping it open.

She watches him creep closer to the dumpster. They should see the Infected by now or it should sense them, unless it's a small child, perhaps a toddler. The idea of seeing a little baby come screeching out of that mess, jaw gaping, makes her insides coil.

Derrick leans forward and moves some of the debris. He cries out and she tightens her grip on the door. Was that a good cry or a bad cry? She can't tell and she's almost about to race toward him when he reaches into the garbage.

"It's okay," he coos, bending down. "Come here, little fella."

Little fella?

He picks up a scraggly dog, plucking him from the crumpled food wrappers and cans. The dog squirms in his grasp, wagging its tail faster than a fan blade, its fur matted and covered in dirt.

Derrick has a giant smile on his face as he turns to her. He holds the dog close to his chest as it lifts its muzzle to lick his face.

She comes over, unable to stop laughing even when it mixes with tears. She runs her hand along the dog's back, feeling each vertebra. The poor thing is nearly skin and bones, but they have Dinty Moore beef stew and time and love to share.

"Can you believe it?" he asks.

"No," she says, shaking her head, but it's here and so are they, reveling in this moment and in this space.

And it's beautiful.

ABOUT THE AUTHOR

HJ Ramsay has an MFA in Creative Writing from Antioch University, Los Angeles, and lives in Northern California with her husband and three children where they can be found regularly on a golf course or a tennis court.

She's had a life-long fascination with zombies and staunchly believes that if there ever was a zombie apocalypse, she'd survive.

HJ loves hearing from her readers.

facebook: facebook.com/@hjramsay

instagram: @hjramsay

www.BOROUGHSPUBLISHINGGROUP.com

If you enjoyed this book, please write a review. Our authors appreciate the feedback, and it helps future readers find books they love. We welcome your comments and invite you to send them to info@boroughspublishinggroup.com.

Follow us on TikTok and Instagram, and be sure to sign up for our newsletter for surprises and new releases from your favorite authors.

Are you an aspiring writer? Check out www.boroughspublishinggroup.com/submit and see if we can help you make your dreams come true.

Love podcasts? Enjoy ours at

https://boroughspublishinggroup.com/podcast

Made in the USA
Monee, IL
06 March 2025

13176178R00142